Young Lionz

C. J. Hudson

URBAN
BOOKS

www.urbanbooks.net

Urban Books, LLC
300 Farmingdale Road, N.Y.-Route 109
Farmingdale, NY 11735

Young Lionz Copyright © 2020 C. J. Hudson

ISBN 13: 978-1-64556-012-8
ISBN 10: 1-64556-012-0

First Trade Paperback Printing March 2020
Printed in the United States of America

10 9 8 7 6 5 4 3 2 1

*This is a work of fiction. Any references or similarities
to actual events, real people, living or dead, or to real
locales are intended to give the novel a sense of reality.
Any similarity in other names, characters, places, and
incidents is entirely coincidental.*

Distributed by Kensington Publishing Corp.
Submit Orders to:
Customer Service
400 Hahn Road
Westminster, MD 21157-4627
Phone: 1-800-733-3000
Fax: 1-800-659-2436

Young Lionz

Young Lionz

by

C. J. Hudson

Acknowledgments

First of all, I have to give thanks to the Lord Almighty for even giving me the talent and skill to complete this novel and continue on my journey as an author. Without you, I am nothing but a speck of dust.

To my wife Margo, who has been forever patient and understanding. I love you and all the sacrifices you make for our family. You hold us down and life us up, and I appreciate you to no end!

To my sons, Deonte and Aaron. You young men have a great future ahead of you. Continue to strive and grow.

To my mother, Joanna Willis, who has instilled in me the never give up, never quit attitude that I have today. You taught me the value of hard work, and I am forever grateful.

To Urban Books and Carl Weber. Thank you for giving me a chance to showcase my talent to the world.

To N'Tyse, the super literary agent! Thank you for believing in me. You probably had quite a few authors to choose to represent, and I feel honored that you chose me.

To Tresssa Azarel Smallwood and Live Changing Books. You gave me my first book deal, and even when I branched out on my own, you continued to help and guide me. I truly appreciate all that you have done for me.

To Kwan Foye. What can I say, dawg? The things you have taught me about this business have been invaluable! You told me when I did something good and let me hear

Acknowledgments

about it when I was messing up. You will never know how much your mentoring and friendship has meant to me.

To Raynesha Pittman. Boy, do I ever appreciate you! You included me in a project at a time when I had pretty much lost my will to write! You lit a fire up under me, and I truly thank you for it!

Athea Cranford, my test reader. Words can't express how much I appreciate you taking time out of your busy schedule to read my work.

Last but not least, I would like to send a shout-out to the streets of Cleveland! Wade Park, St Clair, Superior, Hough! C-Town in the house!

Chapter 1

After kissing the Cleveland skyline for much of the day, the sun had finally decided to descend and leave what was left of the earth's twenty-four-hour loop to the moon and stars. That wouldn't have been so bad, had it not been for the dark clouds starting to roll in. They were followed by light thunder, which preceded a moderate drizzle.

The thumping sound on the top of Antwan's hood nearly drove him crazy. He and his friends Niko, Chris, Temp, and Bishop all sat in his 2006 Buick LeSabre, passing the blunt and waiting for the right time to spring into action. But one of them was having second thoughts about their intended heist. It wasn't that he was scared. There was something else on his mind. They had discussed this heist many times before, and now that the time was near for them to execute it, he was starting to get cold feet.

"What? Man, fuck that bullshit you talkin' 'bout! It ain't yo' fuckin' job that we putting in jeopardy. It's mine," Bishop shouted into the back seat. He was nervous enough and wasn't in the mood for Temp to be questioning his manhood.

"Man, please! Yo' ass only work part-time," Temp laughed.

Bishop worked at the convenience store on the corner of 153rd and Lakeshore. At 17, he was the youngest of his crew. He was the only one holding down a steady job. With both of his parents deceased, Bishop lived with his grand-mother. He attended school on a semi-regular basis and committed petty crimes. He never minded it before, but when his boys approached him about robbing his place of employment, he hesitated. It was only when his fellow hoodlums started questioning his heart and courage that he gave in and agreed. Now that the time had arrived, he was having serious second thoughts.

The fact that his job didn't pay much made no differ-ence to him, but he had a pretty good relationship with his boss, Mr. Hanley. It was Mr. Hanley who had offered him a job one day when he caught him stealing.

"Son, you don't have to steal for a living. If you need to keep a few dollars in your pocket, you can come and work for me, after school of course," the old man had told him.

Bishop had grown quite fond of Mr. Hanley, and the last thing he wanted was to hurt him in any way. He was now kicking himself in the ass for telling his crew about the stacks of $100 bills he'd seen in the safe. From the very minute he'd told them, they'd been riding him to get the combination to the safe. But even though Mr. Hanley liked Bishop, he didn't trust him enough to allow him to get close enough to see him turn the safe dial.

When Bishop reported to his crew that he couldn't get the combination, Temp came up with the idea to rob the place. At first, Bishop refused to go along with the plan, but when Temp started talking about going in the store with guns blazing, Bishop figured that the only way to ensure that Mr. Hanley didn't end up getting hurt was to submit to their plan. He still didn't want to do it, but at least if he was there, he could see to it that his boss and friend didn't get hurt.

But now that the moment of truth had arrived, Bishop just wanted to turn around and head for home.

"Yo, Bishop, let me holla at you for a second."

Without waiting for a response, Antwan got out of the car and waited for Bishop. When Bishop got out, the two of them walked a few feet away from the car in silence. Then without warning, Antwan grabbed Bishop by the shoulders and spun him around so that they were face-to-face. When Antwan was sure that he had his friend's undivided attention, he began to speak.

"Look, man. I know you got love for the old dude. I understand that he gave you a job and put some change in ya pocket. But we've been planning this shit for two weeks, dawg. And from the way you described it to us, it's gotta be twenty-five Gs in that safe. And to be honest with you, man, Temp has a point. That old muthafucka is makin' a ton of bread off the people in the neighborhood. But how much is he payin' you? Fuckin' seven dollars an hour? Man, that's a slap in the fuckin' face! They takin' advantage of you, man!"

"Man, I just don't want the old dude to get hurt. I mean, I do owe him—"

"First of all," Antwan said, cutting him off, "you don't owe that muthafucka shit! And second, man, ain't no-body gon' hurt old school. The most we gon' do is slap the shit outta him if he don't open that damn safe. And like I said, from what you told us," Antwan said as he pointed his index finger directly at Bishop's chest to let him know that he was just as involved as the rest of them, "it's gotta be mad loot up in there, son. You mean to tell me that you wouldn't slap that old muthafucka for five grand? Nigga, I'd slap yo' ass for five grand," Antwan said, laughing. "A'ight, playa, it's getting late in the day. What you gon' do? It's time to shit or get off the pot."

Bishop looked at his buddy and flashed a wicked grin. "Fuck it, bro. Let's go get this paper," he said.

***

"Nigga, stop acting like a bitch. You got the most important job of all," Temp said to Bishop.

Bishop had had an attitude ever since Antwan told him that he was going to be the getaway driver. Bishop would much rather be inside with the rest of them to, if nothing else, ensure that nothing happened to Mr. Hanley. Antwan, on the other hand, didn't want Bishop to inadvertently screw up the plan because he had love for the old dude.

At 8:50 p.m., the crew decided it was time to make their move. Since the store closed at nine, the place was pretty much empty, save for one half-drunken old man staggering out of the store with a fifth of Absolut in his hand. The parking lot was somewhat small, which would work to their advantage when it came time to make their getaway. They would only have to run about fifteen feet to where the car was parked.

With Antwan and Temp leading the way, they slid out of the car and made their way across the empty parking lot. Just before he got to the glass double doors, Antwan stopped. Leaning his head forward slightly, he peeked in and saw Mr. Hanley sweeping behind the counter. With his back turned and a broom in his hand, he had no idea what was in store for him. Before Mr. Hanley knew what was happening, Antwan had his .22 pressed against his head.

"A'ight, ol' man. Turn the fuck around. And get ready to check that muthafuckin' bread in. And don't try no slick shit, or I'm gonna have to put this heat to yo' old ass."

Mr. Hanley slowly turned around to face his robber. Had his hair not already been white, it would have surely turned that color once he stared down the barrel of the pistol Antwan was aiming at him.

"Okay, son. Take it easy. No one has to get hurt here," Mr. Hanley said, trying to remain calm.

While Antwan and Temp pushed Mr. Hanley toward the cash register, Chris and Niko watched the front door. Mr. Hanley nervously watched as Temp stuffed all the money into a black duffle bag held by Antwan. After he was done, Temp turned to Mr. Hanley and glared at him. The puzzled look on the old man's face incensed Temp.

"Ol' man, I know damn well this ain't all the money you got up in here. You betta run that shit here real quick or we gon' have a problem," he said, cocking his pistol.

"Ease up, dawg," Antwan said, trying to calm his hot-headed friend. "Look, ol' dude. We ain't got time for games. You think we don't know you got a safe around here somewhere? It would be in yo' best interest to take us to it and stop bullshittin'."

"I don't know what you're talking about. That's all the money I have in the—"

Crack!

Mr. Hanley never got a chance to finish his statement as Temp slammed the handle of his gun into his face.

"Now, let's try this again, muthafucka! Take us to the fuckin' safe," Temp screamed. Antwan looked over at Niko and Chris. He knew that at any moment someone could be trying to enter the store, so he had to think of something quick. The clicking sound of Temp's gun caused Antwan's head to snap back around.

"Pops, if you don't hurry up and take us to that safe, I swear on everything I love, I'ma put one in you," Temp warned.

"Yo, dawg, chill the fuck out," Antwan said.

"You," Antwan said, pointing at Niko. "Come over here for a second, man," Antwan ordered.

"What's up?" Niko asked.

Antwan whispered something into Niko's ear, then quickly walked back over to where Temp still had his gun trained on Mr. Hanley. Antwan then pulled out his gun and cocked it. He could see in the old man's eyes that he didn't want to die, so he decided to take advantage of that.

"A'ight, muthafucka, I'm through playin' with yo' ass! Either you take us to the safe right now, or I'ma put so much lead in yo' ass, Superman won't be able to see through you."

"Okay, man, just calm down," Mr. Hanley said, fearing for his life. The old man trembled as he led the robbers back to the safe, while Bishop patiently sat behind the wheel and played his part as the getaway driver.

Chapter 2

Eddie was so aroused that he almost busted a nut in his pants right then and there. After months of him begging, pleading, plotting, lying, and scheming, his girlfriend had finally given in and told him that she was going to give him the pussy. Eddie and Joy had been together for three months, and the closest she'd ever come to being sexual with him was letting him suck on one of her enormous tits. His friends thought he was an idiot. Some old heads labeled him a fool.

The moniker fit him well, seeing that the only time she wanted to be bothered with Eddie was when he was dishing out cash or taking her shopping. But tonight, as he listened to her talk dirty to him on his cell phone, Eddie felt like a king. He was on top of the world. But his royal fantasies were about to come to an abrupt end. Eddie had been so engrossed in the lightweight phone sex that Joy was providing, he never saw Temp creep up beside him. It was a mistake he would soon come to regret.

The fact that he was sitting on the safe and blocking the money only served to enrage Temp that much more. Eddie's gap-toothed smile disappeared in a flash as Temp cracked him square in the mouth. Teeth and blood flew from his mouth and landed onto the marble floor a few feet from the safe. Eddie's phone fell out of his hand and crashed to the floor as he instinctively reached for his mouth. Slightly dazed, he dropped to the floor.

"Get yo' bitch ass out the way," Temp yelled.

Antwan then kicked Eddie's phone into the wall, breaking it instantly. He wanted to make sure that whoever was on the other end of the phone could not hear what was going down.

"A'ight, pops. Before we go any further, take that muthafuckin' surveillance tape out of the recorder and give it here," Antwan ordered. "And before you tell a lie and say you ain't got one, I done already peeped the cameras in the corner out there."

Mr. Hanley muttered a curse under his breath. On his way to the recording machine, he walked past Niko. Because the ski masks hid their identities, Mr. Hanley couldn't see their faces, but to him, it looked like Niko was smirking behind his, which infuriated him. He briefly thought about trying to overpower the young thug and take his weapon, but being that he was in his early sixties, with a bad heart, Mr. Hanley knew that having good sense would have to prevail, so he kept walking. He glanced over at Eddie, who was sitting on the floor in a corner, shaking like a crap game. Mr. Hanley shook his head. *Fuckin' coward. Just because he's scared doesn't mean that he has to act scared.*

"Hurry the fuck up, Grady," Temp screamed at him.

Hearing the teenaged thug insult him gave Mr. Hanley more courage than it should have. He began to think about how he'd worked his fingers to the bone for the last twenty-five years on his previous job as a machinist just so that he could own his own business. He's always wanted to work for himself, and now that he'd become somewhat successful, these young punks, who had probably never worked a day in their lives, were ordering him to give up his earnings.

The room containing the surveillance equipment was rather small. It took an effort for all five bodies to fit comfortably inside. None of them were no more than five feet away from each other.

"Yo, man, I ain't gonna tell you again to hurry up," Temp warned.

"Go fuck ya'self, lowlife. Why don't you just go back to the gutter where you came from?" Mr. Hanley spat. He was scared shitless but wasn't going to give them the satisfaction of knowing it. It took all of one short step for Temp to be in his face.

"What? Who the fuck you think you talkin' to like that?" Temp yelled. Before the old man could respond, Temp punched him in the stomach and knocked the wind out of him.

Mr. Hanley went down like a ton of bricks. Temp drew back to hit him again, but Antwan grabbed his arm. "Ay yo, that's enough of that shit, man. We ain't got all night."

Antwan then proceeded to drag Mr. Hanley across the floor. He came to a halt right in front of the safe. "Open that shit up! Right now," Antwan said as he cocked his .38 snub-nose and pointed it directly at the store owner's head.

While holding his stomach with his left hand, Mr. Hanley reached for the safe dial with his right. He was still gasping for air when he clicked the last number. As soon as the safe popped open, Temp roughly pushed him to the floor. Antwan then walked over to the safe and started emptying the money into a black duffle bag. After the bag was filled, Temp put his gun to Mr. Hanley's temple.

"Old man, I'm gonna give you five seconds to run that tape, or you're gonna be the quietest muthafucka in church this Sunday, feel me?"

Still holding his stomach, Mr. Hanley limped over to a desk and opened a drawer. He pressed eject on the VCR and took out the tape. Temp rudely snatched it out of his hand.

"You two," Antwan said, pointing at Niko and Chris, "take old dude back out there with that other punk-ass nigga and tie both of them muthafuckas up."

Chris passed Niko the duct tape he'd been holding. It took Niko less than three minutes to bind and gag Eddie. Antwan smiled as he removed the last remaining stack of bills.

"You punks got what you came for. Now get the fuck outta my establishment!"

"Muthafucka, what the fuck you say to us?" Temp barked.

"You heard me! You got the money! Now go crawl back under your fuckin' rock!"

Niko and Chris started laughing hysterically.

"Ain't this a bitch?" Antwan asked in amazement. Even though they were robbing Mr. Hanley, he had to admire the old man's bravery and "take no shit" attitude.

"Whatever, old fart. Let's be out this bitch, y'all," Antwan said, laughing at the comments. As Antwan, Niko, and Chris headed for the back exit, Temp didn't budge.

"You know, you talkin' a gang of shit, ol' man."

"Temp, come on, man," Niko called out to him.

"Just get the fuck out, asshole!" Mr. Hanley spat.

That did it. In one swift motion, Temp pointed his gun at Mr. Hanley and fired. The other three jumped at the sound of gunfire erupting from the barrel. Mr. Hanley slumped down to the floor, holding his midsection. Blood seeped through his fingers and onto the floor. Mr. Hanley stared up at Temp with disbelieving eyes. He never once thought that the young thug would really pull the trigger. But now that he was looking into Temp's eyes, he suddenly realized that he'd made a big mistake. Temp's eyes had the look of death in them.

"Man, what the fuck you doin', bro?" Antwan's words seemed to snap Temp out of his satanic state. "Come on, man! We need to get the fuck outta here! Now!"

As the four of them ran out the back door, Eddie reached up and ripped the tape from his mouth. It hurt like hell, but he couldn't worry about that at the moment. Amid the confusion, Eddie had spotted a partially hammered-in nail on the floor that he'd used to tear the tape from his wrists. He quickly got up and ran to the front of the store. Throughout this whole ordeal, he'd wondered why no customers had come in the store. Now he knew why. The door had been locked, and the CLOSED sign had been hung up. Without a second to waste, Eddie dialed 911.

Meanwhile, as soon as the rest of his crew got into the car, Bishop peeled off down the street. He bent the corner so hard that Temp fell over on him. His gun, pack of Newports, and a blunt fell out of his pocket onto the driver's side floor. Temp reached down to pick up his items, but Bishop beat him to it. Temp snatched his things out of Bishop's hand.

"Man, just drive," he yelled at Bishop.

"And slow the fuck down before you get us knocked," added Antwan.

"Where the fuck we goin', Twan?" Bishop asked.

"We goin' to my crib."

After getting the rest of his crew settled in the basement, Antwan went into his bedroom and picked up the twenty sack of weed that was lying on his dresser. He looked over at his woman, Tangie, who was lying there snoring lightly. Antwan had been with Tangie a little over a year. Tangie was three years his senior, and the house they resided in belonged to her late grandmother. The grandmother had stepped in and raised Tangie when Tangie's mother, Evelyn, had gotten stabbed to death by a jealous wife.

Evelyn was a good woman who had gotten caught up with a married man. Since the man never wore a wedding ring and had allowed her to come over pretty much whenever she wanted, Evelyn assumed that he was single. That all changed when the wife came home from a business trip two days earlier than expected and caught the two of them in bed together. Evelyn had tried to explain to her that she didn't know the man was married, but she didn't believe Evelyn. Nor did she give a damn. Unable to convince the woman, Evelyn tried to surprise her and wrestle the switchblade away from her. But the woman was much stronger than anticipated.

Evelyn ended up getting stabbed twice in the neck. She remained in a coma and on life support for three weeks until she finally passed away. Tangie's grandmother then took her in and took care of her until a stroke sent her home to be with the Lord. She did, however, leave Tangie a trust fund that was to be given to her on her twenty-fifth birthday. That along with an insurance payout of $15,000 was enough to convince Antwan to wife her. She wasn't particularly attractive, but when Antwan saw her, all he saw were dollar signs, although over time he had come to care about her.

Tangie, who already had low self-esteem, became extra vulnerable when her grandmother died. She met Antwan at a bar one night while she was out trying to clear her mind. Antwan, horny and half drunk at the time, provided her with a shoulder to cry on. Tangie, like so many women with low self-esteem, spent her money like water, praying that Antwan would want to be bothered with her for more than one night. Antwan had just been kicked out of his parents' house and saw this as a golden opportunity for a quick come up. He moved in with her the same night and had been there ever since.

Antwan looked at the clock and noticed that it was only ten thirty. The way that Tangie was sleeping, if he didn't know any better, he would have thought that it was two in the morning. Antwan shrugged his shoulders and walked out of the bedroom. On his way to the basement, he stopped by the refrigerator and grabbed a six pack of beer. When he got back downstairs, he saw that Temp had already dumped all the money onto the table. Antwan's eyes lit up at the sight of the cold, hard cash lying on the table.

"Now, that's what the fuck I'm talkin' 'bout." Niko beamed as he rubbed his hands together. "A brother can eat good off this kind of bread. Feel me, dawg?" he asked, cutting his eyes toward Bishop.

From the time they'd left the scene, Bishop hadn't said a word. He didn't care about many people, but his boss was one of those he did like. Antwan had told him that everything went off without a hitch, but Bishop was skeptical. He didn't want to believe that Antwan would lie to him. He looked up to Antwan. He wanted so badly to pull out his cell phone and call the store. But a move like that would be considered soft, and the pack of wolves he ran with would definitely look down on him for it, so he decided that he would do it when he went to the bathroom.

"Let me get one of them cold ones, my dude," Temp said, reaching for a beer. After drinking the beverage in ten seconds flat, Temp opened his mouth and let out a loud belch. He then frowned and grabbed his stomach.

"The fuck wrong with you, dawg, pregnant?" laughed Antwan.

Temp gave his friend the finger, set his gun on the edge of the table, and bolted for the bathroom. When Antwan sat down, he bumped the table, causing the gun to fall off onto the floor.

"Damn, man, what the fuck!" Chris yelled.

The rest of the crew jumped as they anticipated the gun going off and shooting one of them. After staring in the direction of the bathroom for a few seconds, they all looked at each other and shook their heads.

"Man, that fool careless as hell! You need to talk to that muthafucka," Niko huffed.

Bishop reached down and picked up Temp's gun. After setting it back on the table, he, along with the rest of the crew, started counting the stolen money. When they were halfway done, Temp came out of the bathroom, rubbing his stomach.

"Damn, nigga, did you just funk up my bathroom?" Antwan wrinkled up his nose and started fanning in front of it.

"Sorry, dawg. It musta been some shit I ate."

"Nah, my dude, that's just yo' rotten-ass guts," Niko joked.

As the crew continued to count the money, Bishop reached for a beer. After taking a few sips of it, he seemed to mellow out a little. Going to the bathroom to call the store seemed to drift from his mind.

"It's about time you stopped actin' like a bitch," Temp teased him.

"Man, fuck you! And get this piece-of-shit-ass gun off the damn table. I thought yo' ass had better sense than to leave it sittin' here like this, but I see that yo' ignorant ass don't know no betta."

Chris and Niko both snickered at the comment while Temp's face turned beet red. He could dish it out with the best of them. His problem was when he had to take it. Antwan, seeing the anger on his friend's face, decided to nip this shit in the bud real quick.

"Temp, don't even look like that, man. You started fuckin' with him first, so don't try to get all mad and shit now."

Temp slowly dug in his pocket and pulled out a blunt. After inserting the ganja stick between his lips, lighting it, and taking a long puff, he smiled and passed it to Bishop. Bishop took the smile as a friendly gesture. Antwan knew better. He knew Temp better than anyone else in the crew, and his gut instinct told him that Temp was thinking about how he would feel when he found out that his boss had been shot.

"Yo, Chris, roll something up. That one blunt that Temp and Bishop over there babysittin' ain't gon' be enough for all of us," Antwan said as he threw the sack of weed to him.

The crew continued to smoke weed, bullshit with each other, and count money deep into the night. When it was all said and done, the crew had clipped off close to thirty grand from the store. Each one of the youngsters smiled and rubbed their hands greedily as the money was divided up equally.

"Okay, now that we done took care of the business, somebody need to tell me what went on in there," Bishop said.

Niko and Chris both looked at Temp, while Antwan and Temp stared at each other.

"Well?" he asked again.

"Dude, stop fucking worrying. That shit went down smooth as butter," Antwan lied.

"So, Mr. Hanley's okay? He didn't try to resist, did he?" Bishop asked, expressing legitimate concern.

"Man, ain't nothing wrong with that muthafucka," Temp yelled.

"Muthafucka, I wasn't asking you," Bishop yelled.

"Bishop, he's okay, man," Antwan said, praying that he was telling the truth.

After that, Antwan dropped each one of them at home.

Chapter 3

"Yo, man, why y'all going in so early?" Niko asked. As usual, he was stalling, but his friends never picked up on his reluctance to go into his own home.

"Early? Man, it's two o' clock in the muthafuckin' mornin'! The fuck you on, son?" Bishop asked.

"Yeah, man. You pull this same shit every time Twan drops us off," Chris concurred.

"The fuck you scared to go in yo' house for? The rats raping yo' ass or somethin'?" Everyone in the car cracked up laughing at Chris's joke.

"You know what? Fuck y'all then," Niko said as he got out of the car and slammed the door. Once inside, Niko just shook his head. The farther he got inside, the harder the smell of nicotine attacked his nose. Before he could make a right and head upstairs to his bedroom, he heard his mother spring off the couch.

"Where the fuck you . . . Oh, it's just yo' li'l crumb-snatchin' ass," his mother berated him. She was obviously disappointed that it was her son instead of her no-good, womanizing boyfriend, James.

"Yo, ma, you okay?" he asked, ignoring her contempt for him.

"The fuck you mean, am I okay? Yeah, I'm okay, and don't start askin' me no stupid-ass questions! My business is my business, so stay the fuck out of it!"

Niko watched as his mother stomped back into the living room and fell back onto the couch. It was hard for him to tell from his angle, but he could have sworn that he saw her eyes glistening. It pissed Niko off to see his mother in such pain. Although she was abusive and very cruel at times, he loved his mother just the same.

Doris Wallace was hopelessly in love with James. They'd been together since Niko was 10 years old. When they first met, Niko was away at summer camp. Doris thought that it would be a good idea for him to be around other kids while he coped with the death of his biological father, Curtis. After dating James for only one week, she figured she'd give up the good-good and capture James's heart. But in the process of giving herself to him, Doris got sprung. After only two weeks, she was madly in love.

She started dropping subtle hints about wanting to get married and start a family. She never seemed to notice that whenever she would bring up kids, James would slyly change the subject. Doris never once even brought up Niko. Truth be told, him being at summer camp was a break for her. When she finally did decide to tell James about her son, she made the mistake of introducing him personally instead of telling James that she had a son beforehand. James was so angry he went ballistic. He accused Doris of trying to trap him and threatened to leave her.

Doris freaked out. No man had ever made her feel the way James had, and she would be damned if she was going to let that slip away. James confessed to her that he was living with a woman who treated him like a king, and he wasn't going to leave that for something equal or less. James then told Doris that the woman he was with had required him to keep a job, but he was tired of being treated like a slave and like shit by racist employers. If they were going to be together, then she would have to take care of him for a little while.

That little while turned into seven years as Doris fell for James's bullshit hook, line, and sinker. She had no way of knowing that James was lying through his teeth. James did live with another woman. But the woman was his sister, who had given him three months to find a job or vacate the premises. After James moved in, Doris brought up marriage one more time. James left and stayed gone for a week, using money that he'd stolen from Doris to camp out at a hotel. Doris missed him so much that, upon his return, she pretty much became his slave, fearing that if she angered him again, he would leave for good next time. James made it clear that he didn't want to get married or have any kids with Doris, and he wasn't at all thrilled that she already had a child.

As the years went by, the bond that Doris was hoping would form between James and Niko never materialized. In fact, it was just the opposite. The two men in Doris's life soon grew to despise each other. They barely spoke, and whenever Doris wanted to spend any time with her son, James took it as a snub and disappeared for a day or so.

Doris then started to blame the troubled relationship on Niko and commenced beating him whenever James hurt her. Niko sighed. He knew it was just a matter of time before his mother found something to get upset about and take out on him. Slowly he trudged up the steps and dragged himself into his bedroom. After hiding his gun in his closet, he lay down on his bed. He was so tired from running around with his boys that he passed out without even taking his clothes off.

Shortly thereafter, he was awakened by his mother slinging open the door and barging into his room. "Didn't I tell yo' ass to go to the store and get some fuckin' bread today, Niko? Yo' little ass ain't doing shit in school! You might as well make yo'self useful around here!"

"But, Ma, you told—"

"Oh, so now you talkin' back to me, muthafucka? You tryin'a be a smart ass?"

Doris had her hand behind her back. Niko didn't need three guesses to know what lingered behind her. "Muthafucka, answer me," she screamed, raising an extension cord high above her head.

Rage and furry combined in her eyes as she brought the weapon down across Niko's body. Niko covered up as best he could. He took the blanket that was on his bed and quickly wrapped himself up in it, but it made no difference. The wallop from the extension cord cut through it with ease. The cord hit the blanket with a resounding thud. Niko screamed at the top of his lungs. He had learned a long time ago that the quieter he was during the beatings, the longer they would last. Hearing her son yell out in agony gave Doris a twisted sense of pleasure.

When she was good and worn out from beating him, she went back downstairs and waited for James. Niko got up and went down the hall to the bathroom. On his way back, he heard his mother crying. As badly as he wanted to go and check on her, he knew from experience that that would have been a mistake. Instead, Niko just shook his head, went back into his room, and fell asleep.

Chris walked down the hallway to his bedroom, but instead of retiring for the night, he made a sharp left and headed for the door directly across from his. He closed his eyes and slowly walked toward it. Momentarily he hesitated, as he stood just a few inches from the door. After getting up his nerve, he proceeded to open the door and walk in. With tears threatening to break free from his eyes, Chris sat down beside his baby sister and stroked her hair. For as hard as he was on the street,

Chris went through great lengths to nurture his mother and sister. The smile that appeared on her face tugged at his heartstrings. His steely resolve cracked as she reached out and touched his arm.

"Hey, big brother," she said, opening her eyes.

"Shit, sis, I thought you was asleep."

"Now you know I can't go to sleep until you get home."

"Did you take yo' medicine today?"

"Yeah, but it was my last dose."

Chris looked into his sister's light gray eyes and saw that she seemed to be worried about when she would be able to get her meds. Although Chris had never let her go without, Tracy was always concerned that she would not get them. His mother, Vivian, was doing the best she could with her disability check, but she had other things to pay for, such as food and rent. It didn't help that Chris's sorry-ass father didn't have the guts to stick it out with his mother and help her take care of their sick child.

Apparently, the lure of a 21-year-old hood rat with a killer body was too much of a temptation for him to resist. After his father walked out on them, Chris came home one day and found his mother curled up in her bed, crying like a newborn baby. She was cradling his sister in her arms, and she too had tears flowing down her cheeks. From that day forward, Chris vowed that no matter what he had to do, he would take care of them both until his dying day. He wasn't going to let his family suffer because his father wasn't shit.

"Don't worry 'bout it, sis. You gonna get yo' meds."

Chris then kissed his sister on the forehead and headed for the door. No sooner had he walked through it did he turn and see his mother walking down the hallway. Vivian Brown walked slightly slumped over due to the herniated disk in her back. Years of bending over at a stamping plant had taken its toll on her.

"I see you finally decided to come home, son."

Vivian hated that her 17-year-old son had decided to drop out of school and go to work in order to see to it that she and her daughter had a decent life. But with the small amount of money disability was paying her and the large amount of bills she'd accumulated over the years, she had little to no choice but to accept it. Plus Chris had made it clear that he was going to get a job and do his part, period. Of course, there was no legitimate employment. The only job that Chris had was terrorizing the streets and strong-arming citizens out of their hard-earned money.

Vivian never questioned where he worked or how much he made. She was too concerned about her daughter to worry about anything else. Besides, she thought, Chris would be 18 in a few short months and he would just drop out of school anyway.

"How is she?" Vivian asked when she got close enough to Chris smell him.

"She's doing okay. She told me that she was out of meds, though."

Vivian dropped her head and nodded. "Yeah, she is. And I don't have a drop of money. I don't know what we're going to do either, chile."

"Mama, did you forget I got a job?"

With overwhelming pride, Chris reached into his pocket and pulled out his portion of the money he'd earned from the robbery. Vivian's eyes almost popped out of her head as she eyed the bankroll her son was holding. Her smile suddenly turned to a frown as she cocked her head to the side.

"Chris, you didn't do anything illegal to get this money, did you?"

"Huh? Why would you ask me something like that, ma?"

Vivian looked at the money and then back up at Chris. "Because, son, that ain't chump change you got in your hands."

"Ah, ma, I—"

Vivian threw up her hands to stop his words. "Look, Chris, I'm not accusing you of anything. But remember this: if you go to jail for doing somethin' bad, then me and Tracy don't have anyone." She stared at him for a few seconds to let the severity of her words sink in. "The medicine costs four hundred dollars."

Chris's mouth fell open. "Four hundred dollars? But we ain't been paying but sixty dollars for it."

"I know. But the insurance no longer covers the medication. Said something about it's too expensive for them," she said as she laughed mockingly.

"Ain't that 'bout a bitch?" Chris mumbled under his breath.

"Boy, what did you say?"

"I said, 'Ain't that a trip,'" he lied.

"Uh-huh."

Chris then peeled off $1,500 and handed it to his mother. "That should take care o' the rent, the food, and Tracy's medicine."

Vivian took the money and stuffed it inside the pocket of her robe. She looked at her son and smiled. "Thank you, Chris. I knew I could count on you."

After Chris and his mother embraced, he watched her go into the bedroom to be with his sister. With mixed feelings, he went into his bedroom and walked over to the window. It made him feel good to be able to do things for his family.

He quickly checked to make sure that his mother wasn't coming, reached into his pocket, and pulled out a blunt that he'd snuck out of Antwan's house. Quietly opening the window, he lit it and took a long puff. He took another couple of puffs, then blew the smoke out of the window and turned in for the night.

Chapter 4

Bishop woke up to the sound of his sister, Carla, and her boyfriend, Jason, arguing. That Jason even had the guts to say anything back to her at all was surprising. Carla treated Jason like shit. She took most of if not all of his money, drove his car whenever she wanted to, and talked to other men right under his nose. Bishop despised Jason for being such a wimp. He didn't know if Jason was afraid to stand up to his sister because he was there, or if it was because he was madly in love with her.

Either way, every time Bishop looked at him, he saw SUCKER stamped across his forehead. Bishop looked at the clock and saw that it was one in the afternoon. His head felt like someone had hit him with a sledgehammer. He didn't drink beer that much, but because the crew was celebrating their big come up, he drank more than he normally would. Bishop was now living with his sister because of a huge fight that he'd gotten into with his mother.

At the end of the argument, she made it clear to Bishop that if he was going to live under her roof, then he would have to abide by her rules. Bishop walked out, slammed the door, and went straight to his older sister's house. Carla had been on her own for a few years by that time, and since she and her mother had never gotten along, she saw letting her little brother stay there as the perfect way to irk the hell out of her.

Carla didn't have a lot of rules for Bishop to follow. As a matter of fact, the only hard rule that she had for him was for him to stay out of her business. She only charged him $100 a month for rent and told him that he had to buy his own food. She didn't care where he got the money from. She just wanted to get paid when the rent was due. Every now and then, Carla would go up to the store where he worked during his shift and ask him to turn his head so she could steal a few things. Although Bishop liked his boss, the last thing he wanted was to piss his sister off and get kicked out of the house. She didn't even care if he went to school. The only thing she was accomplishing by letting him stay there was hurting her mother, in which she took great pride.

Bishop stumbled out of bed and staggered down the hall into the bathroom. When Carla spotted him, she called out to her baby brother.

"Yo, bruh. Settle this argument between me and this fool."

Bishop hated when she did this. It was okay for him to get in her business when she felt she was right, but any other time was off-limits.

"Yo, why the fuck you gotta always be disrespectin' me, Carla? How you gon' talk to me like that in front of yo' brother?"

"Muthafucka, if you don't like it, you can take yo' ass on."

Jason took a deep breath and shook his head.

"Yo, sis, you told me to stay out o' yo' business, remember? That was the one rule you gave me when you let me move in here."

Before Carla could say anything, Bishop disappeared into the bathroom. He giggled to himself as he thought about the look on Jason's face when Carla basically told him if he didn't like it, he could get to stepping. After taking a piss, he walked back out of the bathroom and saw that his sister was staring at the bathroom door. Bishop tried to hurry up and slide back into his room, but Carla ran and blocked him.

"Bishop, settle this fuckin' argument. And I don't wanna hear that bullshit about a rule I made. I make the rules, which means I can break them muthafuckas."

Carla stood there defiantly with her hands on her hips. She was tall and lean. Her golden brown hair hung just above the top of her ears and was curled under. She was light in color with fierce light brown eyes.

"Is it or is it not okay for a man to cook for his woman?"

"Shit, I don't know, sis, I guess." Bishop was saying what he thought his sister wanted to hear. All he wanted to do was get back to his room and lie down a little longer.

"That's what the fuck I told this bonehead muthafucka!"

Bishop didn't know why they were talking about something like that. All they ever did was eat out anyway. Neither one of them knew their way around the kitchen that well. As the two of them continued to argue, Bishop went into his bedroom and closed the door. He had almost drifted off to sleep when his sister burst through the door.

"Oh, I almost forgot to tell you. Eddie's punk ass called late last night. I started to cuss that muthafucka out until I heard him crying like a bitch over the phone."

A bad feeling erupted in Bishop's gut. He leaped off his bed and grabbed his cell phone. He wasted no time calling his job. The phone rang four times before someone answered it.

"Hello?" a sweet-voiced honey said on the other end.

"Hey, Wendy, is Mr. Hanley in today?" Wendy was the store's assistant manager. She ran the place on the days Mr. Hanley wasn't working.

"Boy, where the hell you been? Eddie said he tried to call you three times last night and couldn't reach you!"

"I had a few things to do last night."

"Well, while you was out doin' whateva the fuck you was doin', Mr. Hanley was shot!"

"What? The fuck you mean he was shot?" Bishop immediately got heated. Antwan had lied to him. "Fuck! Ay yo, is he all right?"

"Nah, he ain't all right, Bishop. He's in critical condition. They sayin' he might not make it."

Bishop fell back down to the bed. Feelings of betrayal crept into his soul. Antwan had told him that his boss wouldn't be hurt, but now he found out that Mr. Hanley was in a hospital bed fighting for his life. Bishop jumped up and threw on his clothes. After getting dressed, he ran downstairs and bolted out the door.

Antwan and Temp sat on Antwan's front steps sharing a blunt. Temp was still hyped up about the amount of money they'd taken from the safe. At least three times, he took a wad of money out of his pocket and thumbed through it. It wasn't like he'd never been around a few thousand dollars before. Temp just always got a thrill holding large sums of cash in his hand. That was just the way Temp was.

"Man, why the fuck you keep flashing that bread like that? You tryin'a get us knocked or somethin'?"

"Man, I don't see no police 'round here," Temp said, looking from one end of the street to the other. "Damn, don't be so scary, my G."

Antwan stared at his comrade for a few seconds. During that time, he realized that Niko was right. Temp was careless, and if he didn't speak on it, it would not only come back to haunt him but the entire crew as well.

"Let me tell you somethin', homie," Antwan started off. "My heart ain't neva pumped Kool-Aid, so don't even come at me with that sucka shit. I ain't scary worth a fuck. All the dirt we done rolled in together, you oughta know that shit by now."

"Twan, I'm just sayin', man. We got all this loot, and you expect a nigga to just sit on this shit? Man, I got big plans for my ends, homie, starting with coppin' me a weed package so I can flip that bitch."

"What? Man, yo' baby-makin' ass need to be puttin' some of that money back so you can pay for them abortions. Plus we really need to lay low for a few days, man. The last thing we need to do is to start splurgin' and shit. With that dummy move you pulled last night, the cops gon' be all over this shit."

"What dummy move?" Temp asked as if he really didn't know.

"Nigga, I'm talkin' 'bout that dumb-ass move you pulled when you popped that ol' dude, that's what."

"Man, fuck that ol' ancient-ass muthafucka. He shouldn'ta been talkin' shit."

Antwan just looked at his friend and shook his head. "And what about Bishop?"

"What about him?"

"Man, I gave him my word that we wasn't gon' hurt the ol' dude."

"I don't know why the fuck you told him some shit like that. You know as well as I do, whenever you pull a caper, shit like that can happen."

"Temp! The muthafucka wasn't even strapped, man!"

Antwan was growing increasingly irritated with Temp. The two of them had done more dirt together than worms. But Temp's carefree attitude was starting to weigh on him. Antwan had a major moneymaking scheme up his sleeve. His plan was to bring his four comrades along for the ride so they could all make some dough, but he had to first decide if Temp was going to be an asset or a liability.

"Dude, you really need to—" Before Antwan could finish his sentence, Bishop came storming across the street.

"The fuck wrong with his ass?" Temp asked when he saw the look on Bishop's face. Antwan mean mugged Temp as he got up to go and meet Bishop in the front yard. Temp shrugged his shoulders and took the last hit off the blunt before flicking it over the banister.

"Yo, li'l homie, I know what you about to say, but the ol' dude reached for somethin' and I had to plug him," Antwan lied. "It was either him or me, dawg, and I would much rather it be him."

Antwan knew that if he'd told Bishop that Temp was the trigger man, the two of them would have had a major falling out. He also knew that Bishop looked up to him, so it would be much easier for Bishop to forgive him about the incident.

"Twan, how come you ain't tell me this shit last night, man? Why the fuck you lie to me, fam?"

"'Cause, my dude, I didn't want you getting all bent outta shape about the shit, dawg. But like I said, he reached. So I had no choice."

Bishop looked up on the porch at Temp, who was busy rolling another blunt. Then he looked into Antwan's eyes in search of the truth. But that maneuver was useless, and Bishop knew it. Antwan could lie to Jesus Christ and not blink. "But I don't think he even owns a gun, man."

"What makes you say that?"

"'Cause, man, Mr. Hanley doesn't even like guns."

"Man, you believe that shit? That muthafucka probably got more guns than he know what to do with. How many muthafuckas in this neighborhood ain't got a strap? Plus he owns a store. Man, you think he got hisself naked out there like that in this neighborhood? Come on, young blood. Wake up and smell the weed."

Bishop thought about it for a second. Antwan was making sense. No one in their right mind would own a business in this area without some form of protection.

"Man, fuck it. What's done is done, dude. Is the ol' man okay?"

Bishop then cocked his head and looked at Antwan. He thought it was weird that he would ask about Mr. Hanley's condition after saying that Mr. Hanley had tried to fire on him. Before he could form another thought, his cell phone rang. After answering it and hearing Eddie's voice on the other end, Bishop listened intently. A large smile came across his face.

"A'ight cool. Thanks for the update," he said. Bishop then hung up and proceeded to answer Antwan's question. "That was Eddie's punk ass. He said that Mr. Hanley has been upgraded to stable condition."

"Good! Now can y'all stop sweating that bullshit?" Temp yelled from the porch. Neither Antwan nor Bishop knew that he was even listening. "Now come on up here, and let ya boy Temp put y'all up on another moneymaker."

Antwan and Bishop looked at each other, walked up on the porch, and took turns hitting the blunt that Temp had rolled while they listened to his master plan.

Chapter 5

Niko heard the rumblings from his inside his room but didn't budge. The scene was not new to him. Time and time again, he'd heard his mother and James arguing over stupid shit. Well, it was stupid to him. Twice a week, his mother would hit James with the usual barrage of questions. "Where you been?" "How come you didn't call?" "What bitch you out there fuckin' around wit?" To him, the solution was simple: kick James's cheating ass out and get on with your life. Why his mother chose to put up with a man who obviously didn't give a shit about her was beyond him.

Niko may have been young, but he was nowhere near naive or stupid. He knew for a fact that James was fucking around on his mother. One day while he was ditching school with a shorty, he ran into James at the movies with a thick, dark-skinned chick on his arm. The girl was young enough to be Niko's sister and James's daughter. Niko's first thought was to hop on his jack and call his mother. Then he came to his senses. From previous experience, Niko knew that instead of getting mad at her no-good man, his mother would have turned her anger toward him. "Why the fuck you ain't in school?" she would have said, as if she really gave a damn. Niko had long since told himself that as long as James didn't hit his mother, he was going to stay out of it. But the minute he touched her in a harmful kind of way, it was going to be on and popping.

Niko pulled the covers back over his head. He wasn't in the mood to hear a bunch of nonsense. He had no idea what time it was. All he knew was that he wanted to get some more sleep.

He had almost drifted back to sleep when his door burst open. Niko looked up just in time to see James coming at him with a lead pipe. His mother was right behind him, waving her belt.

"Muthafucka, did you go in my fuckin' wallet?" he screamed.

"What? Man, what the hell you talkin' 'bout? Ain't nobody gotta steal shit from yo' broke ass!"

Before James could even swing the pipe, Doris ran around him and started beating Niko with her belt. "Ma, what the hell you doin'?"

"Boy, don't talk to your fuckin' mother like that," James screamed. Without saying another word, James brought the pipe down across Niko's knee.

Niko screamed in pain. Instinct caused him to roll out of bed and onto the floor. James then brought the pipe down once again, narrowly missing his leg a second time.

"Hey, muthafucka, you was just supposed to scare him with that damn pipe, not assault my fuckin' child," Doris yelled.

For her words, she received a backhanded slap to the mouth. Doris fell to the floor, bleeding profusely. James raised his hand to hit Niko again, but Doris grabbed his leg. Although this was a fucked-up situation to be in, Niko never loved his mother more than at this very moment. She had finally stepped up and remembered that her child was more important than a piece of dick.

"Run, Niko baby! Get the fuck outta here," his mother screamed with tears coming down her eyes.

"Oh, you want some too, bitch?"

James then turned his vengeance on Doris. Violently, he swung the pipe toward her head. Doris threw her arm up at the last instant and blocked the blow from crushing her skull. But in doing so, the pipe shattered three bones in her wrist. The pain was excruciating. Her face twisted into a mask of anguish as her high-pitched screams nearly shattered the windows. Her body began to shake uncontrollably, as if she were going into convulsions. Tears ran down her face and crashed onto the floor. With his knee aching and his temper flaring, the only thing that Niko could think about was making it to his closet to get his heater.

Chris and his mother walked into Rite Aid and made their way back to the pharmacy. Chris looked at the smile on his mother's face. It made him feel good to be able to put a look like that on his mom's grill. Just as quickly, the smile faded as he saw some locals that he and Niko had gotten into it with a few weeks ago. Not wanting them to see him with his mother, Niko tried to think of an excuse to get away from her. The last thing he wanted was for his mother to get caught up in a beef and get hurt because of his actions.

"Yo, ma, I'll be back in a minute. I gotta go use the bathroom," he said as he pulled out a knot of cash and passed it to her. Before she could speak, he was gone. Chris hated that he had to duck down from his enemies, but there was no way he was going to risk the safety of his mother.

He quickly ducked into the bathroom and held the door ajar. He held his breath when he saw the troublemaking thugs walk past his mother. He became nervous when they stopped and eyeballed her.

Quick as a flash, Chris pulled out the pistol he'd stashed in his waistband. He'd already made his mind up that if one of them even looked at his mother cross-eyed, he was going to put a couple of hot ones in them. Just as he was about to step out of the restroom and confront his two adversaries, one of their cell phones rang. He couldn't tell what the dude was saying, but after his conversation, he clamped his phone shut, and the two of them hurried out of the store. Chris breathed a sigh of relief. Not because he was afraid, but because he couldn't bear to think that something may have happened to his mother. He quickly stuffed his gun back into his waistband, pulled his white oversized T-shirt over it, and walked out of the bathroom. He was just about to tell his mother that he was back when his cell phone rang.

"What up," he said when he saw that it was Antwan on the other end.

"Yo, what up, partna? I'm 'bout to send Bishop to come pick you up. We got some shit to discuss."

"Gimme about thirty though. I'm at the store with my moms."

"A'ight, dawg. Hey, call Niko and let him know about the meeting."

"A'ight, I got you," Chris agreed. "Peace." Chris didn't know what Antwan wanted, but he hoped that it had something to do with making money.

With great effort and pain, Niko continued to crawl toward the closet. He didn't know if his kneecap had been shattered, but it sure as hell felt like it. Sick laughter filler the air as he made his way to the closet. If he could just get there, he would have a good chance of saving his mother from serious harm, but with every inch he moved, his knee felt like it was being ripped from the socket.

He looked back just in time to see James lift his mother up by her collar and backhand her to the floor. Seeing his mother's blood fly from her nose gave him an extra shot of adrenaline. He pulled open the door from the bottom and reached to the right. After taking the lid off the box that contained his pistol, he reached in and yanked it out. He turned around just in time to feel the bones in his hand crack behind the force of James's lead pipe, causing the gun to fall harmlessly to the floor. Niko was in so much pain it never even occurred to him to pick up the gun with his other hand.

Helplessly, Niko looked up to see James lifting his pipe to deliver one final blow. As the weapon seemed to travel downward in slow motion, Niko started thinking about his mother. He wondered what would happen to her without him being around to protect her from this monster.

Just as the fatal blow connected with his skull, Niko sat straight up in his bed. He quickly scanned his room to spot intruders. He jumped at the sound of the cordless phone ringing. Ever so slowly, Niko started to regain his bearings. He took a deep breath and relaxed when he saw that it was all a dream. He jumped slightly at the sound of his Lil Wayne ring tone. Ignoring the still-ringing house phone, Niko reached past it and grabbed his cell.

"Hello?" he answered sleepily.

"Damn, bro, you still asleep?" Chris asked. "It's damn near three o' clock in the afternoon."

"And? The fuck that gotta do with me gettin' some Z's?"

"Whateva fool. You need to get the fuck up. Me and Bishop on our way to pick yo' ass up. Antwan and Temp got another plan to come up on some more bread."

"That's what's up," the money-hungry Niko responded. "I'll be ready when y'all get here."

After ending the call, Niko looked around cautiously. The dream had seemed so real, he had to check to make sure that James wasn't hiding in the room. He glanced down and examined his hand to make sure that it was still intact.

"Damn," he said as he got up and went to the bathroom to get washed up. Still not convinced, he looked over his shoulder a couple of times before entering the bathroom. After coming out, he threw on an oversized pair of sagging jeans and a wife beater. He didn't feel like brushing his hair, so he left his doo rag on. As he walked through the hallway, he passed the living room. James was sitting on the couch with his legs propped up on the coffee table. His shabby beard and blotchy skin had Niko wondering what his mother saw in him. Their eyes met in a defiant stare as Niko refused to be intimidated by the older James.

"If you lookin' for yo' mama, she ain't here, young blood. She went to the store," James said, breaking the silence. Niko gave him a sinister sneer as he headed for the door.

"How come you ain't in school today, young blood?" James asked.

"The same reason yo' ass ain't at work, ol' school," Niko shot back.

Niko, Chris, and Bishop pulled into the parking lot of the Arabian store on the corner of Holmes and St. Clair. It was late afternoon, and the crew was about ready to get their drink on. The Arabian store wasn't a conventional liquor store, but they did have a license. They also appealed to the masses because they stayed open until ten on weeknights and twelve on weekends. It was a popular spot for underaged drinkers. All they had to do was hit the cashier off with a little extra bread and they would get served alcohol until they couldn't stand up straight. Twice, the ATF had tried to send in undercover agents posing as buyers, but both attempts failed.

Neither Bishop nor anyone else in the crew had any problem copping the booze. They were regulars at the spot. It also didn't hurt that they were heavy tippers. Bishop picked up a fifth of Absolut, a fifth of Seagrams, a gallon of orange juice, and some Styrofoam cups, and walked to the counter. He nodded at the cashier as he placed his items on the counter. The cashier, Raj, smiled as he put the items in a bag.

"Raj, my dude, what's the good word?"

"You tell me," Raj said in his Arabian accent.

"I can do better than tell you. I can show you," he said, dropping a $20 bill into a glass jar sitting on top of the counter.

Because Bishop was a regular, Raj knew that he wasn't ATF. But in order for any other teenager to buy liquor, they had to know the procedure, which was to put $10 or more into the tip jar. That was the cashier's fee for illegally selling liquor to minors. If they wanted to drink, they would have to pay for it. They would also have to come in with someone Raj knew the first time they wanted to buy alcohol. That way, he would feel comfortable selling to them the next time they came in alone.

On the way to Antwan's house, Chris told his partners about the two dudes in Rite Aid.

"Yo, what up then, son? Let's go see about them bitch-ass niggas," Niko suggested.

"Man, let's just see what Antwan talkin' 'bout first. Shit, my rent is due. And with my boss being in the hospital and shit, I need this bread."

Niko and Chris looked at each other.

"Yeah, muthafuckas, I know Antwan popped my boss."

"Huh?" Niko said, confused.

"Man, come off that bullshit! I already know," Bishop said as he pulled into Antwan's driveway.

Niko stared at Bishop for a couple of seconds, then turned his head and looked out of the window. After Bishop parked, all three of them gazed up on the porch. Antwan's girl Tangie was sitting there getting blazed with her best friend, Veronica.

Veronica was as thick as fog on the lake. Niko's dick got hard as she wrapped her succulent lips around the blunt and inhaled. Word around the hood had it that she loved to mess around with young boys, but Antwan and his crew couldn't tell. All she did when she came around was throw them shade and act like she was above giving any of them the time of day. Antwan never tried. He was a firm believer of "never shit where you sleep." Besides, he had plenty of other side bitches. Niko had a slight crush on her, although he denied it ferociously. Bishop looked slightly confused. Tangie hadn't been on the porch when he left to go pick up Chris and Niko.

"Yo, what's up, Tangie? Where the fuck yo' man go?"

"Them niggas in the basement. I guess Temp had a notion to lose his money."

The three of them walked past Veronica and Tangie and into the house. Neither one of them wanted to speak to Veronica because they didn't want to seem like they were sweating her in front of the others. Veronica, wearing a short denim skirt and black high heels, uncrossed her right leg and then crossed her left. She snickered as Niko almost walked into the door trying to catch a peek of the sunshine that was between her legs.

She said, "Yo, Bishop, I'ma be leavin' in a minute, so don't stray too far 'cause I'm gonna need you to move the car."

"Yeah, whateva," Bishop said. He kept walking toward the basement and didn't even turn around. The crew never brought it up, but they knew why Bishop was tight with Veronica. He'd run into her at the store one day and tried to crack for some ass. Veronica laughed his ass out of the store, telling him that he was too young and that his bread wasn't long enough to get with a thoroughbred bitch like her. Bishop had been tight at her ever since.

"Come on, boo, don't be like that," she called out before he disappeared down the steps. Chris looked at Niko and shook his head.

"The fuck you shakin' yo' head for, nigga?"

"'Cause, man, yo' ass be killin' me, actin' like you ain't sweet on that bitch."

"Muthafucka, please. Ain't a bitch been born can capture my blood pumper, fam."

From the top of the stairwell to the bottom, dice could be heard dancing across the floor. In true G fashion, Temp was down on the floor, rattling the ivories in his right hand.

"Yo, what's the point?" Bishop asked.

"Eight," Antwan said as he watched Temp slide nine across the floor.

"Let me get some o' that action, son," Bishop said.

Bishop set down the bag of alcohol, cups, and orange juice and pulled out his money as Temp threw a $50 bill down in front of him.

"Damn, y'all high rollin' today," Niko observed as he reached into his pocket.

"You damn right," Temp bellowed as he threw his point and picked up his cash.

"Fuck! Ain't this a bitch?" Bishop complained. His money hadn't been on the floor for more than thirty seconds before it was lost. Temp couldn't help but brag after that.

"I keep tellin' y'all muthafuckas, I ain't new to this. I'm true to this. Which one of you niggas gon' be the next contestant on *The Money Is Lost?*"

The other four looked at each other skeptically. They all knew from experience that when Temp got hot, he could literally stay on the dice for an hour straight.

"Fuck it," Niko finally said. "I got you faded. What the fuck you shootin', fam?"

Feeling himself because of his previous success, Temp crumpled up a $100 bill and tossed it onto the floor. "Catch that shit, dawg." It was obvious he was trying to play the role of a big shot.

"Oh, nigga, you ain't said a muthafuckin' thang," Niko yelled, undaunted. "Let's do this shit then!"

Temp rolled the dice for another ten minutes before anything of significance happened. That's when his luck ran out and he crapped out on four-trey.

"Fuck!" he screamed as Niko bent down to pick up his winnings. Temp frowned and looked at Chris.

Chris looked to his right then his left. "The fuck you lookin' over here for, dawg?"

"Man, yo' ass is bad muthafuckin' luck! Every time you bring yo' ass around when I'm tryin' ta shoot craps, I lose!"

"What? Man, get the fuck outta here with that bullshit! Yo' ass just hit a point on Bishop about fifteen minutes ago, and I was standing right here! Explain that shit, silly muthafucka!"

"Yeah, man," Bishop chimed in. "You always tryin'a blame somebody else when yo' ass lose."

"Whatever, nigga," Temp said, heated that he'd lost his money.

"Temp, you be on that bullshit," Niko said, adding his two cents.

"Y'all always on some fuckery," Antwan said, laughing.

The others looked at Antwan and saw that he was holding a bottle of tequila.

"What the fuck, Twan? You had me buy all this shit and you already got liquor up in this muthafucka?"

"This is for a special occasion, my dude, so be cool," he told Bishop.

Antwan handed each one of them a shot glass and then filled it to the rim. After he held the shot glass up, the rest of the crew followed suit. When everyone had their glasses in the air, Antwan started to speak.

"Yo, check this shit out. Y'all my dawgs for life, so let's make this pact right now. If one of us rises, then we all come up. But if one of us should fall, then we all go down together! If you with me on this shit, take this shit to the head."

Just before tossing his drink back, Antwan stared each one of them directly in the eye so they could see that he was dead serious. At 20 years old, he was the elder statesman of the clique and knew that the rest of them respected him as such. Antwan downed the liquor quickly. The rest of the crew followed him. Antwan thought about the brief argument between his friends a few seconds ago and smiled. He then held out his fist and said, "Young Lionz for life." One by one, each one of them did the same.

"Now," he said as he pulled out an already-rolled blunt and set fire to it, "Temp is about to break this plan down to y'all about how we gon' come up on some more paper."

Chapter 6

The sun rained heat down on the Cleveland streets, causing the masses to take cover under shaded trees or seek protection behind fans or air conditioners. Open fire hydrants splashed endless gallons of water onto the hot pavement as shirtless and shoeless kids ran back and forth through the refreshing H_2O. Loud laughter could be heard coming from porches. As usual, cluttered debris was strewn from one end of the street to the other. Potholes routinely caused hundreds and sometimes even thousands of dollars' worth of damage to unsuspecting vehicles. It was a stark reminder of just how little the city cared about how the inner city, or the hood as most people referred to it, looked.

Jermaine and Erik rolled through the hood in Jermaine's gold Nissan Pathfinder. The booming sounds of Kendrick Lamar poured out of the vehicle as each one of them bopped their heads. They were both past their prime, players turned wannabe thugs. Although they tended to act big time, selling a little weed here and there, they shied away from the hard stuff. They were pretty boys who weren't built for prison, so they sold just enough weed to floss but not enough to bring serious heat down upon themselves.

Erik, a long and lean brother whose skin was the color of butter, had just touched down two weeks prior after a short stint in the county for assaulting a police officer. At least that's what the charge was. Anyone who knew Erik knew that he didn't have the heart to raise his voice to a cop, let alone hit one. The cop was just pissed off because he was dating Erik's sister and she dumped him for a thug. To get even with her, the cop pulled Erik over on a bullshit taillight violation, beat his ass, and then had his partner back him up in court by saying that Erik attacked him first.

Jermaine was slightly heavier and just a half shade darker. He too thought that he was God's gift to women. Right before he started dabbling in weed, he fancied himself a pimp. He had developed a decent stable of girls until he made the mistake of pushing up on a real thug's cousin. The girl went back and told her folks that Jermaine had tried to con her into selling pussy for him. Her people found him in a local bar, dragged him out, and beat him senseless. After that, Jermaine moved to weed and had been slinging it ever since.

"Man, I'm hungry as fuck," Erick whined. "Let's stop at that gyro place and get some grub."

"Bet," Jermaine quickly agreed. "I can put something on my stomach myself."

Figuring that he knew a quicker way, Jermaine bent the corner and drove the wrong way down a one-way street.

"Nigga, what the fuck you doin'?" Erik shouted. "This is a one-way street."

"Nigga, I ain't goin' but one way."

Both men laughed at the joke until Jermaine slammed on the brakes and looked out the window.

"Man, what the fuck wrong with you?"

Jermaine ignored his friend's question and pulled over to the curb. Without saying a word, he hopped out of the car and strolled across the grass. When Erik saw what he was doing, he smiled and followed him.

***

Veronica and Tangie sat on the porch drinking malt liquor out of Styrofoam cups. No sooner had Chris, Niko, and Bishop walked down the stairs than Veronica broke out into laughter.

"Now, why you do that shit, bitch?" Tangie asked her.

"Do what?"

"Bitch, please! You think I didn't see yo' nasty ass uncross and recross yo' legs when they came up on the porch?"

"Ho, please," Veronica said, waving her hand in a dismissive gesture. "Ain't nobody thinkin' 'bout them young-ass boys."

"Then why the fuck was you tryin'a catch they attention, slut?"

"I don't know what the fuck you talkin' 'bout," Veronica said, smiling coyly.

When Veronica lifted her cup to take a sip from it, she thought about how she had embarrassed Bishop that day at the store. She also thought about what Tangie had just said about her trying to catch their attention. She realized that her friend was right. It hadn't dawned on her until just then that since she'd shot Bishop down and he'd starting ignoring her, she was trying to make him notice her. She hadn't given Chris a second thought. The boyish crush he had on her turned her off. But Bishop represented a challenge, and if Veronica wasn't careful, she was going to find herself on her back with her legs resting on the top of Bishop's shoulders.

"Hey, V, ain't that yo' sister walking down the street hand in hand with some nigga?"

Tangie's statement snapped Veronica out of her day-dream. Her eyes narrowed into slits as she focused on her 17-year-old sister Dana making goo-goo eyes at the handsome young man she was walking with. Dana was so captivated that she never even saw her sister or Tangie sitting on Tangie's porch.

"Dana! Girl, what the hell do you think you're doing?"

Dana's dark skin turned a shade darker when she spotted her sister staring at her. "Huh? Oh, hey, sis. I was just walkin' with Jay and—"

"Do Mama know where yo' li'l fast ass is at?"

Dana was busted. She was supposed to be over at her friend Tracy's house doing homework. Veronica took one look at Jay and decided that it would be best if her baby sister came up on the porch with her. The look in his eyes all but confirmed his intentions. If he had his way, Dana would be taking an oral exam the minute he got her alone inside his house.

"Yeah, that's what I thought! Get yo' li'l fast ass up here! And Jerry or Jay or whateva the hell yo' name is, you can kick rocks, 'cause you ain't gon' be hittin' no ass today! At least not hers," she said, pointing at Dana.

Jay walked off in a huff, mad now that he didn't take the shortcut through the field like he'd started to do. Dana walked up on the porch with an attitude. She couldn't believe that her cock-blocking sister had just stopped her from getting her first piece of dick. She'd been talking to her friends about it, and they had all convinced her that if she didn't give it up to Jay, some other girl would. They had also been telling her how good it felt, so she wanted to try it firsthand.

"I don't know what the fuck you got an attitude for," Veronica said when she saw her sister's face. "I know you didn't think I was just gonna sit back and let you take a chance on getting knocked up by that clown-ass nigga."

"Wasn't nobody gon' get knocked up," Dana said, sucking her teeth.

"How do you know? You don't know if you was gonna get pregnant!"

"I do know that!"

"How the fuck can you know?"

"'Cause, we wasn't gonna do nothing," Dana lied. She was dying to get her first taste of meat.

"Girl, you must think I was born yesterday!"

"You may not have been planning to do nothing," Tangie added, "but that li'l nappy-headed-ass Jay damn sure planned on gettin' him some ass today! You see the way he stomped off mad as fuck?"

Tangie was giggling but stopped when Veronica cut her eyes toward her. She didn't think it was funny. Tangie, on the other hand, thought it was hilarious. She remembered Veronica being the exact same way when she was that age.

"I don't know why you think this is so fuckin' funny, Tangie."

"Because I remember how yo' ass was," Tangie said, putting her on blast.

"See, that's that bullshit right there," Veronica said, pointing her finger at Tangie. "I wasn't nowhere near this hot when I was her age," she said, jerking her head toward Dana. "And even if I was, we ain't talkin' 'bout me. We talkin' 'bout li'l Miss Hot Ass here."

"Sis, you need to just chill the hell out! Shit, it ain't like you my mother. You just my fuckin' sister!"

Tangie and Veronica looked at each other in shock. Their mouths fell open at the same time.

"Li'l girl, who the fuck you think you talkin' to like that? I'll slap the piss outta you."

Dana leaned back and crossed her arms in a defiant posture. Seeing that her sister wasn't moved by her threat, Veronica decided to bring out the big guns.

"Okay, smart ass," Veronica said, taking out her cell phone. "Let's just see what Mama has to say about this shit!"

Dana's confident smirk evaporated in two seconds flat. "Okay, sis, you win. My bad. I'll go home. You ain't got to call Mama." The last thing Dana wanted was for her mother to find out that she was trying to creep over to some boy's house. She would get skinned alive, and she knew it.

"Nah, Miss Bad Ass! You tough shit, remember?"

"Veronica! Don't you dare snitch on that girl," Tangie intervened.

Veronica continued to hold the phone up as if she were going to dial. She wanted her baby sister to know that she meant business. Dana stood there, scared to death. After torturing her for a few more seconds, Veronica finally clipped the phone back on to her hip.

"Listen, li'l girl. The next time I catch you tryin'a creep with a boy, I'ma—"

"Excuse me, ladies," Jermaine interrupted, "but y'all look like y'all could use some company up there."

Tangie and Veronica looked at each other and rolled their eyes at the same time. "Nah, dude, we ain't looking for no company," said Tangie.

"Y'all sure?" Erik chimed in. "We got some smoke and some drink," he said, holding up a twenty sack of weed and a bottle of Hennessy. "We can have ourselves a nice li'l party."

"The fuck these two yellow-ass niggas come from?" Veronica asked Tangie. They had been so preoccupied with Dana that they never saw Jermaine pull up in front of the house and park.

"Look, homie. You and ya man there need to roll out. I got a man, and I'm sure he wouldn't appreciate y'all pushin' up on us like this."

Jermaine and Erik looked around and shrugged their shoulders. They doubted very seriously if either of the ladies had a significant other. In their flawed logic, there was no way the two ladies would be sitting on the porch alone if they were single. They saw Dana standing there, but to them, she was a nonissue. Whether she was the child of one of them didn't matter. They weren't trying to play daddy anyway. All they wanted to do was hit it and quit it.

"Man? Where? Baby, I don't see no man," Jermaine said, holding his palms up.

"Come on, pretty lady, let us come up there and party with y'all," Erik said. He was almost on the porch when he looked up and saw Antwan.

"My dude, if you don't get the fuck off of my steps, I'ma have a party on yo' ass!"

The two men looked at Antwan's boyish features and chuckled lightly. "Ay yo, this yo' li'l brother or somethin'? Go somewhere and watch a rap video, li'l nigga. This here is grown folks' bidness," said Jermaine.

"Yeah, li'l nigga. Ain't you got some homework to do?" Erik joined in.

The two old heads burst out laughing. The giggles came to a dramatic cessation when they glanced in the doorway and spotted Antwan, his pistol dangling in his right hand. Antwan walked out onto the porch, closely followed by the rest of the Young Lionz.

"Oh, so y'all two of them joke-tellin' muthafuckas, huh? Well, I got a joke for yo' ass," Antwan said, walking up on Jermaine. "What do you call a nigga who just wrote a check his ass can't cash?"

Before Jermaine could respond, Antwan smashed him in the middle of the forehead with the butt of his gun. "Laugh at that, muthafucka!"

Jermaine stumbled backward and tumbled down the steps. "Ay yo, hol' up, my dude. We ain't lookin' for no—"

Before he could finish his sentence, Chris slapped him viciously across the face with the barrel of his gun. Blood poured from the one-inch gash left by Chris's heater.

"Tell us some more jokes, bitch-ass muthafucka," Chris spat.

The two old heads scrambled to their feet and staggered to their vehicle. The Young Lionz didn't know if they going to get guns, but each one of them stayed at the ready, keeping their eyes on the truck in case they had to dodge bullets and return fire.

"Damn, y'all on some real-live gangsta shit," Dana commented.

No one had noticed, but she hadn't taken her eyes off of Chris since he'd come outside. A plan started to formulate in her mind. Since her sister was so dead set against her seeing Jay, she would just have to find a suitable replacement to pop her cherry. Hungrily she eyed Chris's tattoo of a black panther on his shoulder.

His flesh was inviting to her as she imagined what it would be like to let the thugged-out youngster be the first to invade her sweetness. When Chris finally did realize that she was looking at him, he gave her a slight smile and a wink. It would be just his good fortune to come along when she was finally ready to give up the goods.

Tangie looked at Veronica, who was busy checking out Bishop. Then she looked at Dana, who was doing the same thing to Chris.

"Sister see, sister do," she mumbled to herself.

Lucky sat back on his couch and counted the money he'd made for the week. He was the local numbers man, and his pockets were almost as long as the sideburns running down the side of his face. Lawrence "Lucky" Crawford had been gainfully employed at Drummond's sheet metal plant when he slipped on an oil spill one day and tore his left ACL. Being that the place he worked at didn't have a union, the foremen tried to save the company a few dollars by firing Lucky before he could file for workers' compensation.

Lucky promptly sued the company and settled out of court for $150,000. His knee never did heal right, so after two surgeries on it, the State grudgingly granted him disability. Being that he had a hustler's mentality to begin with, Lucky started thinking of a master plan that involved making his paper grow more. Then it hit him. While he was working at Drummond's, he would occasionally play the lottery with a guy named Barry, who ran numbers.

Since Barry paid 6-to-1 and didn't take out anything for taxes, the workers would much rather play with him than play with the State. After hitting one day for $4,000, Lucky laughed as he collected his winnings. Barry, who was a notorious braggart, laughed right back at him. Lucky was confused. He'd just hit this dude for a nice chunk of change, and here he was laughing like it wasn't shit to him. When Barry left the lunchroom, Lucky scratched his head.

"I don't know what the fuck he's so happy about," he'd said. "I just lit his ass up for four Gs."

An older white guy named Brett, who'd been there for nearly forty years, just looked at Lucky and shook his head.

"What?" Lucky had asked, still confused.

"Lawrence, how long have you been working here?"

"About ten years."

"And how long have you been playing with Barry?"

"Probably about eight years."

"Now," Brett said, "here's the important question. How much do you spend a week on numbers?"

"Shit. Brett, man, I don't know. About a hundred dollars a week, I guess."

Brett then got up and started walking toward the door. Just before he walked through it, he looked back at Lucky and said, "You do the math, kid. He's paying you with your own money."

Lucky sat there for a minute and let Brett's words soak in. Then he grabbed a calculator and did just what Brett told him to do. Lucky soon discovered that by playing an average of $100 a week, he'd spent over five grand a year in numbers. Sure, he would get the occasional hit, but for the most part, they were only a few hundred dollars. When he thought about the eight years he'd been playing and the amount of money he'd spent, he felt like a straight sucker. That's why when he got his buyout from the company, the first thing he did was put the word out that he was paying 7-to-1 on hits.

Once word got around the hood that he was paying that kind of money, people flocked to him in droves. That was three years ago, and now Lucky was the man to see if you wanted to test your luck in the numbers game. Lucky smiled as he thought about how far he'd come in this game. Although he still walked with a limp, it was more than worth it to him. He'd rather limp with a pocket full of money than walk straight broke any day.

By the time he'd finished counting his take for the month, he'd netted just over $25,000. Lucky then arranged the bills neatly, put them into a brown briefcase, and closed it. After locking it, he set it on the counter.

"Hey, Darlene, what the fuck taking you so long in there?"

Darlene was Lucky's flavor of the month. He had a different girl every month and never let any of them stay more than three nights in a row. Since tonight would have been the fourth night for Darlene, she had to go.

"Damn, Lucky, I'm coming. Give a bitch time to get in here."

Lucky looked at Darlene's thick frame and thought about having his way with her one more time before he dropped her off at home. He quickly shook the thought off, preferring instead to stand by his plan of dropping her off and then heading to the bank to deposit his cash. The bank he belonged to normally closed at six, but since he was such a good customer, they would stay open a little later for him if he was running late.

"I'm ready, baby," Darlene said in her high-pitched voice. "When can I come visit again?"

Lucky had heard this so much he'd started to expect the question. It was no secret around the hood that Lucky was making large bread, so every woman he allowed to spend a few days with him thought she was special. In their minds, they were going to be the one who would tame the infamous Lucky and get him to settle down. Her question was met with the same response he'd given every other one.

"I'll let you know, baby. I got a few things goin' on right now that I need to take care of, but when I get the time, I will definitely hit you up again. Your pussy definitely make a nigga wanna call you again."

Lucky had said those same words to so many other females that it should have been his trademark. Nevertheless, the compliment left Darlene feeling good inside. Being the perfect gentleman, Lucky led her through the kitchen to the attached garage. He opened her door and helped her inside of his cherry red BMW. After throwing his briefcase on the back seat, Lucky let the garage door up and proceeded to pull out. He reached down to change the station on the radio and was startled when he heard Darlene scream.

"Oh, my God, Lucky, stop!"

Lucky slammed on the brakes and looked at Darlene. "Damn, woman, what? You forget yo' lipstick or somethin'?" he joked.

Unable to speak, Darlene simply pointed to the driveway. Lucky peered out and cringed when he saw what appeared to be the body of a teenage boy lying face down. Lucky and Darlene carefully got out of the car and approached the young lad.

"Is he . . . dead?" Darlene asked.

"Nah, I don't think so. It looks like he's still breathing." *I wonder if he got any bread in his pockets,* Lucky thought sinisterly. Lucky didn't want to look like an uncaring monster in front of Darlene, but had she not been there, he would have surely gone through the boy's pockets.

Slowly, Lucky turned him over. The boy looked to have some kind of Halloween mask on his face. Lucky had turned the lad almost completely over when Niko took his hand from under his shirt and stuck a chrome-plated .380 in his face.

"Trick or treat, muthafucka."

Darlene started to scream, but the words got caught in her throat when Antwan slid up beside her and jammed a TEC-9 in her ribs. "Bitch, if you make a sound, I'ma put all kinds of lead in yo' ass. Get y'all asses back in that house."

As Niko and Antwan forced them back into the garage, Bishop, Chris, and Temp all stepped from the side of the house and joined them. All of them wore Halloween masks. Antwan reached into the car and took the briefcase out of the back seat. After forcing Lucky to open the door and let them into the house, Antwan slammed the briefcase onto the table. "Open it," he said calmly.

Lucky looked at the young faces and wanted to burst out laughing. He couldn't believe that he'd been caught slipping by these juvenile delinquents. When he hesitated, Temp cracked Darlene in the head with his gun.

"Muthafucka, you think we playin' wit' yo' ass? Open that muthafuckin' briefcase, nigga!"

"'Cause you hit that bitch? Nigga, you got me fucked up. I ain't opening up my shit just 'cause you hit a bitch in the head."

"Damn, bro, you got a point," Antwan said just before he reached back and crashed the handle end of the TEC-9 into Lucky's jaw. Bones broke instantly.

"Feel like openin' up that muthafucka now?" Niko said, laughing.

The amused thoughts that Lucky had originally were now 100 percent gone. The blood pouring from his mouth told him that these young cats meant business. But although Lucky did have much more money in the bank, he just couldn't see giving up $25,000 to some kids.

"Fuck . . . you," he said as blood ran from the side of his mouth and down his chin.

"Lucky, please just give them what they want," Darlene said. For her input, she was rewarded with an uppercut to the gut.

"Bitch, ain't nobody ask you for yo' muthafuckin' opinion," Temp snarled.

Darlene doubled over in pain. She had no idea that this was personal for Temp. Darlene was Sonya's mother. Sonya was one of Temp's former girlfriends he still screwed around with from time to time. Just like her mother, she was a sack chaser who was out for the dollar, so much so that she set Temp up to be robbed. After visiting Sonya one night, Temp walked out of the house only to be robbed at gunpoint when he got halfway down the street.

The very next day, Temp spotted Darlene shopping out of control at the mall. From what he knew about her, she never did have much money, so when he saw her spending what he assumed was his hard-earned money, he swore that he'd get even with her one day. That was the only reason he was still fucking around with Sonya: to wait for an opportunity to exact his revenge. When Sonya let it slip that her mother was bumping uglies with Lucky, Temp saw it as a way to get revenge and make a come up all in one fell swoop.

"Yo, this muthafucka think we playing with his ass," Chris spat. He took aim and shot Lucky in the shoulder. Lucky screamed in agony.

"Now you got two choices, muthafucka," Antwan told him. "Either you can open this fuckin' briefcase, or we can body yo' ass and take it anyway. Yo' muthafuckin' choice."

Lucky thought about it. He was terrified that if he gave them the briefcase, they might just kill him anyway. But on the other hand, if he didn't give in to their demands, chances were greater that they were going to send him to meet his Maker and still take it.

"Okay, man, okay," he said, relenting under the pressure of living or dying. Bishop grabbed the briefcase and shoved it into Lucky's lap.

"Hurry up, muthafucka! You got ten seconds!"

Lucky opened the briefcase and slid it across the floor to Antwan. He didn't know who these kids were, but it was evident to him that Antwan was the leader. Antwan picked it up and set it on the table.

"Jackpot, boys," he said as he eyed the crisp bills. All of them smiled as they walked over and looked at the money.

Suddenly, Darlene made a break for the front door. She was in no way convinced that they were going to let her go after they had the money. She was halfway to the door when fire shot through her back. Darlene crumbled to her knees as a result of the bullet piercing her thick frame.

"Oh, shit," Bishop screamed. "Man, what the fuck is wrong with you?" he asked Temp.

Temp lowered his gun and looked at Bishop with a crazed look. "Nigga, is you getting soft?"

"Nah, man, but did you have to shoot the bitch?"

"Would you rather she got the fuck away and called the police?"

"How do you know she was gonna call the cops?"

Temp looked at Bishop like he'd lost his mind. "Nigga, what the fuck you think she was gon' do, go shopping? Twan, will you please school this li'l muthafucka, man?"

"Yo, we ain't got time to be talkin' 'bout this shit! We need to get the fuck outta here!" Antwan pointed his gun at Lucky's head and pulled the trigger.

Bishop looked at Antwan and twisted up his face.

"I had to, man. This silly muthafucka here called out my name."

The crew walked out of the house and through the field and got into Antwan's car. Twenty minutes later, they were back at Antwan's house, dividing up the money. During the ride, it occurred to Bishop that Temp was getting a little too comfortable with pulling the trigger when they were just trying to get paid. He didn't like it, and he planned on addressing it with Antwan.

Chapter 7

Antwan lay stark still on the couch. Although his eyes were closed, he was hardly asleep. He knew that Tangie was probably in the bedroom waiting for him to come on blow her back out, but he needed some time to himself. That's why he declined when his crew asked him about getting blazed and tossing back a few drinks. After dropping them off, he hurried back home just for this reason. Cashmere thoughts ran rampant through his mind. Things were finally starting to come together for him. In another day or so, his cousin Thaddeus would be calling him.

Thaddeus, a mid-level drug dealer who resided in Harlem, New York, had come to Cleveland over six months ago on business. While he was in C-Town, Thaddeus made it a point to look up his relatives before he left. The only one he was able to get in touch with was Antwan. After getting tired of answering questions about their family, Antwan made it very clear that the only family he had was Tangie and the four young wolves he ran with. Antwan also expressed to his cousin that he wanted to dip into the dope game.

At first, Thaddeus, who was six years older than his cousin, balked at the request. But after seeing the drive and determination in Antwan's eyes, he decided to put his blood on. "Get you some bread together, and we'll talk about it again in six months, cuz," he'd told Antwan. Now the time was near for him to start making the kind of paper he felt he deserved. Antwan didn't feel the need to tell the rest of his crew. Knowing them like he did, he was positive they would have bugged the hell out of him if he had told them.

As he lay on the couch, he thought seriously about dipping back out of the house and hooking up with his side chick, Rhonda. Rhonda was a short, thick freak who lived across town. Whenever Tangie was on the rag or was acting shitty, Antwan would slide out of the house and kick it with Rhonda.

The thought was cut short by his buzzing cell phone. He picked it up off the coffee table and smiled when he saw the message that was attached to it. The more he read, the harder his dick got.

Hey, baby, what's takin' u so long out there? u no I'm w8n 4 u 2 cum in here and wreck this pussy. Cum on, baby. Bring mama that big dick.

Antwan's feet barely touched the floor as he jumped up off the couch and power walked to his bedroom. Once inside, his loins turned to fire. The only light in the room came in the form of two strawberry-and-cream-scented candles burning. Slow, soft music emitted from the miniature boom box that sat on the nightstand. Antwan was never much of a romantic type of guy, but the sweet aroma of the candle aroused his soul.

"Hey, baby," Tangie purred in a low, sexy voice. Her naked frame seemed to melt into the bed. "You ready to give mama some good lovin'?"

Antwan really didn't know if he'd been that busy or if he'd just not been paying attention to his woman, but it suddenly dawned on him that Tangie had lost ten or fifteen pounds. She looked better than he had ever remembered seeing her. To make the mood even more erotic, Tangie had rubbed herself down with an exotic oil that smelled like coconuts. Antwan could hardly contain himself as he stripped down to his birthday suit and sauntered over to the bed. Tangie's scent was intoxicating.

Ever the cool cat, Antwan slowly and gingerly lifted Tangie's right leg in the air. Then he tenderly started licking on her toes. Tangie panted softly as Antwan ran his tongue along the inside of her thigh. When he got to the inside of her knee, he sucked softly. By the time he got within six inches of her sweet spot, Tangie was ready to explode. Antwan wasn't as skilled in the art of pussy eating as he was with his cock game, but he knew enough to make a girl cum. He had just started flicking his tongue across Tangie's clit when several loud, aggressive knocks came through the door. Tangie's face contorted into a mask of anger as the knocking continued.

"Yo, who the fuck is that?" Antwan wondered aloud.

With the lifestyle he lived, Antwan wasn't taking any chances. He reached between the mattress and box spring and pulled out his 9 mm. He quickly threw his pants on and headed toward the living room. Tangie had thrown her robe on and was right behind him. In her hand was the .22 he'd bought her for protection. Just as they got to the door, a voice rang out.

"Tangie! Girl, open the door, it's me, Veronica!"

"The fuck she doin' knockin' on that damn door like that?" Antwan asked. He was pissed.

"I don't know, but her ass betta have a good-ass excuse!" Tangie stuffed the gun in the couch cushions and stomped toward the door. She was also pissed. She wanted him inside of her in the worst way, and now her best friend had fucked it up.

"Bitch, what the fuck wrong with you, bangin' on my damn door like that?" Tangie yelled. When she opened the door, Veronica barged right in.

"Girl, I need to stay here tonight. I done fucked around and locked my keys in the damn car, and now I can't get in the fuckin' house."

"Girl, do you have any idea what you just fucked up?"

Veronica looked at Tangie and then at Antwan. Just then, Veronica realized that Antwan was shirtless. "Oh, shit. I'm sorry, y'all," she said when it occurred to her what she'd done. "I didn't mean to fuck y'all's groove up," she said honestly. "But hey, I'm really in a fucked-up situation right now. Can I please spend the night?"

"Yo' ass can sleep on the damn porch," Antwan said nastily.

"Antwan!" Although Veronica did mess up her plans, Tangie wasn't about to let her friend sleep on the porch. "Girl, you know you can stay here if you need to."

"Ain't this about a bitch?" Antwan mumbled as he went back into the bedroom and slammed the door.

"Sorry, Antwan," Veronica yelled out when he was gone. "I'm sorry, girl," she said to Tangie.

"Girl, don't worry about it. I'll just suck him off in the morning to make it up to him."

As the two women sat in the living room talking, Antwan lay back in his bed, seething. He wanted to kick himself in the ass for not following his first mind and hooking up with Rhonda.

Chris and Niko walked along the sidewalk on the way to the store. They were both too jacked up to go home after the big come up they just made.

"Man, I'ma buy me a nice-ass ride with this dough we just came up on," Niko said. "Then I won't have to worry about getting a ride home from Antwan all the fuckin' time." Niko looked at Chris, who staring off into space. "Yo, Chris, where the fuck yo' head at, dude?"

"What? Oh, my bad, dude. I was just thinking about some shit at home."

Niko had heard his friend say these same lines before. He didn't want to pry, because he figured that if his friend wanted him to know his business, he would have told him. But the look in Chris's eyes told Niko that maybe he should at least ask if something was wrong. "Yo, what's good with you, fam? Is everything a'ight?"

Chris thought about what his friend was asking him. Even though he and the rest of the crew were a tight group, he'd never even thought about telling them about his sister's sickness. The last thing he needed was for the crew to start treating him like a charity case.

"Yeah, everything okay, playa. I can handle it."

Niko shrugged his shoulders. He wasn't going to press it. The two friends walked into the store and bought a box of Dutch Masters. The girl at the counter gave Niko a sly smile. She was a new employee and drop-dead gorgeous. Her skin was the color of wheat bread. She had long black curly hair that hung to the nape of her neck. Her full lips were coated with black lipstick, and her voice was deep but sexy, like Anita Baker's. She didn't have an overly thick body, but she was meaty in all the right places. Chris gave Niko a subtle shove in the ribs.

"I have to go get some change," she said sexily to Niko. "I'll be back in a minute."

As soon as she left, Chris turned to Niko with a screwed-up look on his face. "Man, what the fuck wrong with you? That bitch settin' that ass out for you, son. You betta hop aboard that caboose, my dude."

Niko stared at the girl as she walked back over to the cash register. As soon as she gave him his change, he went into mack mode. "What's up, baby? What's yo' name?"

"Regina," she said, staring at him.

"My name's Niko, baby, and this is my boy Chris."

"What's up, girl?" Chris said to her.

Niko was about to ask her if she had a man but decided against it. He really didn't care if she did, so in his mind, there was no point in asking. But Regina had no problem asking him such questions.

"You mackin' awfully hard, boo. Ain't you scared yo' girl gonna come in here and start actin' a fool?"

"Nah, I ain't worried about that. I ain't got nobody right now."

As the two of them continued to talk, Chris went outside. Feeling good about the money he was now holding, he reached into his pocket and took out the pack of cigarettes he'd stolen from the store when Regina wasn't looking. After peeling the seal off, Chris shook one out and inserted it between his lips. He lit it and inhaled.

"The fuck takin' him so long?" he mumbled. "He coulda been done fucked that bitch twice, as long as he takin'."

Chris was just getting ready to go into the store and tell Niko to bring his ass on when he was suddenly approached by two rough-looking dudes dressed in all black.

"Yo, what's up, nigga? You remember us?" the shorter of the two asked. He wore a brown bandana and had various tattoos stamped on his arms from wrist to shoulder. Chris looked at the two of them and immediately recognized them as the two dudes he had the beef with days earlier.

"Should I, nigga?" Chris responded.

"Oh, so now yo' ass got amnesia, huh, muthafucka?" The other thug just stood there, smiling and cracking his knuckles. Seeing this caused Chris to chuckle lightly. "Ay yo, you see somethin' funny, nigga?"

"Just you and ya clown-ass partner. Yo, dukes, you need to stop cracking yo' ashy-ass knuckles like that. Yo' ass gon' have arthritis when you get old."

"Oh, I see you think shit sweet, huh?"

The dude who was cracking his knuckles suddenly made a move toward Chris. Before he could effectively take two steps, Chris hit him with a right cross to the nose. The youngster staggered back and had to use his arm to keep himself from falling on the ground.

Chris took a quick look inside the store and tried to get Niko's attention. *This muthafucka don't see me out here scrappin'.* By the time he turned back around to go after the other dude, he was staring down the barrel of a pistol.

"Shit," he mumbled to himself.

The dude he'd hit exacted his revenge on Chris by punching him in the stomach. Chris doubled over in pain. His insides felt like marshmallows as he dropped to one knee.

"Yo, let's take this bitch-ass nigga in the alley and punish his ass," the shorter thug, whose name was Truck, said.

Truck and his partner, Dillon, dragged Chris by his heels into the side alley and started roughing him over. Just when he thought he was going to black out, he heard a voice from afar.

"Nigga, take yo' muthafuckin' hands off my homeboy!"

Chris opened his eyes to see Niko standing there with his gun trained on the two assailants. The one who'd pulled the gun on Chris thought about reaching for the gun he'd tucked back into his waistband, but Niko was a step ahead of him.

"Go ahead, nigga! Reach for that burner so I can turn yo' muthafuckin' ass into Swiss cheese."

The dude reluctantly let his hand fall back to his side. It took Chris a few seconds to catch his breath after being pounded to the body so relentlessly.

"You a'ight, my G?" Niko asked him.

"Yeah, I'm straight, dawg," he said. "These clowns hit like a coupla bitches anyway."

Niko removed the guy's gun from his waistband and clobbered him over the head with it. The guy went down like a ton of bricks. Niko walked over to the other goon and pistol whipped him until he was unconscious.

"Damn, man, it sure did take you a long time to come to the rescue."

"Man, how the fuck was I supposed to know that you was out here getting yo' ass kicked?" Niko said, laughing.

"Whateva." The two friends walked away, leaving their adversaries lying there bleeding and knocked out cold.

After getting blown for half the night, Niko went home to try to sleep it off. He had promised Regina that they would go to the movies the following day, and he wanted to get some much-needed rest. The lights in his living room were on, causing him to shake his head. He already knew what it was before he went in the house. He mentally prepared himself for his mother's tirade.

Niko was trying to stay out of his mother's relationship situation. But the more time went on, the more he wanted to lure James somewhere and body his ass. That way, his mother could cry, grieve, get over it, and find someone who would treat her with the respect that Niko felt she deserved.

Niko walked up on the porch and sighed. As he stuck the key into the lock, he braced himself for the hurricane. He hadn't gotten five feet inside the door before she was on him.

"Boy, what the fuck is wrong with you, tellin' my fuckin' man to get a job just because he asked yo' li'l ass about goin' to school? Have you lost yo' gotdamn mind?"

"Mama, he started with—"

Niko's mother stopped his words with a slap to the face. "Shut the fuck up when I'm talkin'!"

Instinctively, Niko grabbed his stinging face. He looked to the right and saw James sitting on the living room couch, smirking. It took every bit of strength he had in him to keep from pulling out his gun and shooting him in the face. Without saying a word, Niko stormed up the stairs and went into his room. He slammed the door so hard it threatened to come off the hinges.

"And don't be slammin' no muthafuckin' doors in here," his mother yelled. "This is my fuckin' house, and if you don't like it, take yo' li'l crumb-snatchin' ass someplace else!"

For the first time ever in his life, Niko was starting to dislike his mother. It crushed him that his mother, the woman who gave him life, could choose someone over him. Niko made up his mind right then and there that the next time his mother mistreated him because of James, he was going to mount up his crew and make James disappear.

Chapter 8

Yolonda was a short, dumpy-looking girl who Temp had gotten drunk and smashed one night while at a party. She'd been up in his face all night long. For the most part, he ignored the hell out of her. But he couldn't resist when she offered to buy him one last drink. He had no way of knowing that she'd slipped him an e-pill. As soon as the pill started to take effect, she dragged him into the bathroom and bounced up and down on his dick for twenty minutes.

The effects of the e-pill combined with the power of the alcohol had Yolonda looking like Halle Berry. When he sobered up and saw her the next day, she looked like Chuck Berry. Two months later, when he found out that Yolonda was pregnant, he hit the roof. He didn't have to stay mad for long, however. Before he could even broach the subject of abortion, she was begging him for money to get rid of the kid. As it turned out, Yolonda's father had a shit fit when he learned that his precious daughter had gotten knocked up by who he saw as a loser thug.

He demanded that she get rid of the kid or find somewhere else to stay. Yolonda had nowhere else to go, so she consented to her father's wishes and agreed to an abortion. Not that she would have been the best mother in the world anyway. The only reason she even wanted a kid was so she could get on welfare and try to beat the system. She didn't sweat the abortion too much though. Her pot of gold would slip from between her legs one day, she reasoned.

Temp pulled up in front of her house in his blue 2018 Chevy Lumina. It was an okay car as far as he was concerned, but Temp had dreams of driving something much more expensive in the near future. Temp blew the horn twice and watched as Yolonda came out of the front door of the apartment building she stayed in. Her baby bump was just beginning to show, which caused a disgusted look to come on his face the minute he laid eyes on her.

"I'ma have to start strapping up," he mumbled to himself. "I'm getting tired of payin' for these muthafuckin' abortions." It was common knowledge that Temp didn't like to use condoms. He was also terrible at pulling out, which was why he was now about to pay for an abortion for the fourth time.

Yolonda took her sweet time getting to the car.

"Girl, hurry up!"

When Yolonda got to the car, she threw her hands on her hips and just stood there.

"The fuck you waitin' on? Get yo' ass in the car!"

"You ain't gonna open the door for me?" she asked with a smirk.

"What? Girl, you betta quit playing with me and get yo' ass in."

Yolonda laughed out loud as she opened the door and got in.

"You know what? Yo' ass is startin' to play too muthafuckin' much."

"Yeah, whateva. But for real, Temp, I need to talk to you 'bout somethin'."

"Talk to me about what?" Temp asked. He was barely listening to her. He had other plans as soon as he dropped her off, and they consisted of lying with another broad. Temp had been driving for roughly ten minutes before Yolonda came to a decision.

"You know what? I think maybe you should take me back home."

Temp's head snapped around so fast he almost caught a cramp.

"The fuck you mean, take you back home? The fuck you talkin' 'bout?"

"I'm sorry, Temp. I just changed my mind, that's all."

"Changed yo' mind? Nah, bitch, you done lost yo' fuckin' mind!" Temp was beside himself. He didn't want any kids to begin with, and he sure as hell didn't want one with this lumpy-looking broad.

"Nigga, who the fuck you callin' a bitch?"

Temp suddenly realized that he needed to be somewhat nice to her if he was going to get her to have an abortion. "Look, baby, I'm sorry about that. I didn't mean that shit. I'm just a little thrown off 'cause I coulda sworn that we talked about this. Didn't yo' pops tell you not to bring no babies in that house?"

"Yeah, he did. But I ain't got to worry about him no damn more. Mama caught another bitch in the house and put his ass out!"

Temp pulled into the parking lot of a now-shut-down grocery store. "I gotta clear my head," he said as he got out of the car and walked away from it. Not knowing what to do, he reached in his pocket and pulled out a blunt. He looked back at the passenger's side at Yolonda, who seemed to be staring off into space. Temp shook his head, fired up the weed, and blew the smoke into the air.

"Ain't this 'bout a bitch?" he said out loud. Temp figured that he would try to talk to her one last time. He then beckoned for her to get out of the car and join him. Yolonda slowly got out of the car and walked over to Temp.

"What?" she said with an attitude.

"Calm down, baby. Ain't no need to cop no attitude," he said, trying to smooth things over with her. The only chance he had was to try to talk her out of having the baby. Temp started talking fast and furious. But twenty-five minutes later, he still hadn't convinced Yolonda to get rid of her unborn child.

"I'm sorry, Temp, I just can't," she told him.

"I'm sorry too, Yolonda," he said, and he punched her in the stomach as hard as he could.

Just to make sure that he got the job done, he hit her again. Yolonda fell to the ground, writhing in pain. For good measure, Temp picked up his foot and stomped her in the gut a total of five more times. Blood started to seep from her vagina and stain her white capri pants. Temp stood there and watched her for a minute and then calmly walked away.

Antwan woke up at three o' clock in the morning. He was beyond pissed off that Veronica had fucked up his flow the previous night. Antwan looked over to the other side of the bed and saw that Tangie hadn't come to bed yet. He figured that the two of them had gotten either drunk or high and both and fallen asleep on the couch. Not wanting to get any angrier than he already was, Antwan decided not to even go into the living room.

For one brief moment, he thought about going out there and dragging Tangie into the bedroom to finish what they had started earlier, but he didn't want to get into an all-night argument. He rolled out of bed and stumbled sleepily to the bathroom. He held his hands above his head and stretched as he relieved himself. After washing his hands, he opened the door to walk out of the bathroom and ran smack into Veronica. Antwan mean mugged her as he walked past her.

"Sorry," she said after seeing the ticked-off look on his face.

"Whateva," he said as he kept walking.

Antwan got back in his bed. He was almost asleep when he felt a hand riding up his thigh. Knowing that it was probably Tangie trying to make up for him having a nutless night, Antwan relaxed. His penis started to grow as he felt a tongue snaking its way toward his testicles.

"You like that, baby?" Tangie asked him.

"Hell yeah, baby, do that shit."

Antwan grabbed the back of her head and guided it up and down on his now rock-hard member. He finally opened his eyes to see his girlfriend's head bobbing up and down. Just as he was about to bust his nut, he looked up and was shocked to see Veronica staring at the two of them, rubbing herself through her clothes.

"Oh, shit," he yelled out as he released his babies into her mouth. Veronica then tiptoed back into the living room. Tangie smiled as she crawled up beside Antwan and snuggled in his arms.

"Damn, baby, that shit was the bomb."

"Just wanted to show you how sorry I was, boo."

"Shit, I can't believe you just did that with yo' friend in the other room."

"Oh, don't worry about her. Her ass is dead to the world in there."

That's what you think, Antwan thought.

When Antwan woke up the next morning, Tangie wasn't in bed beside him. He looked over on the nightstand and saw that she'd left him a note telling him that she and Veronica had gone to breakfast. Antwan shrugged his shoulders and smiled.

"I wonder if she told you that she was watching you suck my dick last night," he mumbled to himself.

Antwan thought back to the look in Veronica's eyes the previous night. There was something in them that told him she wanted to join in. Veronica was a certified dime piece, so it had traveled through his mind as to what the pussy would be like. Antwan then shook his head vigorously from side to side. He may have stepped out on Tangie on occasion, but he wasn't going to disrespect her by sleeping with one of her friends. He continued to shake his head as he went into the kitchen and poured himself a bowl of Frosted Flakes. He was just about to chow down when his cell phone rang. Antwan smiled. This was the call that he'd been waiting for. Feeling excited, Antwan jumped up and ran into the living room.

"Yo, what's up, cuz?" he asked, thinking it was his cousin Thaddeus on the phone.

"Nah, this ain't Thaddeus," a rough-sounding voice spat through the other end. "This is his friend, Jabba. Thaddeus told me to call you and tell you that he ain't gonna be able to get with you for a minute."

Antwan was shocked. He didn't know what was going on, but he was damn sure about to ask. "Damn, what the fuck happened?"

"Dem boys got him. Charged him with possession, with intent. He gonna probably be down for a good li'l while."

Antwan felt the air go out of his chest. This was the move he'd been waiting for, and now it had been snatched from him in the blink of an eye. "Fuck," he screamed into the phone.

"I feel you, man," Jabba said. "We was about to make some major moves with that coke."

Antwan held the phone up and looked at it with a screwed-up face. *Damn, this muthafucka talkin' reckless as fuck,* he thought. *No wonder my cousin's ass is locked up. If his boy is that careless, maybe he is too.*

"A'ight, man. Tell him to get up with me when he can."

Antwan hung up without saying another word. He wasn't about to get hemmed up because the clown on the other end of the phone was talking like a damn fool. Antwan sat down on the couch and took a deep breath. He fell forward and let his head rest in his hands. He was so close to making the come up that he'd been dreaming of. Antwan lifted his head and noticed that either Tangie or Veronica had left half a blunt in the ashtray.

Feeling that he was going to need that and much more to mellow out his mood, he got up, went to the kitchen, and grabbed a bottle of vodka off the top of the refrigerator. Before he even got back to the couch, Antwan had taken a long swig. After dropping back down on the couch, he relit the blunt and took a drag. For the next hour, Antwan proceeded to get as fucked up as possible.

Bishop woke up with the sole intention of going to see Mr. Hanley. Since the shooting occurred, the store had been closed, but Wendy made sure that Bishop knew what was going on with their boss. Of course, the morning would not have been complete without an argument between Carla and Jason. Bishop didn't know what they were arguing about this time, but he was too tired to be bothered with it. His head also pounded like someone had cracked his skull with a sledgehammer.

He slowly dragged himself to the bathroom and got himself ready for the day. He thought about asking his sister if he could use her car to go to the hospital, but then he changed his mind. He would rather catch the bus than hear about her latest fight with her man. Carefully, Bishop tiptoed down the steps and past the living room. Jason saw him leaving, but his sister didn't. Seeing that Jason was tired of Carla putting her brother in their mix in the first place, he wasn't going to tell her anything.

Bishop started a light jog once he got outside in case she tried to come out and stop him. He got to the bus stop just in time as the bus was coming down the street. The bus came to a stop, and Bishop was about to jump on when he realized that he had stuffed his gun in the small of his back. "Shit," he said as he felt the cold, hard steel pressing up against his backbone.

"Are you gettin' on or what?" the snotty bus driver asked him.

Without even acknowledging her, Bishop jumped off the bus and ran back down the street. He couldn't believe he was about to make the mistake of carrying a loaded gun into a hospital. Once he reached his house, he ran up the steps two at a time. When he opened the door, he heard someone crying. Bishop eased down the hallway and looked in the living room. His mouth fell open at the sight of Jason sitting on the couch with tears streaking down his face. It took everything in him not to start laughing. *This bitch-ass nigga sittin' up here cryin'! The fuck wrong wit' this wimp-ass nigga? My sister be runnin' all over his ass.*

As Bishop listened, Jason kept repeating over and over again that he was sorry. Bishop walked up to his room, shaking his head. By the time he reached the top step, his smirk had turned into full-blown laughter. The ha-ha's stopped when he walked past his sister's room and saw her sitting on the bed, holding a washcloth filled with ice to her face.

Bishop stormed in the room and grabbed Carla's arm. He snatched the cloth away from her face and looked. Bishop's blood started to simmer when he noticed the black eye Carla was sporting. The blood that seeped from her nose caused it to reach a boil.

"Ah, hell nah. I know that muthafucka didn't put his hands on you!"

"It's okay, Bishop. I hit him first. I did kinda bring this shit on myself."

Bishop didn't want to hear that. Even though Carla treated Jason like shit, she was still his sister, and he would be damned if Jason or any man would beat on his flesh and blood.

"Fuck that!" Bishop yelled as he ran out of Carla's room. With fire in his eyes, he bolted down the steps.

"Bishop, wait!" Carla called out to him.

Bishop had blacked out. All he could think of was getting to Jason and cracking his head wide open. When Bishop got downstairs, Jason still had his head in his hands, mumbling that he was sorry. He never saw it coming as Bishop hit him directly on top of the head. A large knot formed immediately as Jason fell to the floor, holding his head. He didn't even have time to scream as Bishop hit him again.

Carla came running down the steps just in time as Bishop had cocked the gun and was about to blow Jason's brains out.

"No!" Carla screamed as she jumped between the gun and Jason's laid-out frame.

Blood poured from the top of his head like a fountain. Carla grabbed a shirt that was lying nearby and dabbed the top of his head. Bishop stood there, shocked. As badly as she treated Jason, Carla was willing to jump in front of a bullet for him.

For the second time in less than five minutes, Bishop went back up the stairs, shaking his head. After putting his gun away, he walked downstairs and got ready to walk out of the house. Just before he did, Bishop looked into the living room one last time. Carla had Jason in her arms, caressing his face. Bishop walked out of the house, stunned.

Chapter 9

When Bishop walked into Mr. Hanley's hospital room, his heart sank. His boss was hooked up to all sorts of machines. An IV slowly dripped medication through a clear tube. The medicine not only served to soothe his aches and pains, but it also gave him peace of mind. As long as he heard their constant beeps, he knew that he was still alive. Eddie, who was sitting beside the bed when Bishop walked in, snorted and turned his head when he saw Bishop. Mr. Hanley's skin was dry and crusted from his stay in the hospital. His lips looked as if they needed a case of ChapStick. Mr. Hanley woke up just in time to see Bishop walk in. He smiled as Bishop approached the bed. Bishop ignored Eddie and went to his boss's bedside.

"Bishop. How are you, son?"

"I'm okay. I'm sorry I didn't get here to see you earlier," Bishop said, feeling guilty. His boss had been laid up for a couple of weeks, and this was the first time Bishop had gone to see him.

"It's okay, son. I know that you're a busy young man, going to school and trying to work, too."

Bishop felt like shit. He'd forgotten all about the lie he'd told Mr. Hanley about going to school. Eddie let out another loud snort, giving Bishop the urge to punch him in the face.

"So, Bishop. Who do you think it was who robbed the store?" Eddie asked him with a sly grin on his face.

"Nigga, what the fuck you askin' me for?" Bishop snapped.

"Why the fuck you gettin' so defensive? You act like you had somethin' to do with that shit." Eddie had always believed that Bishop had a hand in Mr. Hanley's store getting robbed. He couldn't prove anything, but he'd seen Bishop hanging out with the other dudes before.

Bishop walked up on Eddie with his fists balled up. "What the fuck you tryin'a say, punk-ass muthafucka?" The two of them were starting to get loud.

"That's enough," Mr. Hanley said weakly. "I don't want the two of you fighting over something that neither of you are at fault for. I'm going to need you two to get along since it seems that I'm gonna be laid up for a while. I told Wendy to open the store back up. No sense in losing money."

Right about then, the nurse walked in. "I'm sorry, but you two are going to have to leave. It's time for his medication, and he needs his rest."

After saying their goodbyes to their boss, Bishop and Eddie walked out of the hospital, glaring at each other. They didn't say two words to each other all the way out the door. But as soon as they got outside, Eddie tried to start up.

"Nigga, I know you had something to do with Mr. Hanley's store getting robbed!"

Bishop looked at Eddie's mouth and cocked his head to the side. This was the first time he'd seen his coworker since the heist. "Look, I'm gonna tell yo' bitch ass this shit just one damn time. I ain't have shit to do with the store being robbed, but you know what? I wish I did know who robbed the store. I would hit 'em off with some bread for knockin' yo' muthafuckin' teeth out."

Eddie was pissed. He took a step toward Bishop and was rewarded with a hard push. "Nigga, get the fuck outta my face! Don't you ever run up on me!"

Eddie threw up his hands and got in his boxing stance. "See, now you done fucked up," he yelled. "I'm about to beat the brakes off yo' punk ass!"

"Bring that shit then, duke!"

Before either of them could throw any punches, two large security guards came rushing out the door. "What's the problem here?" asked the taller of the two. Both of them looked like they were getting ready to retire to an old folks' home. Not wanting to get caught up in any legal drama, both Eddie and Bishop backed down.

"Ain't no problem, dawg. We cool," Eddie said. He started to walk away and then looked back at Bishop. "Catch you around, homie."

"Yeah, whateva, bro," Bishop said, giving him the finger as he walked away.

After returning home from her breakfast with Tangie, Veronica called a locksmith. She had to wait for the better part of an hour before the greasy-looking fat man showed up and opened her car for her. But to Veronica, it barely seemed like ten minutes. Her thoughts were otherwise occupied by the visions she kept having. When she was spying on Tangie giving Antwan head, she kept seeing herself and Bishop playing out the same scenario. As much as she tried to deny it, Bishop giving her the cold shoulder made her see a stronger, more grown-up side to him. Although she hated to admit it, whenever she was around him, she became aroused.

Veronica was an unusual woman. Her reputation of sleeping around with different guys was partially created by her own tongue. She'd never had a good relationship with her mother, so it was her aunt she confided in most of the time. And it was her aunt who had told her that if she didn't satisfy her man, someone else would.

Somewhere in her mind, Veronica had turned that into, "If a man thinks that other men are after you, the more he will want you." Her friend didn't know it, but the only reason she wore the type of clothing she did was she thought that it would help her find a quality man.

When Veronica finally did get home, she decided to put something in the Crock-Pot for dinner later on. After taking out the pot roast, carrots, and onions, she discovered that she was out of potatoes. Since potatoes were her favorite vegetable, there was no way on this earth she was going to cook without them. She promptly grabbed her keys, walked out the door, and headed to Giant Eagle food market.

As soon as Veronica walked into the supermarket, she wanted to turn around and run back out. The last person she wanted to see stared her in the face.

"Veronica? Girl, is that you?" her mother's nosy friend called out.

"Hey, Miss April," Veronica said with a fake smile. April Daniels was Veronica's mother's best friend and also one of the nosiest people in the city of Cleveland.

"Girl, I ain't seen you in a month of Sundays," she said as she slid her slight frame over next to Veronica. Her hair was dyed black, although it took very little effort to see the gray peeking through the roots. Her newly bought porcelain teeth shined as she gave Veronica her warmest smile. Taking a handkerchief out of her pocket, Miss April proceeded to polish the same red-rimmed glasses she'd worn for the past fifteen years. "Girl, how yo' mama doin'?" she asked.

"She's doin' okay, Miss April."

Miss April just stared and shook her head.

What the hell is wrong with her ass? Veronica wondered.

"Now how would you know how she doin', chile? She said that she ain't seen you in nearly two weeks."

Then what the fuck you ask me that shit for? Veronica wanted to ask. "Well, I been kinda busy, Miss April."

"I undastand, chile. When you work a lot of hours like you do . . . Oh, wait, that's right. You got fired, didn't you?"

Veronica wanted to slap the old woman's teeth out. She also wanted to tell her mother off for discussing her business with other people. That was part of the reason she hated visiting her mother. "No, Miss April. I still have my job. It was just a little misunderstanding, that's all." Veronica was pissed. If her mother had waited before she started spreading fake gossip, she would have known that it was a case of mistaken identity.

Miss April looked confused. She hated it when she got screwed-up information. Slightly embarrassed, she changed the subject. "When you gon' give Irene some grandkids? She's been itchin' to be called Grandma, you know."

"Miss April, I ain't even dating nobody right now, so I know I ain't about to have no kids."

"Uhmm hmm," Miss April said with a twisted-up face.

"Uhmm hmm what?" Veronica asked, offended.

"Oh, nothin', chile. I was just thinkin' to ma'self."

"I gotta go, Miss April."

Veronica quickly rushed down the aisle that was closest to her. Had she stood there a second longer, she would have surely told the old bat off. She was a grown-ass woman and didn't like being interrogated by the likes of April Daniels. After gathering up the potatoes, Veronica made a beeline to the liquor section. Since she didn't have any weed to smoke, she grabbed a bottle of Three Olives Mango Vodka.

She needed something to settle her nerves after the inquisition from Miss April. Veronica crept back down the aisle, trying at all costs to avoid a second encounter with Miss Nosy. She peeked around the corner and smiled devilishly as she saw Miss April chatting with Reverend Bernard Dawson from the First Sky Baptist Church. Bernard Dawson was by all accounts a crooked man. He'd been accused on more than one occasion of stealing money from the church. But since there was never any proof against him, he was allowed to keep his position.

He was also a notorious skirt chaser. He never took the chance of stalking women while at the church, but the second he hit the streets, it was on and popping. Veronica hadn't been to that church since her father's funeral. But when she was younger, she attended on a regular basis, so she knew a thing or two about Reverend Dawson. Like the fact that he had a wife. Veronica didn't know if he would remember her, but she was going to make damn sure that Miss April paid for her actions earlier. Barely able to contain her excitement, Veronica walked toward the reverend and extended her hand.

"Hey, Reverend Bernard. Long time, no see. How are you?"

"Uh, I'm fine, miss, but do I know you?"

"Come on, Rev. You know me. I'm Veronica Campbell. Irene Campbell's daughter. My father's funeral was there."

"Oh, yes, of course. I'm sorry. How have you been?"

"Fine, just fine. How is your wife doing?" Veronica made sure that she put the emphasis on "wife" when she said this. She looked Miss April square in the face.

"Uh, she's fine, Veronica. Thanks for asking."

Taking advantage of his nervousness, Veronica looked back and forth at the Reverend and Miss April. "Oh, I'm sorry. I didn't mean to interrupt anything. I'll be on my way," she said as she walked away.

"Veronica, wait," Miss April called out to her. She wanted to tell her that she and the reverend were old friends, but Veronica had already scampered off to the checkout line. Miss April just stood there, disgusted by the taste of her own medicine.

After paying for her items, Veronica walked out of the supermarket and laughed all the way to her car. She was extremely satisfied with the payback that she'd just inflicted. Miss April was a royal pain in the ass, and although it may have been a bit disrespectful to do what she did, Veronica didn't regret it for one second. She laughed all the way home as she thought about the look on Miss April's face.

Her inner thighs became moist as flashbacks of Tangie giving Antwan head replayed in her mind. Veronica didn't have a dick to suck on, but she planned on giving her vibrator a hell of a workout once she got home. Five minutes later, Veronica pulled into her driveway.

As soon as she got out of her car, the plastic bag burst wide open. Her potatoes fell to the ground and rolled down the driveway. "Shit," she screamed as she tried to run them down. The last one was on its way to the street when it was scooped up and tossed back to Veronica. She was silent for a moment, caught off guard by the appearance of Bishop and his willingness to help. She half expected him to let it go into the busy street and get crushed.

"You're welcome," Bishop said sarcastically as he kept walking.

"Wait! Thanks," Veronica said, embarrassed that she'd momentarily lost her manners. Bishop just nodded and kept it moving.

"Wait! Where you headed?"

"To the house."

"You need a ride?" Veronica asked, trying to get in good with the youngster. Veronica was tired of trying to deny it. She liked Bishop. She had no idea when she started liking him. But somewhere between her laughing at him in the store and him tossing her potatoes back to her, she became interested in him. But Bishop was skeptical. The rejection had hurt him more than he'd let on, and quite frankly, he didn't have time to play these games.

"Nah, I'm straight," he said.

"Well, could you at least give a sista a hand with somethin'?"

"A hand with what?"

"My back door is stuck," she lied. "I can't get it open for shit. Can you try to get it open for me?"

"Your back door is stuck? Are you serious?"

"I'm dead ass."

Bishop really didn't feel like being bothered. All he wanted to do was go home, sit on the back porch, and fire up a blunt. Plus he didn't have his hammer, and Bishop didn't like to be out in the streets too long without being strapped. He made a screwed-up face, and Veronica sensed that she was losing him.

"I'll pay you for your services, Bishop."

"Oh, word? Shit, let's go then!"

Bishop followed Veronica into the house. After making a stop in the kitchen, she led him to the back door. On the way there, she figured she'd try to make things right about the store incident.

"Bishop, I just wanna apologize for what happened at the store that day. I didn't mean to laugh at you. The whole thing just caught me off guard."

"It's cool. Don't worry 'bout it," Bishop said, playing it off. He was actually shocked that she even offered an apology, but he accepted it nonetheless.

When they got to the back door, Bishop saw immediately that there was nothing wrong with it, but he decided to play along. He walked over to it and jerked it a couple of times.

"Got it," he said, after opening the unstuck door.

Veronica stared at Bishop's muscular frame. She'd never really noticed how good he looked until that very moment.

Bishop turned around and caught her looking. "What?"

"Nothin'. Thank you. I've been tryin'a open that damn door for a week and a half now."

"Is that right?"

"What? You think I'm lyin'?"

"Ain't nobody say you was lying." Both of them just stared awkwardly at each other for about five seconds before Veronica broke the silence. "Oh, my bad. I guess you wanna get paid now, huh?"

"Somethin' like that."

Veronica then led him back into the kitchen. She reached in the cabinet and took out two glasses. She opened the refrigerator and took out a carton of mango juice. Bishop just stood there with his arms folded. He was wondering when she was going to go into her purse and get his bread. After pouring two drinks, Veronica handed one to Bishop and kept one for herself.

"The fuck is this?" he asked.

"Payment."

"Payment?"

"Yep. I never said I was gonna pay you in cash," Veronica said, smiling.

Bishop started to get mad, but there was something about the way she smiled at him that warmed him over. He looked at her banging body, and his loins started to heat up. Just then his stomach growled, reminding him that he hadn't eaten anything all day.

"Damn, is that yo' stomach?"

"Yeah," he said, laughing. "I ain't ate shit all day, so I guess my stomach wanna know what the fuck is goin' on. But yo, I'ma roll out and hit up Mickey D's."

The mere mention of McDonald's food made Veronica's stomach turn. "Ah, hell naw, boy, that shit'll kill you. Have a seat, homeboy."

Veronica went back into the refrigerator and took out a plate of fried chicken. After warming it up in the microwave, she set the plate down in front of him. The succulent aroma caused his stomach to howl out again. Bishop tried not to appear greedy, but after the first bite, he was gone. In less than five minutes, the bones were as clean as a baby's ass.

"You want some more?" she asked.

Bishop didn't want to come off as a glutton, but before he could answer, Veronica made the decision for him. "You know you do," she said as she took his plate. "So," she said in a sexy voice, "are you a breast, leg, or thigh man?"

Catching the sensual tone in her voice, Bishop came right back at her. "I like it all, baby."

Veronica smiled as she put a breast and leg on his plate. After heating it up, she set it down in front of him and poured herself another drink. Afterward, she sat down across from him and watched him eat.

"Where you get this chicken from, that new place up on Lakeshore?"

"What? Nigga, you must done fell and bumped yo' head! I got mad skills in the kitchen, dude!"

"You cooked this?" he asked with surprise in his voice.

"Hell yeah!"

Bishop didn't know whether to believe her. He didn't want to insult her, so he just kept on eating.

"What, you don't believe me?"

"I didn't say that," he said as his voice went up an octave, indicating doubt.

Veronica's mouth flew open. Her eyebrows rose as she put her hands on her hips. "I can show you betta than I can tell you," she said as she got up and walked toward the kitchen counter. Bishop continued to eat as she peeled and sliced up the potatoes. She washed them off and put them in a bowl. After that, she took the pot roast out of the refrigerator and seasoned it accordingly. Bishop watched silently as she dumped the food into the Crock-Pot.

"Now, in two hours, get ready for a treat."

Temp sat in the Shake 'Em Up lounge tossing back shots of Jack Daniels. Although he was only 19, he could easily pass for 21, so he had no trouble accessing any bar he wanted to frequent. Temp partially felt like shit for what he'd done, but being a father was not in the cards. He didn't want to be responsible for anyone other than himself. Still, his conscience was beating on him like Ike Turner. He could almost smell the blood that had poured out of Yolonda's womb.

Temp was careful to make sure that there were no witnesses around when he assaulted her. If she called the police later on, he would just deny it. At worst he would have to spend a night or two in jail, but with no one there to see it and with him denying it, it would be her word against his. The judge or the jury, if it even got that far, would surely have to throw the case out.

As he downed another shot, Temp wondered where his life was headed. A high school dropout at the age of 16, he knew that he didn't have the necessary skills to get a high-end job. Working at a fast-food place was definitely not an option for Temp. He just couldn't see taking orders from people or letting them talk to him any kind of way for the small piece of change that kind of job would pay. Of all the Young Lionz, Temp had the most freedom to roam. He didn't have a steady girlfriend to hold him down or nag him.

His father was a retired postal worker who was now a full-time drunk. From the day Temp was born, Richard Green doubted that he was indeed the child's father. Temp's mother, Sandra, was the neighborhood whore, and it had been widely spread that she had slept with three different men on the night that Temp was conceived. But until her dying day, she held steadfast that Tempton David Green was Richard's son. Sandra was also a heavy drinker, a trait that seemed to have been passed down to Temp. And although she died from cirrhosis of the liver, it did nothing to deter Temp from drinking.

Starting to feel his stomach bubble, Temp ordered a dozen wings. When they came, he scoffed them down in record time. Feeling his bladder about to burst, Temp got up and stumbled to the bathroom.

After relieving himself and washing his hands, he made his way back to the barstool. Sitting two stools down from him were two of the finest women he'd ever seen. Both of them appeared to be in their mid-twenties. The shorter one had a cropped haircut. She had butter-light skin and a few freckles on her cheeks. The other one was honey brown. Her hair was sandy brown and pulled back in a ponytail. Temp pretended not to eavesdrop on their conversation, but in reality, he was listening to every word being said.

The taller woman was telling her friend that she couldn't stay out that late because she had to be at work early the next morning. Meanwhile, the other one was complaining that her man was cheating on her and that they hadn't had sex in three months. A sly smile eased onto his face as he saw an opportunity to get some ass. He slowly made his way down to where they were sitting. No sooner had Temp sat beside them than the woman who said she couldn't stay late got up to leave.

"I'm sorry, Deb, but I gotta go, girl. I'll holla at you tomorrow."

"Fine. Take yo' square ass on home then, Pam," Deb said, waving her off.

"Whateva, bitch," Pam responded before walking off.

"Damn, it looks like a partna just bailed on you," Temp said, attempting to make conversation.

"Yeah, I know. Bitch."

Temp noticed that she didn't have a drink in her hand, and seized the moment. "What you drinking on, pretty lady?"

"Well, since you being all gentlemanly, I'll take a Long Island Iced Tea. Thanks."

"Don't worry 'bout it. My name is Temp, baby," he said, extending his hand.

"Debra," she said, receiving it.

"You mean to tell me that yo' man let you out looking like that?"

"Looking like what?"

"Looking fine as fuck," Temp said, licking her lips.

Debra blushed as she let her eyes roam over Temp's frame. "You think I'm fine, huh?"

"Damn right. You the finest muthafucka in here."

For the next forty-five minutes, the two of them proceeded to get better acquainted. Even though they weren't the only people in the bar, that didn't stop Debra from openly groping Temp, causing his soldier to stand at full attention. Debra then leaned over and whispered in his ear. "Hey, baby. Why don't you let me take you in the ladies' room and give you some special attention?"

Temp almost burst in his pants. She didn't need to tell him twice as he grabbed her hand and pulled her in the direction of the women's bathroom. Once they were inside, Debra wasted no time dropping to her knees. With lust in her eyes, she hungrily unzipped his pants. She pulled out his dick and licked her lips while stroking it with her right hand.

"Damn, baby, you could choke a bitch with that shit you packing," she said, gassing him up. A warm sensation overtook him as she engulfed his tool. Temp moaned in pleasure as Debra expertly performed the art of fellatio. Temp felt his nuts tightening up, signaling that he was close to cumming. Shortly after that, he felt something cold and hard pressing against his temple.

"Don't move, muthafucka," said Pam from out of nowhere.

Grinning wickedly, Debra got up off of her knees. She smirked at Temp as she stuck her hands in his pockets. Had Temp been paying closer attention, he would have noticed that for every three drinks he tossed back, Debra only had one. The alcohol more than loosened him up and caused his guard to drop.

"Damn, bitch, was you jus' gon' let this bitch-ass nigga squirt his babies in my mouth?" she asked her partner.

"Hell nah! Then I woulda had to shoot his punk ass. Ain't nobody cummin' in yo' mouth but me, baby." The two women shared a quick kiss before continuing with the jack move.

Ain't this a bitch. I just got caught slippin' by these broads. "Yo, what the fuck is this bullshit?" he asked. His answer came swift and hard in the form of a blow to the head.

"Now ask me another stupid-ass question, nigga!" Pam spat.

After robbing Temp of more than two grand, the women ordered him to turn around and get on his knees. Their faces were burned into Temp's memory forever. He promised himself that he would get his revenge on them if it was the last thing he ever did. That was his final thought before pain shot through his skull and his world went black.

***

"Hey, buddy, you okay?"

That was the first thing Temp heard when he came to. His head felt like a cracked egg. "What the fuck?" Temp said to himself as he looked around. The images he saw were foggy. He shook his head a couple of times, trying to clear the cobwebs. Temp slowly messaged his temples. It was all he could do to try to get the room to stop spinning and the pain to subside. As his vision started to clear, his memory began to return.

"Ah, hell nah," he said, disgusted with himself as his memory fully returned. Temp ran his hand along the back of his head. The bump back there felt like a golf ball had been glued to his scalp.

"Damn, what the hell happened in here?" asked the bartender, whose name was Joe. "The last thing I re-member seeing was you and that cutie pie getting real chummy at the bar. I went to the back to replace a bottle, and when I came back, both of y'all was gone. Shit, man, I thought maybe you had gotten lucky or somethin'.""

"Nah, man, that bitch set me up. She and her girlfriend set my ass the fuck up!" Temp looked around and saw his watch lying on the floor. *I wonder why them thieving-ass hoes didn't take that.*

"Let me help you up, buddy," Joe said, reaching down to grab Temp's arm. It wasn't until that second that he realized he was still on the floor. With Joe's help, Temp got to his feet. Although his head was clearing, he was still slightly wobbly.

"Maybe I should call an ambulance," Joe suggested.

"Nah, man, I'm straight."

Temp half walked, half staggered out of the bathroom and went back into the bar. The place was empty, and most of the lights were turned off, leaving Temp to surmise that the place was closed. He shook his head, trying to clear the rest of the cobwebs. When he felt his head was completely out of the fog, he started for the door. Just before he walked out, he thanked Joe for his assistance. Temp then hopped in his car and pulled off down the street. He drove with the windows down. The blast of air hitting him in the face brought his senses all the way back. Temp was almost home when he realized that he'd left his watch lying there on the floor.

"Fuck!" he screamed. The watch held sentimental value for Temp. It was one of the last things his mother gave him before she died.

He bent two corners and headed back to the bar. He only hoped that the bar hadn't closed completely yet. With his mind clear, Temp started questioning a few things. There was one thing in particular that stuck in his craw. He made a mental note to ask Joe about it if he got to the bar before it shut all the way down for the night.

"Maybe he gotta clean up some shit," Temp hoped.

Temp was about fifty feet from the front of the bar when he saw something that caused his blood to boil. Standing in front of the bar were Debra and Pam. In between them, with his arms draped around their shoulders, was Joe. Temp couldn't be sure from this distance, but he could've sworn that Joe had his watch on. Instinctively, he reached under his seat for his hammer. Murderous thoughts flooded his mind as he chambered a round. He was all set to do a bloody drive-by when a wicked plan popped into his head.

Chapter 10

Niko sat on the edge of his bed and stared at the wall. On the other side of that wall, his mother and James were engaged in a bitter argument. He didn't know what it was about, but from experience, he knew that it could last for hours. He looked at the clock and wondered what they could possibly be into it about so early in the morning. Niko briefly thought about going to school today, but quickly laughed it off. He hadn't been there in the past three months, and he had no intention of going now. Niko hated school. He just didn't see the point in going to a place where he really didn't want to be.

Suddenly Niko heard a door slam. Then he heard his mother bawling her eyes out. He didn't know what had happened, but he knew one thing: he had to get out of that house. It was just a matter of time before his mother came into the room and started whaling on him because she was upset at James. Niko jumped up and ran into the bathroom. He quickly washed his face and brushed his teeth. After throwing on a pair of jeans, he made a mad dash for the door.

He was halfway out when his mother yanked open her door and headed for his room, yelling his name. Niko didn't even bother to answer her. He just kept on going toward his place of solace. He didn't want to be bothered with anyone, so instead of taking the bus, he jogged to his destination. Once he got there, he walked up the bleacher steps and took a seat. Every so often, Niko would go to the football stadium to think. He would often envision himself scampering up and down the field.

His fantasy life consisted of scoring touchdowns and hearing the cheers of the crowd. The next Todd Gurley was who he wanted to be, but when his mother made it clear that she wasn't going to support him emotionally, let alone pay school fees for him to play, Niko's heart broke. Shortly after that, his heart hardened. The football coach had offered to loan him the money so that he could play, but Niko didn't want to play if his mother wasn't going to be there to watch. Soon after that he started hanging out with the Young Lionz crew and had been one of them ever since.

Niko was fantasizing so hard about making plays on the football field that he didn't notice the figure running around the track at first, but once he did, he had to do a double take. The spandex sport shorts wrapped around her juicy ass caused his dick to jump. Niko watched as the figure made its way around the track quickly. By the time she'd reached where Niko was sitting, she made a right and started to run up the steps toward him. Niko smiled. He hadn't noticed her at first, but the second he got a glimpse of her face, he recognized that it was Regina. Regina smiled as she approached Niko. Light sweat glistened on her face.

"Hey! What are you doing out here this early in the morning?"

"Not much. Sometimes I just come out here to think," he told her. "Look at you, though. You didn't tell a brother that you was a track star and shit."

"You didn't ask. Besides, I ain't no star . . . yet." Both of them laughed as Regina sat beside him. "We still on for the movies tonight?"

"Hell yeah! I'm looking forward to it," he said. "What do you want to go see?"

"I don't know. Let's play it by ear and decide when we get there."

"Cool," he said, shrugging his shoulders.

They stared at each other and smiled. They seemed to be hitting it off good. The two of them made small talk before she hit him with a bomb. "Tell me a little about yourself."

"Huh?" Niko hadn't expected that question, and it threw him off. He also wasn't ready to reveal his derelict lifestyle to someone with whom he had started to connect. When he'd first met her at the store, he just wanted to smash. But now that he was getting to know her a little, he became more interested.

"Ladies first," he said, putting her off.

"Well, if you insist." Regina went on to tell Niko about how she'd won a scholarship for track to Ohio State. She also had a 3.3 grade point average. By the time she was done telling him about her plans for the future, Niko felt like a world-class failure. They were headed in totally opposite directions. She was on her way to becoming either a track star or a pharmacist. He was, for all intents and purposes, headed toward a career in drugs and violence.

"Your turn," she said, letting her chin rest in her hands while her elbows sat on her thighs.

Just as he was about to make up something, a voice boomed out from the bottom of the stands. "Regina! Regina! Girl, why you ain't been answerin' my fuckin' calls?"

"The fuck is that nigga?" Niko asked as the older-looking cat made his way up the steps. He was flanked by a short, cocky-looking dude with dark skin and multiple scars.

"My ex-boyfriend," Regina said as she sucked her teeth. "I wish he would just leave me the fuck alone."

Niko smoothly checked to make sure that he had his hammer with him. He didn't want to get ignorant in the football stadium and especially in front of his new friend, but if someone had to get fucked up, he was going to make sure that it damn sure wasn't him.

"Girl, did you hear me? I been callin' yo' ass for a week!"

"Nigga, you can call for a month, and I still wouldn't answer the damn phone! I told you the shit is over, Ricky."

Ricky looked at Niko and made a thumbing gesture. "Why, so you can hang out with a bitch-ass muthafucka like this?"

"Ay yo, fuck you, cuz! Yo don't know shit about me, so don't be coming at me sideways," Niko warned.

"What you say, li'l nigga?" The dude with Ricky spoke as he tried to step toward Niko.

"Be easy, my dude," Ricky said as he extended an arm across his friend's chest. He subtly stared down at Niko's hand, which had already started to travel behind his back. "We don't want no trouble, homie," he said.

Ricky wasn't as quick to move as his friend. He'd seen plenty of men put their hands behind their backs in a battle, and the end result when it returned was never good. The short, gorilla-looking thug standing next to Ricky flexed his muscles. Niko just smirked and grunted. It always amused him how guys who looked like Mike Tyson actually thought they were Mike Tyson.

"Let's roll, my dude," Ricky said, pulling his friend away.

"Nah, man, I wanna beat the smirk off this punk-ass nigga's face."

"Nah, now ain't the time, dawg, trust me."

"You betta listen to ya homeboy. This shit won't turn out good for you, playa."

"Come on, dawg. We'll catch up with his ass later."

Ricky whispered into his partner's ear. Regina just stood there with her hands on her hips. She stared a hole in Ricky as he walked away.

"Yo, what the hell is up with you and that dude? Is he gon' be a problem?"

"Nah," she said as she twisted up her lips. "He's more talk than anything else."

"Yeah, okay," Niko said, figuring that he would do good to keep his guard up.

Chris walked through the mall with a bop in his step. His gangsta swag was evident as he eyed the stores and tried to decide which ones were worthy of his cash. Chris was in a very good mood. It had nothing to do with the fact that his pockets were fat but everything to do with his sister's health. Earlier in the day, the doctor had given her a clean bill of health. She was now in full remission. To celebrate, Chris promised his mother that he was going to take them both out to eat later. He loved both of them dearly. As a matter of fact, there were only seven people, including himself, that Chris really gave a damn about. The other Young Lionz were the other ones, and in Chris's opinion, everyone else could go to hell. Hard life lessons had taught him to not trust many people.

His buzzing cell phone jarred him from his thoughts. The text message was from Temp, telling him of an urgent meeting later. Chris responded by telling him that he had made plans with his mother and that they would just have to fill him in later.

Knowing that Temp would probably text some smart-assed comment back, Chris told himself that he wasn't going to even look at the next text he sent. He was determined not to let anything fuck up his good mood. Still looking down at his phone, Chris ran right into a young cutie. The impact knocked her to the ground.

"My bad, slim," he said, reaching down to help her up. Chris thought she was going to get mad and try to get fly with him, but instead, she just smiled goofily. "You a'ight?" he asked her.

"Yeah, I'm straight, cutie pie."

The compliment threw Chris off guard. He was all set to keep it moving, but after looking at her for a few more seconds, she began to look familiar.

Chris cocked his head to the side. "Hey, shorty, don't I know you from somewhere?" he asked.

"Uh, yeah," she said, slightly offended that he didn't remember her. "I'm Veronica's sister, Dana."

Warning bells went off in Chris's head. Every instinct in his being told him press on and not even give her a second look. The last thing he wanted to do was have to cuss Veronica out because of her baby sister. But his hormones were telling him something different. He hadn't noticed how fine she was before, but he was damn sure seeing it now. She had a few of her older sister's features, but the two of them really didn't look that much alike. Chris didn't know this for a fact, but if he had to guess, he would say that Dana and Veronica probably had different fathers.

"Oh, shit, that's right," he said. "You was on the porch when we had to straighten them punk-ass muthafuckas out."

"Yeeaahh," Dana said with a gleam in her eye. There was something about bad boys that turned her on. She'd never even thought about hooking up with Jay until she found out that he cut school one day and broke into someone's car.

"The fuck you smiling like that for?" he asked her.

"I don't know," she said, shrugging her shoulders.

Chris looked at her curiously, a thought suddenly popping into his head. "Hey, ain't you supposed to be at school?" he asked.

Dana folded her arms across her chest, leaned back, and stared at him. "I could be askin' yo' ass the same thing," she shot back.

Chris thought about what she was saying and came to the conclusion that she had a point. Here he was questioning her about missing school, and he was doing the same.

"A'ight, shorty, you got that. My bad," he said. Chris started walking away and, just like he figured she would, Dana started following him.

"Where you headed, homeboy?"

"Don't know, really. Just tryin'a get some new gear," he said.

"Yeah, me too," Dana lied. She wasn't about to tell him that she was at the mall scoping out potential suitors to take her virginity. She thought that she was going to give it to Jay, but she counted her blessings when she learned through the school grapevine that he'd given a girl she knew gonorrhea.

Dana was a rarity among 17-year-old girls. She was the only one in her circle of friends who was a virgin. At first, she was proud of that fact. But the more she started hearing about how good it felt, the more she wanted to see for herself. And truth be told, Chris wasn't all that experienced himself. He'd smashed a few honeys here and there, but he wasn't a fuck machine by any stretch.

"You gonna tell me your name?" she flirted.

"Chris," he said without looking at her.

"Chris? Ain't that a girl name?"

Chris slowly turned his head to her and twisted his lips. "Hell nah! Who told you that shit?"

"Nobody. It's just that everybody I know named Chris is a girl."

"Well, not me. I am all male, baby."

The two of them continued to walk until they came
to the food court. It was a little after eleven, and Chris's
stomach was starting to growl. With Dana right on his
heels, he strolled up to the Arthur Treacher's counter and
ordered a fish dinner.

"I guess you want me to treat you too, huh?" he asked.

"Only if you want to."

Normally, Chris would've ordered his food and left her
standing there stuck on stupid. But with the news of his
sister getting better, he was in a good mood and figured
what the hell. It also didn't hurt that she was very pretty,
and he was extremely attracted to her. She smiled as he
told her to order what she wanted.

The two of them sat down and started making small
talk. Out of the blue, Dana looked at him and said, "I
hope you don't think you gon' get some ass for buying me
a fish dinner."

Chris laughed hysterically. "Nah, shorty, I don't think
that. Hell, I hope you ain't that loose that you would give
up the ass for a damn dinner."

Damn, Dana thought as she uncrossed her fingers and
took them from under the table.

"Ooooh, yes. Yes. Oh, my God, yes!"

With each stroke, Bishop dug deeper into the basement of Veronica's sex house. What had started out as
an innocent meal had turned into a steamy sex session.
After devouring the meal Veronica had prepared, the
two off them consumed damn near the entire bottle of
alcohol. Before long, they had started sharing secrets and
fantasies. Bishop had intended to back off, considering
Veronica's reputation. He softened a bit when she confided in him that it was mostly self-generated, although he
didn't fully believe her.

But it wasn't until the liquor started talking and she challenged his manhood that he stepped to her and promised to knock her guts loose. Veronica made the mistake of seeing him as just another young dude who was all talk, until she saw the package he was working with. And although the size was quite impressive for a youngster, she still wasn't fully convinced. But after the second stroke almost touched her spine, Veronica was more than satisfied with Bishop's cock game.

"That's it, Bishop! That's it, baby, right there!"

Veronica then wrapped her legs around Bishop and pulled him in as deep as he could go. She howled in passion as she released onto the sheets. Bishop wasn't far behind as he filled the latex condom to the rim. Veronica's leg shook violently from her orgasm. The 23-year-old vixen had been thoroughly dicked down by young Bishop.

"Oh, shit, baby, that was the bomb."

"Hell yeah," Bishop said as he reached over and squeezed her tits.

"Oooo, baby, don't do that shit. You gon' make a bitch cum again," she said, squirming.

"That's just what the fuck I'm tryin'a do," he said as he crawled back on top of her.

"Oh, baby, wait, wait. Oh, shit," she moaned as he stuck it back inside of her. Just that quick, he'd gotten hard again. He was so amped up he didn't even bother to use a different rubber. For the next twenty minutes, Bishop proceeded to pound her pussy to pieces. New cum pushed the old cum out, forcing it to overflow and gush out of her womb and down her leg.

Bishop rolled over and lay on his back. He was exhausted this time. Afterward, the two of them made the decision to keep their rendezvous undercover for a while. Bishop then got up and got dressed. After saying goodbye, he walked home on wobbly legs.

When Bishop got home, Carla was sitting at the kitchen table. Her eyes were red and puffy. Anger flashed in her eyes when she looked up and saw Bishop.

"You happy now, Bishop? He left. He's gone. Because of you, my man left me."

Bishop didn't know what to say. He thought that he was doing a good thing by protecting his sister. But now he was wondering if he should've gotten involved at all.

"I'm sorry, sis," he said, dropping his head. "When I saw yo' face like that, I just lost it."

"Bishop, I told you that I'd hit him first."

"But still, you're my sister. I couldn't just let that shit ride."

"Sit down, Bishop." When Bishop sat across from her, she looked him in the eye. "Bishop, I know I put you in our shit a lot, and I'm sorry about that. But if you're gonna stay here, then you can't be beatin' up on my man, especially if I brought that shit on myself."

Bishop instantly got angry. "Hol' up! So what you tellin' me is that if I see this clown kickin' yo' muthafuckin' ass, then I should just turn my head and walk the fuck away?"

"Oh, I didn't say that shit now. If you see that nigga puttin' the beatdown on a bitch, you jump in and fuck his ass up!" Both of them laughed slightly. "But, Bishop, you was gonna shoot him."

Bishop thought about what his sister was saying and realized that he could've been in jail right now. He made himself a solemn promise that he wasn't going to get involved in her business unless Jason was damn near killing her.

Chapter 11

Tangie stormed out of her house and stomped up the street. She didn't know exactly where she was going, but the place had to include a shelf with vodka and gin. She couldn't believe that Antwan was showing his ass the way he was. All she asked him was did he feel like taking her out to dinner, and he had a shit fit. "Ungrateful bastard," she mumbled to herself. "After that hellafied blowjob I gave his ass this mornin', the nigga oughta take me out for the next week."

Tangie stopped at the first bar she laid eyes on. She walked in with an attitude, determined to drink away her anger. She looked around and breathed a sigh of relief when she noticed that the place was practically empty. Besides herself, there were only three other people in attendance. There were two half-drunk women sitting at the bar gossiping, and there was also one lonely looking woman sipping on a Corona.

She looked disappointed when Tangie walked in, almost as if she was expecting someone in particular. Tangie walked over and plopped down on a stool. She made sure that she sat far enough away from the other patrons so there would be no casual conversation. With the mood she was in, Tangie did not feel like being bothered. A few minutes after she sat down, the bartender strolled up. He was a heavyset, older man who walked with a slight limp. The look in his eyes told Tangie that he intended to flirt with her as soon as he got to her. But the look in her eyes said, "Don't fuck with me."

"What'll you have?" he asked, taking the hint.

"Let me get a double martini."

While the bartender was busy fixing her drink, her cell phone rang. Without even looking at the screen, she sent it to voicemail. She knew that it was probably Antwan, and she didn't want to talk to him right then.

When the bartender brought her drink back, Tangie downed it in ten seconds flat. The bartender was on his way to wait on the two half-drunk women when Tangie called out for him to fix her another. One of the women popped her lips when the bartender did a U-turn and walked back to serve Tangie.

"The fuck kinda shit is this?" she said to her friend. "We been spendin' mad cheese in here. This bitch just got in here, and he treatin' her ass like she a VIP."

Tangie's head snapped around. "Who the fuck you callin' a bitch?" she screamed. "Ho, you don't know me, so you best mind ya fuckin' bidness!"

"Whoa, wait a minute now. I'm not gonna have that in here. If you ladies wanna fight, y'all gon' have to take that nonsense outside." As the bartender poured Tangie's drink, the other two women and Tangie continued to stare at each other.

The bartender couldn't say it out loud for fear of it getting back to his boss, but truth be told, he really wanted the two women to leave. From the moment they walked through the door, they were causing trouble. Before Tangie arrived, they were snickering and pointing at the other woman, who was doing nothing more than keeping to herself. He'd hoped that by not serving them fast enough, they would get up and leave. But his plan seemed to backfire.

When the bartender set Tangie's second drink down, she sipped that one a little more deliberately. Out of the corner of her eye, she could see the women whispering and stealing quick glances her way.

Thinking that she may have to whoop some ass, Tangie took out her cell phone and called Veronica. The two of them had always had each other's backs, so Tangie knew she could call on her girl. That thought disappeared when her call went straight to voicemail. Tangie tried again and got the same result. "Yo, bitch, get the dick outta yo' mouth and answer the phone," she said, leaving her homegirl a message. Tangie then got up to go to the bathroom but stopped in her tracks. After thinking about it, she snatched her drink off the counter and took it with her. She didn't trust the two women, or the bartender for that matter.

Tangie walked into the bathroom and headed for the first stall. She had to piss so badly her stomach hurt. She set her glass down on top of the toilet paper dispenser, pulled her pants down, and handled her business. She knew it seemed like a nasty thing to do, but she wasn't about to leave her drink unattended.

After relieving her bladder and wiping herself dry, Tangie emerged from the stall. Standing there with screwed-up faces were the two women at the bar. "What's up now, bitch?" one of them said. "Talk that bullshit now!"

Tangie looked at both women who were struggling to stand up, and she started laughing.

"The fuck so funny, bitch?"

"You two drunk, ignorant-ass hoes, coming in here like y'all on some gangsta shit. Get the fuck out my way."

The shorter woman walked up on Tangie, waving her finger. "Bitch, let me tell you—"

That's as far as she got before Tangie threw her drink in her face. The woman staggered back, frantically trying to wipe the alcohol out of her eyes. Tangie then turned her attention to the other woman, but before she knew what was happening, the woman rushed her. The football-like tackle momentarily knocked the wind out of Tangie. She fell back into the stall and landed on her ass. Trying desperately to catch her breath, Tangie began to cover up as the women started throwing wild punches.

By this time, the woman who was the recipient of Tangie's facial splash had reemerged. "Fuckin' bitch," she said, pulling out her switchblade. In one quick motion, she had it pressed against Tangie's throat. "Now I gotta carve yo' stupid ass up," she threatened.

Before she could make good on it, she heard a pistol click from behind her. The woman turned around to see the lonely looking woman aiming a .25 at her.

"Hey, this shit ain't even your business," the other woman said.

"Well, I'm making it my fuckin' business. Let her the fuck go!"

The two women took one look at the seriousness in her eyes and backed off. "This ain't ova, bitch," the woman said as she and her friend walked toward the door.

Tangie had never been so grateful in her life. She didn't know if the woman would have cut her, but she didn't want to find out. "Thanks," Tangie said, still a little out of breath.

"Don't worry about it. Them bitches been getting on my nerves ever since I walked through the door. I'm Cynthia," she said, extending her hand.

"I'm Tangie. Let's get the fuck outta here. I got some liquor at home we can drink. Shit, I just came here to get out of the house." Tangie peeked out of the door just in case the two women were waiting to ambush them. When she saw the coast was clear, she walked out. A few more people had come into the bar since she'd been in the bathroom. Tangie sucked her teeth when she noticed the bartender all up in a strawberry's face. She looked back Cynthia, who just shook her head.

"No wonder his fat ass don't know what's goin' on."

"Hol' up a second. I gotta pay my tab."

"Don't worry about it, girl, I already got it."

"Shit, thanks again." Tangie and Cynthia walked out of the bar and jumped into Cynthia's 2016 Dodge Charger. As the two of them headed toward Tangie's house, Tangie couldn't help but imagine how much fun she, Cynthia, and Veronica were going to have together.

Antwan crept out of Rhonda's apartment on rubber legs. She had fucked, sucked, and drained him dry. He hadn't planned on going to see her, but when Tangie sent his call to voicemail, it pissed him off. Even though he was wrong for going off on her the way he did, Antwan felt that whenever he called, she was supposed to answer. So when Rhonda sex texted him a picture of her dripping wet vagina, he couldn't resist making that trip. The funny thing about Antwan sleeping with Rhonda though was that it totally went against his "never sleep where you shit" rule.

Rhonda and Tangie were cousins. First cousins, as a matter of fact. The two hadn't spoken to each other in three years. The blame rested squarely with Antwan, who got drunk one night and pushed up on Rhonda after running into her at a club. Rhonda, trying to be a good cousin, ran right back and told Tangie. But instead of Tangie believing her own flesh and blood, she accused Rhonda of trying to break up her and Antwan, implying that she thought Rhonda wanted him for herself. Rhonda became enraged. The two of them engaged in a heated argument in which Tangie, who had secretly always been jealous of Rhonda's looks, told her cousin that Antwan would never want a piece of trash like her.

Rhonda's feelings were crushed. She cried for days, but after the crying stopped, revenge crept in. Rhonda promised herself that she would make Tangie hurt just as much as she hurt. She caught up with Antwan at Gordon Park one day and offered the goods up to him. She had planned on recording it and sending Tangie a copy just to show her two things: that her man wasn't shit, and that she could indeed fuck him if she wanted to. But something else happened. She got sprung. And since she knew that Antwan was never going to leave Tangie for her, she became content being the side chick. That wild incident made Antwan adopt his rule.

Antwan thought about the way Rhonda had ridden his dick like a rodeo star, and he got hard all over again. He thought about turning around and going back to get another shot, but then decided that he at least owed it to Tangie to tell her why he went off like that. It really wasn't anything she did. Antwan was just so frustrated that he'd come that close to getting in the dope game and didn't. In his mind, that was his big shot at making a grand come up.

But after visiting Rhonda, his motivation was restored. Antwan stuck in his favorite CD, *Get Rich or Die Tryin'* by 50 Cent, and jammed to it the rest of the way home. He pulled into his driveway and looked at his watch. He had just enough time to eat and shower. Earlier, he'd received a text from Temp calling an urgent meeting over at his house. Antwan got out of his car and walked up on the porch. He did a double take when he saw a car he didn't recognize sitting in front of his house. Instantly, thoughts started running through his head.

"Man, this bitch betta not be stupid enough to have another nigga in here," he said. "'Cause it's gon' be a muthafuckin' problem if she do." He patted his gun.

Antwan eased through the door. He was half expecting to hear moaning sounds coming from the house. But instead, all he heard was laughter coming from the kitchen. Confused by what was going on, Antwan walked into the kitchen to see both women sitting across from each other. They were both slapping the table and laughing hysterically, and both of them had nearly empty glasses of liquor in front of them. His face twisted when he saw a woman he didn't recognize. Wanting to make his presence known, Antwan cleared his throat.

"Oh, hey, Antwan," Tangie said, unenthused. She was still a little upset about his blowup earlier. "I want you to meet my friend, Cynthia."

"Sup," Antwan spoke as he walked straight to the refrigerator.

"Hello," Cynthia responded.

Antwan grabbed a beer and looked at Cynthia again. There was something about her face that was strangely familiar, but he couldn't quite put his finger on it. As Tangie and Cynthia continued to talk, Antwan went upstairs to get ready to meet up with his boys. He tried one last time to remember where he'd seen Cynthia before, but he couldn't. He thought about asking her but decided against it.

"Oh, well," he mumbled. "The shit will come to me sooner or later."

Chapter 12

Temp sat on the top step of his back porch, smoking a Black & Mild. Instinctively he looked down at his wrist and became murder mad when he remembered he didn't have his watch anymore. This had been a hell of a day for Temp. He still hadn't heard anything from Yolonda regarding the beatdown he'd given her. He was so nervous he'd dropped the cigar three separate times. At any minute, he expected the Cleveland Police Department to run up on him and arrest him. When an ambulance drove down the main street, flashing its sirens, Temp nearly jumped out of his skin. He walked through the house to the front door and peered out. After doing that, he walked to the back door and checked to make sure that the door was unlocked. He had fully planned to make a mad dash if them boys came calling.

"The fuck takin' these dudes so long?" he asked himself. Temp turned around and walked toward the kitchen. He looked down at the couch disgustedly. Lying there with his mouth wide open and snoring was his father. As usual, he was passed out drunk. Temp grabbed a beer and headed out the back door. When he got back out there, he saw Niko sitting on the steps rolling a blunt.

"Damn, nigga, when the fuck you get here?"

"A coupla minutes ago. I was just gettin' back here when you went in the house."

"Cool. Put that shit in the air, dawg."

"Damn, can you let me finish rollin' it up first?"

Just then, Bishop came around the corner, startling Temp into jumping. "Nigga, what the fuck you jumping fo'?" Bishop asked.

"Nigga, ain't nobody jump."

"Man, you did jump. Somebody after yo' ass or some-thin'?"

"Yeah, whateva," Temp said.

"A'ight," Antwan called out as he walked around the corner. "What the fuck was so important?"

Once again, Temp jumped. Although they were his boys, Temp didn't want them involved in what he'd done, so he figured the best way to keep them in the clear was keep what he had done a secret between him and God.

"And what the fuck you jumpin' for?"

"Man, I asked his scary ass the same damn question," Bishop said.

"You need me to go and buy yo' timid ass a nightlight?" Antwan joked.

"Man, fuck y'all," Temp screamed. "Anyway, the reason I called you muthafuckas ova here—"

"What up, peeps," Chris said before he could finish. For the third time, Temp jumped. The rest of them looked at each other but didn't say anything. Antwan made a mental note to ask his friend what was going on. He'd never seen Temp so jumpy before.

"I thought you said yo' ass wasn't coming."

"I wasn't, but I changed my mind. Let's get this shit going. I got school tomorrow," Chris said, smiling. The rest of the crew looked at each other and cracked up.

"School? You know damn well yo' ass ain't been to school in forever," Niko laughed.

"Nigga, I know yo' ass ain't talkin'," Chris shot back.

"Yo, dawg, if you muthafuckas are through talkin' 'bout the dumb shit, can we get down to business now?" Temp interrupted them.

"What's up, man?" Antwan asked.

"Yo, man, check this bullshit out. I went to the bar last night to toss a few back and clear my head on a couple things. The next thing I know, I'm being jacked by these two bitches. Now—"

"Hol' up, nigga," Niko cut in. "Did you just say that you got jacked by a coupla bitches?" The whole crew broke out into laughter. One by one, Temp stared at them like he wanted to fuck each one of them up.

"Muthafucka, if y'all would shut the fuck up and listen, it's more to the fuckin' story."

"A'ight, y'all. Chill out, and let's hear what this nigga gotta say," Antwan told the rest of the crew.

"Well, like the fuck I was sayin', me and shorty was feelin' each other. We was goin' at it hot and heavy right there in the bar. Then we took our li'l porno show to the bathroom. Man, this bitch started giving me head, and the next thing I know, her friend put a muthafuckin' hammer to my fuckin' head! The bitches made me turn around, and the next thing I know, the bartender helpin' me the fuck up off the floor!"

"Damn, dawg! Them hoes laid the smack down on yo' ass," Niko said.

"Oh, nigga, that ain't even the worst part."

Eyebrows went up in anticipation of what Temp was going to say next.

"After I left the bar, I was on my way home and forgot that I'd left my watch there on the floor. I thought that shit was kinda funny that they didn't take it. I went back to get it, and that's when I saw all three of them mutha-fuckas standin' in front of the fuckin' bar, laughin'! It was a setup! Them schemin' muthafuckas set me the fuck up!"

"Oh, hell nah! That shit ain't gonna fly," Niko screamed. "We gon' have to tighten they asses up behind that sucka-ass shit!"

"You gotdamn right," Antwan concurred.

"Well, what I was thinkin' was we might as well kill two birds with one stone," Temp said.

"The fuck you mean by that?" Bishop asked.

"What I mean is that we can get revenge for them hoes and that punk-ass nigga jackin' me and make a come up at the same time."

The rest of the crew looked at each other and smiled. All except Bishop. He was getting tired of doing petty crimes for small change.

"The fuck wrong wit'chu, Bishop?" Temp asked.

"Man, ain't y'all tired o' doin' these penny-ante-ass jobs? We need to do something that's gonna bring us a big-ass score."

"Nigga, do you got a plan for this big-ass score you talkin' 'bout?"

"Nah, but—"

"Bishop, let's get this job out of the way first. I got a plan that's gonna net us all a good chunk o' change."

Antwan had one more trick up his sleeve, but now wasn't the time to reveal it. Going to see Rhonda had produced more than a nut.

"Yeah. A'ight, man, whateva," Bishop said.

"Cool. Now let's put our heads together and come up with a plan to put those bitches and that ho-ass nigga in their place."

"No need, playa. I've already come up with one," Temp said, smiling deviously.

Antwan sat in the Shake 'Em Up bar sipping on Jack Daniels. Every now and then he would rock back and forth, pretending to be drunk. Debra and Pam looked at each other and smiled. In Antwan, they saw what they felt was an easy mark. Antwan listened as they repeated the same lines they'd said to trap Temp. Antwan got up and fake staggered to the bathroom. When he came back out, Deb was just getting up to leave. This time it was Pam who would be luring their victim into the bathroom. Antwan looked around and surveyed the bar. There were about fifteen people present, and he wondered how the two women were planning to pull off a robbery with so many other patrons in the bar.

Right on cue, the bartender yelled, "Last call." People looked at their watches and held up their hands. They were obviously confused.

"Sorry about this, people," he said. "I just got an emergency call telling me that my wife has been rushed to the hospital. I'm sorry for your inconvenience, but please settle your tabs because I have to go."

Customers who had tabs rushed to the counter to pay them. Antwan glanced to his right and noticed that Pam wasn't moving. He started to get up and leave, but the bartender got his attention and slowly shook his head, signaling to Antwan that he didn't have to leave. When the last customer had left, the bartender walked over to Antwan.

"You don't have to leave, my man. I just did that because you and this young lady are the only ones spending any money. And I ain't in the business of letting people hang out in here without spending any money."

Antwan knew it was bullshit but kept quiet for the sake of the plan. After a few minutes, Pam started flirting with him. Before another ten minutes had passed, she was all over him.

"Hey, baby, why don't you come in the bathroom and let me give you a treat?" she told him.

Antwan let her lead him into the ladies' room. Once inside, she followed the exact same script her partner had. While she was giving Antwan head, she wondered why it was taking so long for Debra to appear. The last thing she wanted was for Antwan to bust in her mouth. She had no desire to taste a man's sperm. The only thing a man could do for her was introduce her to his sister. When it became apparent that something had gone awry with the plan, she tried to stop. But Antwan wasn't having that. She tried to pull back, but Antwan grabbed the back of her head and held it there.

"Uh-uh, you li'l slick bitch. Finish that shit," he said, taking out his gun. "And if you bite my dick, I'ma blow the top of yo' muthafuckin' roof off."

Pam started to gag. She didn't mind sucking a dick if it meant that she was going to get paid for doing it. But to be forced to do it made her sick to her stomach. She didn't know what had happened to her partner. She just hoped that she was all right. Knowing that Antwan would surely hurt her if she didn't do what he'd told her to do, Pam sucked harder. She wanted to get this over with as quickly as possible. Antwan grunted loudly when he came in her mouth. Pam scooted back and immediately threw up.

Her eyes watered as she continued to feel nauseous. She looked up and became terrified as she saw her partner being led from the last stall at gunpoint by Niko and Bishop. The last stall was equipped with a trap door that ran from the women's bathroom to the back of the building. The owner had it put in a few years ago in case one of the ladies had to make a fast getaway. He also had one installed in the men's bathroom. Closely following them was Temp. When Pam saw his face, she almost passed out. The look in his eyes was pure hatred as he walked up to her, palming a switchblade. She didn't know where her uncle Joe was, but seeing that Temp had regained possession of his watch, it didn't look good for him.

"Sup, bitch? Remember me?" When she didn't answer, Temp hauled off and backhanded her. "I asked you a question, bitch. Do you fuckin' remember me?"

Pam nodded her head slowly. She looked at Debra and for the first time noticed that there was blood coming from her lip. "Yeah, I thought that might jog yo' mutha-fuckin' memory." Temp punched Pam in the stomach, causing her to double over in pain.

"Bitch, did you actually think you was gonna jack me and get away with that shit?" Pam looked up at Temp with fire in her eyes. The look resulted in a vicious kick to the face.

"Bitch, who the fuck you looking at like that? And where the fuck is my money?"

"I don't have it," Pam said weakly.

"Niko," Temp said, looking at his fellow Young Lionz. Niko responded by slamming the butt of his gun into Debra's mouth. Debra slumped to her knees, dazed.

"Now let's try this bullshit again, bitch. Where the fuck is my money?"

When Pam didn't answer fast enough, Chris put his gun in the middle of Debra's forehead and cocked.

"Okay, wait," Pam screamed, holding out her arms. "It's in our car."

"A'ight. Let's go get that shit," Antwan said.

Pam started to get up, but Antwan pushed her back down to the floor. "Not you, bitch. You stay here. Temp," he said, looking at his friend, "me, Niko, and Chris gon' go get this money. You and Bishop stay here. If we ain't back in ten minutes, put a hole in this bitch."

When Antwan and the rest of the Young Lionz went to get the money, Temp looked at Pam and smiled wickedly. He reached down and unzipped his pants.

"Now I'm gonna make you finish what yo' slutty-ass girlfriend started, bitch. Get back down on yo' knees."

When Pam hesitated, Temp cocked his pistol. "Bitch, you think I'm playin' with yo' ass?"

Bishop didn't say a word. Although he understood that Temp was pissed, he didn't agree with him making a bitch suck his dick at gunpoint. When Temp pulled out his penis, Pam looked at it like it was the serpent in the Garden of Eden. Instantly she recoiled.

"Suck it, bitch," Temp screamed at her as he pointed his gun at the middle of her forehead. Hesitantly, Pam crawled back over to Temp and grabbed his dick. She was so angry and felt so violated that she wanted to yank it right off his body. But she knew doing that would mean instant death. The boys looked young in her eyes, but they were also quite dangerous. She made a disgusted-looking face as she wrapped her lips around it.

Pam thought seriously about biting Temp's dick off. Even if his friends blew her brains out, it might have been worth it to her for the humiliation he was causing her. But in the end, she decided that she didn't want to die. She began sucking for all she was worth. She was hoping that either they would return with the money before he came in her mouth or that he wouldn't come at all. She would receive no such answers to her prayers. When Antwan returned with her partner and the cash, it didn't stop Temp at all. He was determined to get what Debra had cheated him out of.

"Man, what the fuck?" Antwan said upon seeing Pam's tear-streaked face going up and down on Temp's knob. Temp held up a finger, indicating for them to wait a second. When Temp came, Pam tried to jerk her head back before any of it got in her mouth. For this, she was rewarded with a face full of semen.

"Damn, bitch, you suck a good dick," he said, zipping up his pants.

"Go to hell!" she screamed.

"You first, bitch." Before anyone could protest, Temp shot Pam in the face.

Bishop rushed over and snatched the gun out of Temp's hand. "Man, what the fuck you doin'? You got yo' fuckin' money back. Why the fuck you shoot her?"

"'Cause, nigga, them bitches played me to the mutha-fuckin' left, that's why." Temp cocked his head to the side and stared screw faced at Bishop. "Yo, nigga, you been actin' like a real-live bitch-ass nigga lately! What the fuck is yo' problem, man? When the fuck did you develop a fuckin' soft spot for hoes?"

"It ain't about having a soft spot for no damn ho. It's about yo' ass goin' off the deep end. Every time we turn around lately, yo' ass is shootin' some damn body!"

As soon as Debra heard this, she immediately pissed on herself.

"Nasty bitch," Chris said.

Antwan wrapped his arm around Bishop and led him away from the rest of the crew. "Dude, you a'ight?" he asked.

"Yeah, man, I'm cool. I just don't understand why the fuck we gotta kill somebody every time we jack they asses."

"Bishop, you gotta realize, man, that when you take from people, you gon' have to look over your shoulder for the rest of your life. Ain't nobody in they right mind gonna just let you take what they've worked so hard for, man. And as far as this situation is concerned, these bitches violated, man. You mean to tell me that you give a fuck about these bitches more than you do your brothers, man? Come on, dawg. We been there through thick and thin, and no matter what happens, you can't go against ya crew, man." Antwan pushed Bishop back with his hands on both of Bishop's shoulders and looked him in his eyes. "Bishop, you gon' have to man up, dawg. Now

I know you ain't scared, but this is survival of the fittest. It's a dog-eat-dog world out there, man. What are you, playa: a pit bull or a mutt?"

Bishop sighed and looked over at Temp. He knew that his friend's pride was wounded badly when the two women stuck him up. He also knew that he'd pledged with the rest of the Young Lionz to be down with them for life. But Bishop was getting tired of killing innocent people for a few dollars. He made the decision right then to start pulling away from his homies. But for now, he would have to sink or swim with them.

While he was thinking about how he was going to break away from his crew, Temp walked around and got behind a crying Debra. She'd been bawling uncontrollably since he'd shot her friend.

"Bitch, shut up," he said, grabbing her in a reverse chokehold. Using his strength to lift her off her feet, Temp squeezed his forearms together as tight as he could until he crushed her windpipe. Debra fell dead on the spot.

"Yo, let's get the fuck outta here," Antwan yelled. The Young Lionz were fast becoming notorious. One by one, they stepped over Joe's dead body as they walked out the back door.

Chapter 13

Detective Tracy Ramsey sat back in her chair and kicked her long legs up on the desk. At six feet one, she was easily the tallest woman on the police force. With a cup of coffee in her hand, she thought back to the grisly murder scene at Lucky's house. The motive didn't appear to be robbery. There wasn't anything missing. It had crossed her mind that it had been a murder/suicide, but her gut feeling told her that this was something else altogether. Even more disturbing was the fact that the woman's daughter was found bleeding to death in a nearby park. Ramsey wanted to talk to the girl, but she was in a coma.

It also saddened Ramsey that the girl was pregnant and had lost her baby during the attack. Although she was a superb detective, she didn't need her training to tell her what had happened in this instance. Too many times she'd seen women get assaulted because sorry-ass men didn't want to be fathers. It sickened her to think that a man could do this to a woman. Before she became a cop, she too was an abused wife. Just because she couldn't get pregnant, her husband took it out on her and pounded her mercilessly. When he packed up his shit and left, it was the best thing that could've happened to her. Last she heard, he'd jumped on the woman he'd left her for, and the woman's brothers beat him damn near to death. Her only regret was that she wasn't there to see it.

Ramsey tapped her French-manicured hands on top of her desk. Her eyes gravitated toward the door as her partner, John Reynolds, walked up to her desk. Shrugging her shoulders, she sat up and looked at him. "She woke yet?"

"Nope. She's still in a coma, partner."

Just as fast as the smile had appeared on Tracy's face, it vanished. She knew that it hadn't been that long since the girl was admitted to the hospital, but she was hoping for some good news. She decided to go back down to the evidence locker and look over what was taken off of the girl. Maybe she'd missed something important, something that would give her the ammunition to sink the bastard who had done this.

Yolonda could hear the nurse's voice in the background, but she couldn't move. All she could do was lie there and cry on the inside of her soul. She knew that Temp was going to be upset when she told him that she didn't want to get an abortion, but she didn't know he was going to try to kill her. When Temp first hit her, she thought it was a terrible dream she was having. The pain soon destroyed that notion.

She would never get to change the child's diaper or listen to its cry. Even if she got pregnant ten more times, nothing could replace the void that Temp had caused in her life. Yolonda may have been in a coma, but her mind was still aware. She couldn't move. She couldn't communicate with anyone. It has often been said that coma victims are aware of everything that goes on around them, but they can't act on it. Their limbs are frozen. Their voices become trapped in their throats. Deep inside her own mind, she swore with every fiber in her being that if she ever made it back to the land of the living, she would make Temp pay with his life.

***

Nearly twenty-four hours after committing a triple murder, Bishop and Chris sat on the couch, each one gripping a joystick intensely. The $100 winner-take-all wager sat on the coffee table in front of them. It only intensified their respective competitive natures. Niko was walking around the room, smiling like he'd won the lottery. His cell phone was pressed up against his ear while Regina whispered sweet nothings into it.

"Look at this love-sick-ass nigga," Temp said to Antwan as the two of them passed a blunt back and forth.

"Man, why you always dissin' our li'l partners, man? You act like they ain't down."

Temp looked around the room and grinned slightly. When his eyes stopped at Bishop, he frowned somewhat. "I ain't worried about all of 'em. Just that cotton-soft-ass nigga over there," he said, gesturing toward Bishop.

"Temp, you know good and damn well that Bishop ain't soft."

"Then he oughta stop actin' like it."

Antwan looked at his friend and sighed. "Temp, yo' ass has been off the hook lately. I mean damn, nigga, you gotta shoot everybody who crosses our path? You gonna get us locked up before we get halfway rich."

"Speakin' of which," Temp said, as he chose to ignore Antwan's statement, "what is this big-ass plan you got goin' on?"

Antwan grabbed the blunt from Temp, stuck it between his lips, and took a long, deep pull. After blowing smoke into the air, he stared at Temp for a few seconds. "First things first, nigga. What the fuck been up with you?"

"The fuck you talkin' 'bout, nigga?"

"Temp, you know what I'm talkin' 'bout, man. Yo' ass was jumpy as fuck in ya backyard, and you been nervous ever since. What the hell you done did, playa?"

Temp looked at Antwan like he was Matlock. He thought about lying and telling Antwan that everything was okay, but he knew his friend would see right through it. "Man, I think I fucked up wit' Yolonda, man."

"Who?"

"Yolonda, man. The broad I told you I fucked around with a coupla months ago."

Antwan looked up in the sky, trying to figure out who his buddy was talking about. Then it hit him. "Oh," he said, popping his fingers. "You talking about that thick bitch with the fat ass!"

"Yeah, that's her." Seeing the look on Temp's face told Antwan that whatever he was about to say was going to be bad.

"Man, what did you do, man?"

After Temp ran the story of his assault of Yolonda down to him, Antwan was shocked. He didn't know whether to respect Temp's gangster move or despise him for his unspeakable act. Temp paying for the women he screwed around with to get an abortion was one thing. But doing what he did to ensure his seed wasn't born was downright despicable.

"Temp, you know you my nigga straight from the placenta. But that shit was just foul, man."

"I know, man. I just fuckin' panicked. That's why I been so jumpy and shit. I been halfway expectin' the cops to come for a nigga any second."

"Did you even go back to see about the bitch, man?"

"Hell nah! You think I was gonna go back there and risk havin' them boys haul my ass away? Fuck that shit!"

"Yeah, that woulda been a dumb-ass move," Antwan laughed.

"Man, I don't know what happened to that bitch. I know it's wrong, but I'm just glad that I might not have to pay no fuckin' child support!"

Antwan looked at Temp like he was retarded. "Nigga, you ain't got no muthafuckin' job no damn way!"

"Man, whatever. I don't remember yo' ass fillin' out a damn W-2 last year either! Now, what about this plan you was talkin' about?"

Antwan sat back and rubbed his chin. He debated back and forth in his mind which one of his comrades he was going to let in on the plan before he divulged it to the rest of the crew. At first, he was leaning toward Bishop. But the more he thought about it, the more he realized that Temp may have had the better temperament to serve as his right-hand man in the dope game.

"A'ight, dawg. Let me break this shit down to you."

Antwan leaned in real close to his friend and told him of his master plan to get rich. Temp smiled as Antwan broke the plan down to him. Dollar signs danced around in his head as he thought about becoming rich at a young age. Temp had no idea that Antwan knew anything about the dope game. He was going to take some of the money that they had made robbing and stealing and buy him a few pounds of weed to turn over, but Antwan's plan seemed much more profitable. Temp nodded slowly as Antwan continued to explain to him how they were going to generate paper. After he finished, he told the other members of his crew that he had to make a run and to let themselves out.

"How the fuck we s'pose ta get home?" Chris asked.

"Here," Temp said, tossing Bishop his keys. "Drop these niggas off. I'll pick my car up later."

Antwan and Temp sat in the parking lot of IHOP staring at Rhonda and her man, Bo, through the window. They had been sitting there for a little over twenty minutes.

"Yo, how you know you can trust this muthafucka, man?" Temp asked.

"I don't trust that nigga. But I trust my bitch." Antwan looked over at Temp. "Nigga, you ain't getting cold feet, is you?"

"Hell nah! You know betta than that shit! I just ain't tryin' to get hauled off to the fuckin' pen fuckin' with some clown we don't even know!"

"Be cool, homeboy. I got the shit under control."

The two of them got out of the car and walked into the restaurant. Rhonda nodded at Antwan to let Bo know that was the person they were waiting for. Bo was a cocky, arrogant son of a bitch whom Rhonda only dealt with to keep her pockets fat. He was constantly in and out of town on dope-man business. He was 27 years old with processed hair slicked back and a thin moustache connected to a goatee. His dark skin tone shined like wet coal, and his gravelly voice sounded like the Undertaker from the WWE. His was a rather thin dude but was extremely tall, standing nearly six feet five inches high.

As Antwan and Temp sat down, Rhonda scooted closer to Bo to give him the impression that she was getting closer to him out of admiration and love. Nothing could be further from the truth. The only reason that Rhonda was even putting Antwan on was she thought that it would eventually cause him to leave Tangie and be with her.

Bo smiled cockily as he wrapped his arm around Rhonda. "Your cousin here tells me that you want to do some business with me."

It took everything in Temp not to laugh in the man's face.

"Yeah, I do," Antwan said dryly. "She tells me that you're the man to come see if you want to get your feet wet and make a few dollars."

"She told you right, playa. Let me ask you something, though. Do you have anywhere to push this product? It makes no sense to have the stuff and not be able to get it off."

"I've done a little research," Antwan said. "I know of a few spots that's dry right now."

"Well, with the amount of product you're talking about getting, my friend, you're gonna need to be in a spot that really pops. But maybe I can help you out with that . . . for a small percentage of your intake."

"Is that right?"

Bo smiled. He liked Antwan's style. "I like you, my friend. You remind me of myself back in the day. Ambitious." Bo leaned in and stared whispering to them. "I just happen to know of a block that's in dire need of some guidance. There is a lot of money to be made on that block, and since the boys who were on it seemed to have disappeared, I need a few soldiers there to ensure the flow of cash."

Antwan didn't ask Bo what he meant when he said that the boys had disappeared. He already knew. Antwan's ear was always to the street, and he'd heard through the hood vine that some cats from Eighty-seventh and Wade Park had tried to beat a certain dope dealer out of some bread. The dealer promptly sent a few of his soldiers to put work in, and those cats were never heard from again. It didn't take a genius to figure out what the deal was as Bo was already known as a major player around that area.

"And since you my girl's peeps, I'm gonna do something that I normally never, ever do. I'm gonna front you and ya man here a couple of keys to get started with."

Antwan sat back and pondered Bo's offer. He didn't want to bite off more than he could chew. Two keys seemed like a hell of a lot of dope to be fronting people he didn't even know. Antwan couldn't help but wonder what his angle was. After thinking about Bo's proposition a few seconds longer, Antwan told him that he was willing to accept his offer.

Rhonda smiled on the inside, thinking that she was one step closer to having Antwan for herself. She would make it a point to teach Antwan how to cook and cut dope.

Chapter 14

After dropping the rest of the Young Lionz off, Bishop made a beeline to Veronica's house. He'd been thinking about her ever since he'd smoked her boots the day before. Just thinking about her pussy made Bishop's dick hard as steel. He couldn't wait to get in between her creamy thighs a second time. As he was thinking about Veronica, his cell phone rang with her on the other end.

"Hey, boo," she said when he answered the phone.

"Sup, girl. I was just about to come ova there and see what was up with you."

"Oh, is that right? You was jus' gon' drop by here unannounced, huh?"

"Shit, baby, I didn't think that you would mind after all the good lovin' I put on yo' ass the other day."

"Damn, nigga, you kinda conceited, ain't you?"

"Nah, just confident, baby, just confident."

"Whateva, nigga, yo' dick game okay."

"Okay," he said, offended. "Oh, I see you tryin' ta challenge a nigga, huh? A'ight then. This time I ain't gonna take it easy on yo' ass. This time I'ma wreck that pussy."

"Well, if you think you can swing it, then bring it, big boy," she said with a hint of seduction in her voice.

Veronica would never admit it to him, but Bishop had left her insides extremely sore. It had taken her the entire day to recover from the pounding. After hanging up with

Bishop, Veronica hurried into the shower. She wanted to be extra clean for her new fuck buddy when he got there. No sooner had she gotten done than her phone rang.

"Sup, bitch?" she said as her hello to Tangie.

"Nothin' much. Just sittin' ova here bored to fuckin' death. Come on through, ho. Let's blow a coupla trees."

"Can't right now, homegirl. I got company coming over."

"Whaattt? Bitch, I knew yo' ass was getting some dick from somewhere! Who the fuck is it?"

"None of yo' business, nosy bitch! Why you wanna know everything a bitch doin'?" Veronica said, laughing.

"Oh, bitch, I know you ain't tryin' ta get secretive on me!"

"Nah, it ain't that, girl. I just gotta hurry up and get ready 'cause he on his way over here."

"A'ight, bitch. But when that nigga get finish blowing yo' back out, you betta call me and gimme the muthafuckin' lowdown on who he is!"

"It's all good," Veronica said just before hanging up. Because she had no idea how her friend would react to her sleeping with her new, young lover, she chose to keep it under wraps for now.

After rubbing her body down with peach lotion, Veronica splashed on some sweet-smelling perfume she'd purchased from Victoria's Secret the day before. She wanted to look and smell as good as she possibly could when Bishop arrived. She went into her closet and took out a sheer red negligee. She had already made her mind up that she was going to attack Bishop as soon as he walked through the door.

She lit a couple of scented candles and inhaled sharply. The intoxicating smell of strawberries and cream caused her to get moist almost instantly. Veronica fanned herself as sexual heat radiated throughout her body. A nervous excitement traveled through her spine. Even she herself was surprised at the amount of anticipation that overcame her. She looked at her bed and frowned. It was covered with the same sheets that were on the bed from the last time. She quickly ripped them off the queen-sized love nest and replaced them with maroon silk ones. She then went back into the bathroom, grabbed a comb off the sink, and got her flowing locks together.

When she was sure that she looked her best, she went into her kitchen and headed toward the refrigerator. She opened it and took out a bottle of Moscato wine. After popping the cork, she poured two glasses full and set them inside the refrigerator to keep them chilled. Just then, she heard a car pull up in the driveway. Not expecting him to arrive in a car, Veronica mistakenly thought that someone else was at the door.

She quickly went to the window and looked out. She was fully prepared to shoo anyone away who she thought was about to come between her and Bishop's lovemaking session. She looked out and was pleasantly surprised to see that it was indeed Bishop who had pulled into the driveway. She didn't remember him having a car, but she would ask about that later. For now, all she wanted to do was get him into her house and devour him.

Veronica watched through the window as Bishop walked up to the door with a swag that caused her to yearn for him even more. She made it a point to open the door before he even knocked on it. Bishop took one look at her voluptuous body and started drooling. His dick almost poked a hole right through his pants.

"Damn," he mumbled as he stumbled through the door. Bishop almost tripped and fell flat on his face as he continued to stare at Veronica's body.

"Damn, boo, you a'ight?" she asked as she chuckled lightly.

"Yeah, I'm straight," he responded, trying to save face.

Veronica walked up to Bishop and threw her arms around his neck. Then she stuck her tongue so far down his throat she almost touched his tonsils. Feeling extremely turned on, Bishop reached behind her and palmed her ass. His dick pressed up against her pelvic area and threatened to insert itself inside of her. Veronica then pushed away from him, although it was a struggle for her to do so, and led him into the kitchen. She opened the refrigerator, took out the wine, and handed him a glass. Bishop, who really wasn't used to drinking anything except beer and liquor, made a face as he looked at the drink.

"The fuck is this?" he asked with a screwed-up face.

"It's wine, negro."

"Wine? The fuck you buy this shit for? You ain't got no liquor up in this piece?"

Veronica just shook her head. She knew there would be issues dealing with someone younger than she, but she at least thought Bishop knew what the hell wine was.

"Bishop, wine is like an aphrodisiac. It sets the mood."

"Oh, okay," he said, not wanting to show his ignorance but being too late to avoid doing so. Veronica took a swig of the sweet juice and motioned for Bishop to do the same. Bishop obliged. To his surprise, it actually tasted pretty good.

"You like it?"

"It ain't bad." He drank a little more. "To be honest, this shit tastes pretty good."

"So do I," she said, taking notice of his full lips.

"The fuck that s'pose ta mean?" he asked. Bishop had a strong feeling that he knew what Veronica was referring to, but he wasn't with that.

"Nothing, boy. I'm just' playin' with you," she said, even though she wasn't. The way he'd responded told her that he was a virgin when it came to fellatio.

It had been a long time since a man had gone down on her, and quite frankly, she missed the feeling. Eating pussy was one thing that Bishop hadn't done at his young age, and he wasn't about to start now. But Veronica wasn't worried. She knew that, in time, she could convince him to munch on her carpet if she played her cards right. She was a seductress, and she knew that if she put her mind to it, she could get Bishop to do her bidding.

After finishing the wine, Veronica led Bishop to the bedroom. As she walked through the doorway, she reached down on her dresser and flipped the on switch to her CD player. The smooth sounds of Her poured through the speakers. Veronica then led Bishop to the edge of the bed. She sat down, grabbed his belt buckle, and pulled him forward. Looking up at him with a lust that spoke volumes, Veronica slowly and deliberately unzipped his fly.

She could barely get it all the way down before his love muscle jumped out at her like a live boa constrictor. But this snake was nowhere near flexible. It was as hard as Chinese arithmetic. Veronica kissed the head of it. Then she started licking the shaft. After getting him good and heated up, she stuffed the whole thing in her mouth. Bishop let out low moans of pleasure as Veronica worked her magic on him like a porn star. Although she was enjoying what she was doing, this was also a trap.

She intended to give Bishop such good head that when she got ready for him to go down on her in the future, she could use this as a bargaining chip. Veronica massaged his balls as she continued to take it deep in her throat. She increased her speed and listened to him wilt under her talents.

"You like that shit, baby? You like it when mama sucks that?"

"Oh, hell yeah, baby. Don't stop," he stuttered.

"You want mama to show you a trick?" she asked him.

"Oooo, shit, go ahead, baby."

Veronica didn't know if Bishop had ever had the pleasure of receiving what she was about to do, but she knew that if he'd been dealing with younger women, he certainly would not have had it this good. Veronica started sucking faster and faster. Spit ran from the corners of the mouth and traveled down the sides of his dick. When Bishop got ready to cum, he tried to pull out and scoot back. Veronica smiled on the inside, knowing that since he was trying to take it out, he'd never had what she was about to give him. She wrapped her arms around his waist and held him in place.

"Oh, shit!" Bishop screamed as he shot his load into Veronica's awaiting mouth. To make it even better for him, Veronica made loud gulping sounds as she swallowed his cum. With his legs threatening to give out on him at any moment, Bishop sat down on the bed and lay back.

"Did you like that shit, baby?" she asked as she continued to stroke his dick.

"Hell yeah, baby, I loved that shit," Bishop said, breathing heavily. It only took Bishop five minutes to become hard again.

Damn, maybe I shoulda been fuckin' with young boys all along, Veronica thought.

She helped Bishop take off the rest of his clothes. For a lad so young, she couldn't believe the girth of his pecker. Once Bishop was completely naked, Veronica got on her hands and knees and told him to hit it from the back. She looked back at him and saw a look in his eyes that she'd seen from a man before. It was not a look she liked.

"Don't stick that muthafucka in my ass," she warned.

"Huh? I'm not, baby. I want that pussy."

"Well, make sure that's where you put it at."

Veronica didn't know if he'd planned on trying to be slick and sodomize her, but she wasn't going to take any chances. She'd had men shoot that line to her before that they'd thought when she bent over, she wanted them to get the ass. She thought it was kind of funny that Bishop had never eaten pussy but had maybe fucked a girl in the ass. Bishop eased the head of his dick into her juicy womb. Veronica cooed like a bird as pre-cum oozed from her womb.

"Oh, yeah, nigga, hit that shit."

Hearing Veronica talk like this only fueled Bishop's aggressiveness. He gripped both sides of her hips and began pounding away. Veronica was up to the challenge as she threw it back at him, giving as good as she got. Bishop then used a move that he'd learned from watching a porno movie. He reached down and grabbed her left leg and lifted it up in the air. He then stepped slightly to the side so he could go in deeper.

"Oh, shit, Bishop, you killing this pussy!" Bishop responded by punishing her womb more. When he finally did slow down, Veronica took advantage of it and quickly turned around, causing him to lose his balance. Bishop fell on his back. Before he knew what was happening, Veronica was on top of him. She reached down and grabbed his still-hard dick and started riding him like a rodeo star. She bounced up and down so fast that Bishop was afraid that she might break his dick. For the second time in less than twenty minutes, Bishop came. But this time it was deep inside of Veronica's sex core instead of her throat. Veronica came with him as she collapsed onto the bed. Smiles were plastered on both of their faces. Neither of them said a word for about five minutes.

"Damn, baby, that shit was the fuckin' bomb," Veronica finally said.

"You ain't lyin'. A nigga can get used to this shit," Bishop said, sticking his chest out.

Veronica jumped as she was startled by the ringing of her cell phone. She looked at her phone and then down at Bishop's still-hard member. She gave her phone the finger and lowered her head back down to Bishop's sweet stick.

Tangie slammed her phone shut so hard the shell almost cracked. It was killing her that she didn't know who her friend was fucking. Plus she wanted to tell her about the surprise birthday cookout that she was planning for Antwan. It would be held in their backyard and would be by invitation only. It was going to also be a grown-folks-only party. Tangie's friends who had kids were not going to be invited. She didn't want to be bothered with the possibility of her friend Bebe's kids running through her house and tearing up her shit. Besides, Veronica was the only one she really kicked it with anyway.

Tangie went to her phone's contact list and started texting Antwan's friends. She didn't want to run the risk of calling them because she didn't want Antwan to walk in and catch her on the phone. She told them that they were free to invite one guest apiece. After texting them, she received a text of her own. It was Cynthia asking her if she wanted to get together for drinks later on. Even though Tangie didn't feel like being bothered with anyone, she figured that she'd take this opportunity to invite her to the cookout. But instead of texting her back, Tangie called her.

"Hello?" Cynthia answered.

"Hey, girl, what you up to?"

"Not a damn thing. I was wondering if you wanted to kick it tonight."

"Sorry, girl, I promised Antwan I was gonna spend a little quality time with him, if you know what I mean," she lied.

"Oh, I feel you on that one, girl. We can hook up some other time then."

"Hey, while I got you on the phone though, I wanted to invite you to a cookout I'm giving. It's for Antwan's birthday."

"Umm, I don't know, girl. I'll have to see if I can get somebody to babysit my son."

There was a momentary awkward silence on the phone. Cynthia was waiting to see if Tangie was going to tell her she could just bring her son with her. Tangie, on the other hand, was debating if she should break her "no kids" rule for someone she'd just met. After carefully considering it, Tangie decided that if she was going to become friends with Cynthia, she could afford to break her rule this one time. But first, there was something she needed to know.

"Tell you what. Does your son like to watch cartoons?"

"Does he like to watch cartoons? Girl, that's all he likes to do," Cynthia laughed.

"Cool. Bring him on over and we can sit him in front of the television while we in the backyard doing grown-up shit. If you want, you can even bring a guest. I mean, if his father is still in the picture, you can—"

"Hell nah, that bastard ain't still in the picture! Wherever he's at, I hope the son of a bitch is pushing up daisies!"

"Damn, girl, sorry I fuckin' asked."

"Shit, I'm sorry, Tangie. I didn't mean to yell at you. I just get so frustrated talkin' 'bout that punk muthafucka sometimes."

"I know the feeling, girl. Most of these niggas ain't shit. But come on through. That way I can introduce you to my homegirl Veronica."

"That's cool. I'ma clear my schedule and make sure that I can make it."

Chapter 15

"Yo, dawg, you need me to take you by Bishop's house so you can pick up yo' ride?" Antwan asked his friend.

"Hell yeah! Man, you think I wanna let that nigga keep my muthafuckin' whip?" Temp laughed.

"So, what you think of my plan, dawg?"

Temp shrugged his shoulders. "Sounds like we stand to make a hell of a lot of cheese if everything goes good. Except for one thing, dawg. Nigga, we rob, steal, and jack! What the fuck do we know about selling rocks?"

"Nigga, Rhonda knows that shit inside and out. For the next week or so, I'ma be hanging out with her. She gon' show a nigga how to cook and cut that shit up. And wait a minute, nigga," Antwan said as he suddenly thought of something. "Didn't you say a few days ago that you was gonna buy some weed and start selling it?"

"Yeah, but it's a big-ass difference between selling weed and slanging rocks. But fuck it. If the shit can get us rich, then let's go for it."

"That's what I wanted to hear, my nigga. If we do this shit right, we can all come up quicker than a bitch on a bad dick!"

The two friends gave each other a pound as they pulled up in front of Bishop's house. "Man, where the fuck that nigga at in my damn car?"

"Shit, he might be out tryin' ta get some pussy," Antwan suggested.

"Yeah, right," Temp said as he snatched his cell phone off his hip and called Bishop.

"Yo, what's up?" he answered.

"The fuck you mean what's up, nigga? The fuck you at with my ride?"

"I'm right around the corner from my house. Meet me over there in about ten minutes."

"Nigga, we sitting in front of yo' house now."

"A'ight, bet. I'll be there in a second."

Three minutes later, Bishop pulled up and parked behind them. He hopped out of Temp's car and jumped in Antwan's. "Sup, niggas?"

Both Antwan and Temp turned around and looked at Bishop. After seeing the look on his face, they both looked at each other and broke into laughter.

"What the hell y'all laughing at?" he asked.

"Nigga, you been somewhere fuckin', ain't you?" Antwan said, ignoring his question.

"Why, muthafucka?" Bishop tried hard to suppress the smile that threatened to break through.

"Look how this fool cheesin', man," Antwan said, pointing at Bishop. "Nigga, spill that shit. You know we boys, so let us in on the pussy you just got."

"Man, fuck all that," Temp said, waving his hands. "What I wanna know is if you think the bitch is willing to do the whole crew?"

Bishop didn't like the comment but didn't show it. He didn't want to look like a sucker for love in front of his boys.

"Man, chill out, man," Antwan said, pushing Temp in the shoulder.

Bishop really didn't want to tell them who he was messing around with. After all, he and Veronica had decided to keep it on the low for the time being. But on the other hand, if he didn't say anything, he would look like he was pussy whipped and he would never live it down.

"Man, if I tell y'all who it is, y'all can't say shit."

"Nigga, who the fuck we gon' tell?" Temp asked him.

"Man, I'm just sayin', this broad got some good-ass pussy, and I wanna get some more of that shit, so don't be fuckin' it up for a nigga."

"Man, go 'head on with that secretive-ass shit," Temp blasted him. "If yo' dick game was on point, you ain't gotta worry about that shit no way. Now spill the beans, muthafucka."

"A'ight, man. It's Veronica."

"Veronica?" they both said in unison.

"Nigga, you fucked fine-ass Veronica?" Temp was shocked. He'd been planning on cracking on Veronica for some ass for a while but had never gotten around to it. Bishop held up two fingers to indicate to them that he'd fucked her twice.

"My nigga, you gotta gimme some dap on that shit, man," Antwan said as he held out his fist. Bishop smiled as he gave his friend a pound. He cut his eyes at Temp, who was slightly mean mugging him.

"The fuck wrong with you, man?" Bishop asked.

"Huh? Man, ain't shit wrong with me, my dude."

For some reason, Bishop didn't believe Temp, but he let it pass.

"A'ight, my nigga. I'm about to hip you to the plans me and Temp been making," Antwan said.

Dana walked out of school with mischief on her mind. Her light blue capri pants hugged her hips and thighs like a second layer of skin. The cutoff T-shirt she had on may have had ANGEL written across the chest area, but Dana was in the mood to act like a devil. Her hormones raged out of control as her eyes searched the area for Chris. He had agreed to pick her up from school and walk her home.

Chris didn't know it, but Dana had much more on her mind than a simple walk home.

This was the day that she was going to lose her virginity. Dana figured that she'd waited long enough. For the past month, her pussy had been on a slow simmer. It gradually progressed to a boil, and now that it was smoldering, she needed a good, stiff dick to cool it down. Dana frowned when she didn't see Chris.

"If this nigga done stood me up, I'ma cuss his ass the fuck out," she said to herself.

"See, that's the problem when you deal with bitch-made muthafuckas. You can't count on them."

Dana looked around and saw Jay's lanky frame coming toward her. He was flanked by Rich and Earl, his two closest friends.

"What do you want, Jay?" Dana asked, sucking her teeth.

"Ease up, baby. I just wanna talk to you for a minute."

"Well, as you can see, I ain't got time right now. I'm waiting on somebody."

Jay looked around and smirked. "Well, whoever the fuck you waitin' on don't look like they coming."

"Jay, take yo' ass on somewhere and leave me the fuck alone. Ain't it a bottle o' penicillin somewhere with yo' name on it?"

Jay's light skin turned bright red. He glanced at his boys, who were obviously trying to hide their smirks. Embarrassed and pissed, Jay rushed up to Dana and grabbed her by the collar.

"Yo, bitch, who the fuck you think you talkin' to like that?"

"Nigga, get yo' fuckin' hands off of me," she said, pushing Jay in the chest. "And who the fuck you calling a bitch? I don't see yo' mother nowhere around here!"

"Oooo, shit," Jay's friends said, instigating. By this time, a small crowd had started gathering around. Determined not to be punked by a girl, Jay ran back up to Dana, grabbed her by the shoulders, and shook her violently.

"Bitch, did you just call my mother a bitch? I'll beat yo' muthafuckin' ass out here," he yelled. All of a sudden, the crowd parted like the Red Sea as Chris stormed through.

"Nigga, if you don't take yo' hands off of her right now, I'ma bust yo' head to the white meat!"

Jay momentarily stopped shaking Dana and turned his heated stare on Chris. Rick and Earl stepped up beside Jay to show their friend that they had his back. If either of them had looked closely, they would have seen the bulge protruding from Chris's white oversized T-shirt.

"Nigga, what the fuck you got to do with it?" Jay challenged.

"Yeah, muthafucka," Earl said. "Don't make us turn that white bandana wrapped around yo' dome red!"

Chris looked at the three school boys and started laughing.

"Nigga, what's so fuckin' funny?" Jay asked while invading Chris's space. That proved to be a big mistake. As soon as he was close enough, Chris yanked his pistol out and hit Jay in the nose. Jay's nose shattered upon impact. Blood and snot flew from his nose and decorated the concrete.

"Damn, he pushed Jay's shit waayy back," an instigator bellowed.

"You two pussies got something to say?"

Rick and Earl looked at each other and backed away, shaking their heads. This was the first time they'd witnessed a violent act of this proportion. They were used to fistfights, but not pistol whippings. Dana looked across the schoolyard and saw the school principal quickly making his way toward the commotion. Not wanting Chris to get in trouble, Dana grabbed his hand and led him away. She almost came on herself as she thought about the hardcore way Chris handled the situation.

As Dana and Chris walked down the street, Dana stared up at Chris as if he were some kind of god. From the time they'd left the school, her coochie had been moist. His thuggish mentality was just what she was looking for. Most high school girls would have been scared to death with what had transpired. But something deep inside of her stirred whenever she was around a young lion who liked to wild out.

Remembering what happened the last time she walked past Tangie's house, Dana made a detour and cut through the field. Chris knew what she was doing, so he didn't object. By the time they got to Dana's house, she was on fire. She couldn't wait for Chris to pop her cherry.

"You should be straight now, shorty," Chris said as they walked up to the porch.

"Can't you stay here for just a little while?" she asked. "Just in case that fool comes over here and starts trippin'?"

Chris smelled a setup. He knew that Dana was feeling him, and if he was being honest with himself, he was feeling her too. But even so, he knew he had to be careful. The last thing he needed was for her parents to come home and catch him long stroking their daughter. Chris had made up his mind while walking her home that, if given the chance, he was going to smash Dana out. Unlike most 17-year-olds, Chris was very experienced when it came to sex, having been exposed to it at the tender age of 12.

Sadly, his babysitter, who was also his second cousin, preferred to keep it in the family, as they say, instead of finding someone out in the world to give her pussy to. She was a twisted human being who took great pleasure in molesting Chris. From anal sex to oral sex, she taught

Chris how to do things that no one his age was ready for. When she died in a car crash, the secret went with her, as Chris promised himself that he would never tell anyone about it. Even though he'd already made his mind up to fuck Dana, Chris decided to see how much she really wanted the dick.

"I don't know, shorty. I got a few things to do today. Plus I don't wanna get caught up in no bullshit if yo' people come home, ya feel me?"

"You ain't got to worry about that, baby boy. My mother don't get off from work until ten o' clock tonight. And my sister don't stay here."

Chris rubbed his chin and looked up in the sky as if he was debating her proposal.

"I'll be right back," she said, breaking his train of thought. Chris stood there and watched her jog down the hallway to her bedroom. Her ass jiggled like jelly, causing Chris to get rock hard. A few seconds later, Dana came back with a blunt in her hand.

"Maybe this will convince you to stay," she said, tossing him that weed-loaded cigar.

"Damn, girl, what you know about this?"

"Boy, please. Do I look like a square to you?"

Chris didn't respond. He simply took out his lighter and flicked it.

"Hol' up! Not in here," she said, wide-eyed. "We gotta go on the back porch." She led Chris through the kitchen and out on the back porch. She tried hard not to look at the bulge in his pants, but she couldn't help it. Chris caught her looking but pretended as if he didn't see it.

"Can I blaze up now?" he asked.

"Do that shit."

Chris sat down on the stoop and flicked the lighter. Instead of sitting across from him, Dana made it a point to sit right beside him. After taking a couple of good, long puffs, he passed it to Dana. Chris was shocked at how expertly she handled the blunt. He could tell right away that she was no novice when it came to smoking weed. Chris started fantasizing about her pussy and head game. She seemed like a down-ass broad who knew what she was doing, but so did a lot of other females whose sex game was garbage. For some reason, Chris started to get paranoid. Dana noticed him looking around and got nervous herself.

"What the hell are you lookin' for?" she asked.

"Ay yo, you sure yo' folks ain't gon' come rushing through here in a few?"

"Nigga, will you stop worrying about that? I told you, my mother won't be home until later."

As Chris started to relax again, Dana smoothly placed her hand on his thigh and rubbed it. Her homegirls had told her that rubbing a man's leg was a turn-on to him. They had schooled her on quite a few things, except for one. Dana slickly inched her hand up Chris's thigh. She didn't stop until she came to what felt like a steel pole. For the first time since she'd made the decision to lose her virginity, Dana got slightly nervous. *Damn, he gon' stick this long-ass thing inside of me?*

"What you doin', girl?" Chris asked.

Before she could answer, he reached over and palmed one of her titties. Dana's sex box instantly started to drip, saturating her panties. "Come on, ma, let's go in the house."

Nervously, Dana led Chris into the house. Despite all the shit she portrayed as far as being ready to have sex, when the time came to put up or shut up, Dana was scared to death. *Come on, girl. You can do this,* she convinced herself.

Once they got into the bedroom, Chris pulled her to him and started kissing her neck. He was very careful not to leave any passion marks. Dana melted in his arms as he began to caress her breasts. She shook slightly as he ran his tongue along the outside of her earlobe. But as he started to undress her, Chris noticed that something didn't feel right. It was almost as if she was afraid to take her clothes off in front of him.

Chris shrugged it off and continued to probe her body. When he finally got her completely naked, he started taking off his clothes. By the time he got his clothes off, a thin layer of sweat had formed on Dana's forehead. Chris paid it no mind as he continued to kiss and fondle her. As they lay on the bed, he wondered why she wasn't touching him that much. He grabbed her hand and guided it toward his dick. But when her hand touched it, she just left it there. *Damn, this bitch don't know how to stroke a dick.* Just as he was about to call her on it, she beat him to the punch.

"Chris, I need to tell you something. I'm a . . . a virgin."

Chris stopped in his tracks. Now it all made sense to him, the reason why she was acting so awkward. Chris opened his mouth to say something, but before he could get it out, they heard a door slam.

"Shit," Dana said, jumping out of the bed and running to the window. A disgusted look formed on her face when she saw Veronica's car in the driveway. "Fuck, fuck, fuck," Dana said as she started putting her clothes back on.

Not knowing what was going on, Chris followed suit. "Yo, I thought you said that yo' moms wasn't gon' be back until tonight."

"She won't. That's my bitch-ass sister. I didn't even know she still had a key. Quick, get in the closet."

Chris quickly gathered up the clothing he didn't get a chance to put on and dipped into the closet. Dana finished putting the rest of her clothes on and plopped down on her bed. She grabbed the *Vibe* magazine that was on her nightstand and opened it. A half second later, Veronica burst through her door. Her eyes darted around the room. It was if she was looking to catch her baby sister up to no good.

"Don't you know how to knock?" Dana asked with an attitude.

"Why the fuck should I have to knock to walk into my own room?" Veronica smirked. She loved to remind Dana that it was her room first.

"It ain't none of yo' damn room! You don't live here!"

Veronica glared at her baby sister. "Watch ya mouth, you li'l heifer! I was walking through this damn house when yo' ass wasn't even thought about!"

"Whateva," Dana said, folding her arms over her chest. She was super tight at her sister for fucking up her groove. "What the hell are you doing over here anyway?"

"That, little girl, is none of yo' damn business!"

"Humph. Yo' ass must wanna borrow some damn money."

"What?"

"You heard me. That's the only time we see yo' ass is when you tryin' ta hit Mama up for some money."

Veronica glared at her before she spoke. "Dana, you don't know what the hell you're talking about. I only borrowed money from Mama one time, and I paid that back."

"Yeah, right."

"You know what? You keep runnin' yo' fuckin' mouth and I just might decide to tell her about the little stunt yo' hot ass was tryin' ta pull the other day! Now, what the fuck else you gotta say?"

Dana was so mad at Veronica she could have cut her throat and not thought twice about it.

"That's what the fuck I thought," Veronica said as she turned around and headed out of her sister's room. "I guess Mama ain't here, or yo' ass wouldn't be cussin' like a damn sailor. When she gets home, tell her I said to call me."

Dana gave her sister the finger behind her back.

"Fuck you too," Veronica said. She knew her sister all too well.

Meanwhile, Chris was relieved that she was leaving. He was starting to sweat in that closet. When Dana heard the front door close, she ran to the front room and peeked out the window. She breathed a sigh of relief when she saw her sister pull off down the street. When she got back to her bedroom, Chris was sitting on the edge of the bed.

"Damn, shorty, you like to live dangerously, don't you?"

"I can't stand that bitch," fumed Dana. Chris was perplexed. He couldn't understand how two people who came from the same womb could dislike each other so much. He loved his sister and would take out anyone who tried to bring harm to her.

"Now, where were we?" Dana said as she started getting undressed again. Before they could finish what they had started before her sister came in, Chris's cell phone rang.

He started not to answer it, but something in his gut told him he'd better get it. He held up his finger to tell Dana to hold on a second. The slight smile he had on his face disappeared in an instant when he got the message from the other end of the phone.

"Yo, I gotta go, shorty!"

"Huh?"

"I gotta go! I got an emergency at home! I'll hit you up later!" Without saying another word, Chris kissed Dana on the forehead, ran out the door, and headed home.

Chapter 16

"Chris! Come home now! I think your sister is dying!"

After hearing his mother's frantic plea, it took Chris only three steps to get to top speed as he leapt off of Dana's porch and hit the ground running. He didn't know what was going on, but the panic in Vivian's voice told him it wasn't good. Chris ran past two bus stops on the way to his house. Even though he kept an eye out for the bus as he was running, he didn't have time to wait for the slow-ass Cleveland transportation system. As he ran, horrific thoughts passed through his mind. Was his sister going to die? How would his mother cope with it if she did? How would he, himself, deal with it? Since the sidewalk was full of pedestrians, Chris had to dodge quite a few of them on the way.

"Hey, watch it," an elderly man yelled as Chris nearly knocked him to the ground. Luckily for Chris, his house was on the same side of the street he was running on, so he didn't have to worry about darting into traffic and getting hit by any cars. By the time he got to the corner of his street, Chris was winded. His frantic sprint had pretty much absorbed all the air from his lungs, but Chris knew that he couldn't rest long. He bent over for a second to catch his breath, but when he stood back up to start running again, his heart skipped a beat.

From the corner, he could see the flashing lights of an ambulance in front of his house. Ignoring his fatigue as well as the cramp forming in the side of his stomach,

Chris sprinted toward his house. The closer he got to his destination, the more his insides knotted up. Images of his sister's chest being pushed in and out to resuscitate her flashed through his mind, causing him to panic. He reached his front door just in time to see the paramedics wheeling his sister out of the house on a gurney. His mother was right behind them, weeping heavily.

"Ma, what happened?" Chris asked, trying to maintain his composure.

"I'm not sure. I went into her room to check on her, and she was shaking real bad. I dialed 911, and by the time they got here, she had gone into convulsions."

"Are you riding with us to the hospital, ma'am?" one of the paramedics asked.

"Yes, of course."

"What hospital y'all takin' her to?"

"We're taking her to the emergency room at Euclid Meridia."

Chris grabbed his mother and hugged her. "Go ahead, Mama. I'll lock up the house and meet you there."

Chris watched helplessly as the ambulance drove off with his sister and mother in tow. After they were gone, he quickly ran upstairs and stuffed his gun under his bed. When he came back outside, several of his neighbors were standing around wondering what had happened.

One woman whom Chris had seen his mother talking to on occasion walked up to him and asked him if everything was okay. With tears starting to leak from his eyes, Chris told her that he didn't know. He offered to pay her and give her gas money to take him to meet his mother at the emergency room.

"Keep your money, Chris. Let's go," she said, leading him toward her car.

***

The light blue sky rapidly turned gray as Chris and his mother sat in the waiting room. Chris glanced at his mother, who had prayed no fewer than three times since they'd been there. Chris's gut feeling told him that his sister's cancer had returned, but he didn't dare say that out loud. His mother was having enough of a hard time dealing with what was happening now. Chris silently prayed to God that he was wrong.

His relationship with his mother and sister was one of the few things he treasured in this world. When the doctor came out, Chris's knees threatened to give out. Vivian's nerves were shot. There was no one else in the waiting room, so when he started walking through the area, he could only be coming for them. The doctor was a tall man with a long, angular head and Middle Eastern features. The name on his smock read DR. TALIB. His eyes were sunken in, and he looked as if he hadn't been to sleep in days.

"How is she, Doctor?" Chris's mom asked before he'd even reached them.

The doctor didn't say a word at first. He just led them to the hard sofa and motioned for them to sit down. He didn't mince words as he rubbed his face and got right to it.

"Your daughter's cancer has returned," he said, staring directly into her face.

"Oh, my God!" Vivian cried as she grabbed Chris for support. "What happened?" she asked.

"At this point, we're unsure, ma'am. We're currently running a series of tests on her to try to pinpoint exactly what occurred."

"Unsure?" Chris jumped to his feet with his fists balled up at his side. "The fuck you mean y'all unsure? That's my baby sister in there!"

"Chris! Stop that, right now," Vivian yelled.

Not wanting to hear anymore, Chris stormed out through the automatic sliding glass doors. He was moving so fast he almost ran into them before they had a chance to open. Once he got outside, he snatched his bandana off and rubbed his head. He turned around and looked back through the glass. His mother's hands were up motioning toward him. Chris could only guess that she was apologizing for his actions. Chris knew he was wrong for going off on the doctor, but that was his little sister lying in that room.

Chris turned his back to the glass and sat down on the ledge. He smiled slightly as he remembered the fun he and his little sister used to have when they were younger. After about ten minutes, Chris gathered the strength to get up and go back inside. When he got back inside, his mother just stared at him.

"Ma, I'm sorry," he said, misreading her look. "I just don't want nothing to happen to my sister."

"She needs an operation, Chris," Vivian said as if he hadn't just said a word. "She needs a bone marrow transplant. While we were talking, another doctor came out and said that they located where the cancer returned in her body. They said they can do the operation, but it's very expensive. The type of insurance we have won't cover it. Oh God, what are we gonna do?"

Chris's mother burst into tears and collapsed in his arms. Never in all of Chris's 17 years had he hated the system as much as he did at this moment. His young mind couldn't or wouldn't understand why the hospital couldn't just do the surgery and save his sister's life.

"They won't do the surgery because the insurance won't cover it?" Chris asked.

"Yes, they will do it, but where are we going to get the money to pay for it? We're barely making ends meet now. It doesn't matter, though. I don't care if we have to live on beans for the next five years, as long as they do whatever they have to do to save my baby."

"How much is the surgery, Ma?"

"The doctor said it could cost as much as three hundred thousand dollars."

Chris had some money from the two heists that he and his fellow Young Lionz had pulled, but nothing close to that. "We'll figure something out, Mama."

"I hope so, son."

Vivian got up to go to the bathroom. As soon as she was out of sight, Chris reached for his phone. He had to make some paper, and fast. He looked at the screen to dial and saw that he had a voicemail message. With everything going on, he never even felt his phone vibrate. He punched in his code and saw that it was from Bishop.

"Yo, what's up, Chris. Hit me back up when you get this message. Antwan done came up on a way to make some major paper."

Chris couldn't believe his luck. Just when he needed money the most, it seemed like fate would fall on his side. His smile soon faded as he thought about the amount of money he would have after they split it five ways. He then shrugged his shoulders and smiled again. *Any money beats no money.*

He started wondering how he and his mother were going to get home when he looked through the hospital glass and saw someone getting out of a cab. Knowing that he needed to hurry, Chris jumped up and sprinted outside. The cab was just about to pull away when Chris called out, "Yo, homie, hol' up. Me and my moms need a ride home."

The cabbie looked around suspiciously. When he didn't see anyone other than Chris, he started to pull off. He'd already gotten robbed at gunpoint once this month, and it had made him leery. But then he heard a woman calling someone named Chris and took a chance that the lad just may have been telling the truth. Yet he flinched when Chris reached into his pocket. His fear was quickly replaced by greed as he eyed the roll of bills in Chris's hand. His attitude changed in an instant as he even got out of the cab to hold the door open for Chris's mother.

During the long ride home, Chris stared at his mother, who in turn just stared out the window. Seeing her like this broke Chris's heart. His mother wanted to stay with her daughter, but the doctor told her that she needed her rest and to come back early the next morning. As tears slowly rolled down his mother's face, Chris became more determined than ever to get the necessary paper.

Chapter 17

Detective Ramsey snapped up in her bed. She'd been reviewing a case she was working on and had just gone to bed two hours ago. To make matters worse, Denzel Washington was just about to enter her when her phone rang and woke her out of her sweet dream. Sleepy and pissed off, she threw her covers off of her. The vibrator she'd used to relieve some tension earlier went crashing to the floor.

"Fuck!" she screamed when she saw the batteries skate across the floor and roll under her dresser.

"Yeah," she said dryly as she answered the phone. Her frown soon turned into a huge smile. She had just been told that Yolonda had come out of her coma and was now ready to talk to the police. She had coerced one of the nurses into promising to call her when and if Yolonda regained consciousness. Ramsey quickly threw on her clothes. She brushed her hair to try to make herself more presentable, but when she couldn't get it like she wanted it, she simply pulled it back in a ponytail.

She grabbed the picture she'd gotten from the evidence locker and looked at it again. She didn't know how she'd missed it the first time. It was a picture of Yolonda and some guy named Temp. She'd never even heard the name before, but a fellow coworker who'd handled juvenile cases took one look at the picture and knew exactly who

Temp was. The coworker remembered busting Temp two years earlier for shoplifting and weed possession.

Ramsey thought long and hard about bringing him in for questioning, but with nothing else to go on but a picture, she decided not to. Besides, the last thing she wanted was the captain crawling up her ass because she brought someone in and couldn't hold them, let alone charge them. She stuffed the picture in her back pocket and headed out the door. By the time she got to the hospital, she could barely contain herself. She felt like a kid on Christmas. She hoped like hell that Yolonda had something useful to tell her.

"Hold that elevator," she said to a nurse with a bowl of salad in her hand.

"Floor?" asked the nurse.

"Third," Ramsey answered.

The nurse looked down at Ramsey's badge and put two and two together. "Oh, you must be here to see that girl who got attacked the other day."

"That's right," Ramsey responded. She wasn't about to hold a lengthy conversation with the nosy nurse. This was police business.

"Yeah, I heard that she had come out of her coma when I came in an hour ago."

An hour ago? And your ass is on break already? Ramsey was relieved when the doors opened, and she didn't have to hear the woman's mouth anymore. She rolled her eyes when she discovered that she and the nurse were going the same way. Just as she was about to ask the nurse behind the desk about Yolonda, nosy ass spoke first.

"Hey, Barb. This is the officer who—"

"Detective," Ramsey corrected her.

"Sorry. This is the detective who's here to talk to Yolonda."

Ramsey couldn't take it anymore. She had to get away from this woman before she choked her. "Excuse me, could you tell me where the bathroom is?"

After giving her a funny look, Barb pointed her in the direction of the ladies' room. She stayed in there checking her messages and reading Facebook posts until she had calmed down enough to go back out. When she came out, the nosy nurse was gone.

"Thank God," she mumbled to herself. She walked back up to the nurse's station and asked Barb to escort her to Yolonda's room. Ramsey's gut tightened up as a somber look fell across Barb's face.

"They didn't tell you? Yolonda's nurse, Rachel, said she was going to call you back."

"Huh? Call me back for what?"

"I'm sorry, Detective, but there was a mix-up. The nurse who called you back got the patients mixed up. There was another patient who came out of a coma. The patient you're referring to died this morning."

"Wait a minute! I spoke with a Nurse . . . Jennings yesterday," Ramsey said as she took out her notepad and flipped through the pages. "I told her to call me when Yolonda was able and willing to talk."

"Well, I'm sorry for the miscommunication, Detective, but Nurse Jennings doesn't work here anymore. She was fired late last night. I'm not supposed to tell you that, but since you're the police, I don't see the harm in doing so."

Detective Ramsey just stood there, stunned.

Tangie woke up hot and horny. She was lying on her stomach with her ass slightly lifted in the air. It was an odd way for a person to sleep, but for what she wanted to do, it served her well. Tangie scooted her knees up so her ass went up even higher.

"Antwan? Antwan, come on, baby. I want you to hit it from the back."

When Antwan didn't respond, Tangie slid her hand along the sheets next to her. To her surprise, she didn't feel anything. She opened her eyes only to discover that Antwan wasn't in the bed with her. She got up, looked around, and got pissed.

"The fuck this nigga at?" she asked herself.

Thinking that he may have just gone to take a leak, Tangie stripped asshole naked and got back in the bed. She waited for another minute before getting out of the bed and stomping to the bathroom. Her mouth dropped when she saw Antwan standing in the mirror, brushing his waves. He was fully dressed in a pair of jean shorts and a LeBron James jersey. On his feet, he sported a pair of white-on-white Air Force Ones.

"What you doin' up so early, and where the hell do you think you goin'?"

Antwan stopped brushing his hair and turned around to face her. "First of all, it ain't that damn early. And second of all, we talked about this shit last night, so don't try to get brand new on a nigga."

"Talked about what last night?" she asked in a confused tone.

"Tangie, I told you last night that I had a hookup with a dude I went to school with," Antwan lied. It slid off his tongue so easily he almost believed it himself.

"What kind of hookup?"

"Yayo, dope, cocaine, and yo' ass said as long as I brought some long paper in here, you was cool with it."

"I said that?" she asked, pointing to herself. If Tangie was honest with herself, she would concede that she couldn't remember much of anything that happened the night before. The most important thing she remembered was that Antwan came in the house rambling about how they were about to get rich. That's all she heard, and quite frankly, that's all she needed to hear. The two of them commenced tossing back tequila and blowing blunts. They ended the night by passing out in bed without a hint of sex, which was the reason Tangie was so horny.

"How long did you say you was gonna be gone?"

"Three days. My nigga Bo wants to show me all the ins and outs of the dope game."

"Oh. Okay," Tangie said sadly.

"What the fuck wrong with you? I know you ain't trippin' 'cause I'm trying to go and get this paper! Yo' ass ain't gonna be trippin' when you spendin' that shit!"

"Boy, stop yellin' like you fuckin' crazy! Ain't nobody trippin' off that!"

"Then what's up?"

"Damn, I just thought you mighta wanted some pussy before you left, but I guess yo' ass ain't got time for this good shit," she said as she walked back into the bedroom.

Antwan thought about it for about half a second before he rushed into the bedroom, bent her over the dresser, and hit it from the back.

The afternoon sunlight poured through the windshield and splashed across Antwan's face as he headed for Bob Evans. Right before he'd left his house, he'd either called or texted each member of the Young Lionz crew and told them to meet him there. Antwan smirked as he thought about the lie he'd told Tangie. There was no way in the world he would have been able to leave without a fight had he told her that it was really her cousin Rhonda who was teaching him how to cook cocaine. The hardest thing for him to do was going to be watching Bo paw all over his side bitch for the next few days.

Antwan smiled as he fantasized about the money he and his crew were going to make once they learned the finer points of slanging dope. Although he realized that it still carried a hefty prison sentence if they ever got caught, he would rather slang rocks than jack people. At least this way innocent bystanders wouldn't be getting hurt, not that he cared that much. He grabbed a blunt out of his ashtray and lit it. He felt good knowing that his dreams of becoming rich were about to become a reality.

Chris looked at his phone and smiled. More than anyone else in his crew, he needed money. It tore him apart to listen to his mother crying all night long. He wanted so badly to go into her bedroom and comfort her. But he also knew that the only thing that would make this situation better was cold, hard cash. He walked over to his closet and took out the money that he'd made from his crew's jack moves. He laid every bit of it on his bed. Then he emptied his pockets and laid that on the bed too. After he was done counting his money up, it came to a little over $8,000.

He put $1,000 in his pocket and put the rest in a bag. He took the bag down to his mother's bedroom and hung it on the door. Chris then got dressed as fast as he could. After receiving the text from Antwan, Temp had called him and told him that he was going to pick up him and the rest of the Young Lionz. Chris stared out of the window until he saw Temp's car coming down the street. With his mind on his money and his money on his mind, Chris left the house on a mission to save his sister at all costs.

***

Niko couldn't wait for Temp to come and get him. For the last hour, all he'd heard was his mother screaming James's name as he pounded her guts. He hated that James could pretty much do what he pleased, including going out and screwing around with other women, and his mother would always turn a blind eye to it. Niko got up from his bed, walked out of his room, and headed toward the front door. He was glad to hear that James was no longer smashing his mother. As he walked down the stairs, he heard his mother's door open.

He thought it was his mother, so he braced himself to hear the mean and despicable things that she always said to him. But instead, he saw James beaming about something else.

"Damn, that bitch got some good-ass pussy for an old broad. That shit juicy as fuck."

Niko stopped in his tracks. He turned around and glared at James, who just smiled at him and headed into the bathroom. Niko quickly walked out of the house and sat down on his front steps. He didn't trust himself to stay in the house with James a second longer. If he had, he was sure that he would shoot him in the face. He waited another two minutes before Temp pulled up.

Temp, Niko, Chris, and Bishop were all quiet as they headed to Bob Evans to meet Antwan. Each one of them had their own issues to deal with, and none of them wanted to talk about it. As soon as Temp pulled into the parking lot and turned off the engine, he looked each one of his friends in the eye.

"Y'all Young Lionz ready to make this money?" he asked as he stuck his fist out.

One by one, each member of the crew put their fists in the middle and gave one another dap. They got out of the car and walked into the restaurant on a cash-getting mission. As far as restaurants went, the place was quaint but cozy. Equal amounts of booths and four-seat tables filled the area. For the lovebirds, there were also a fair amount of two-seated tables. Waitresses smiled as they made their way to and from tables carrying different meals. The four young men all sniffed the air and smiled. Some of their stomachs rumbled as the aroma of bacon, eggs, and sausages wafted through the air. It took a few seconds for his eyes to sift through the sea of bodies seated in the place, but soon Niko spotted Antwan sitting in the back, talking on the phone.

"Yo, there that nigga go right there, Temp."

The four of them made their way back to the booth. When Antwan saw his partners in crime approaching, he hung up with whoever he was talking to and smiled. "*Mi amigos,* what's up?"

"You, dawg," Temp spoke up.

"Let's get to it, dawg. I'm on a paper chase," Chris said.

Antwan smiled some more and motioned for them to sit down. "A'ight, peeps, here it is. This li'l bitch I'm fuckin' with hipped me to the dope game. Her dude, Bo, is some kinda small-time kingpin over on his side of town. Apparently the nigga he been countin' on to sell the shit ain't gettin' the job done, so I had Rhonda talk to him and tell him that she had a cousin who wanted to get put on. Me and Temp went and met the nigga the other day, and he lookin' for somebody to hold down one of the blocks that's starvin' for somebody to serve them fiends. That's where we come in at. I just got off the phone with Rhonda and she done already cooked, cut, and rocked some shit up, so all we gotta do is step in and start grinding. I'm going over there tonight, and she gon' teach me how to cook the shit up."

It was quiet for a minute before Antwan looked at all of them and asked them, "What y'all think?"

"I think we need to hurry up and get this shit poppin', son," Chris spoke up. As much as he needed the paper, he wanted to get on the grind as soon as possible.

"You got that shit right, dawg," Niko concurred. "I'm ready to get paid for real. Fuck all that chump change we been making."

While the rest of his crew was smiling, Bishop sat there with a strange look on his face.

"Nigga, what the fuck you lookin' all confused and shit for?" asked Temp.

Before Bishop could answer, the waitress came over and asked them if they were ready to order. "Nah, we straight," Temp roughly said. The waitress frowned at Temp as she walked away, causing Temp to blow her a kiss and laugh.

"Hol' up a second," Bishop started. "You said something about a cousin or somethin'?"

"Nah, dude," Antwan laughed. "Her nigga, Bo, thinks I'm her cousin. But in reality, I'm beatin' that pussy to pieces, my nigga."

"That nigga gonna find out and split yo' muthafuckin' wig," Bishop laughed.

"I wish that punk muthafucka would. I'll beat the perm out his muthafuckin' head."

The five friends all cracked up laughing. When the waitress came back over and asked them if they were ready to order, Temp caught an instant attitude. "Man, let's hurry up and order before this broad blows a gasket."

The waitress once again frowned at Temp.

"Ay yo, I don't know what the fuck yo' problem is, but you can quit mean mugging me like that."

"Temp, chill out, man," Antwan said, trying to calm his friend down. After placing their orders, the five friends continued to discuss how they were going to go about getting paid.

"Okay, dawg. So basically we're going to dive into the dope game, right?" Niko asked.

"You damn skippy, my nigga," Antwan answered.

"What the fuck are we gonna be doing?" Bishop questioned.

"Everything, my dude. We're gonna learn how to mix the dope, cook it, and cut it up. We're also gonna learn how to sell it in powdered form, by weight," Antwan explained.

Chris paid special attention. His friends didn't know it, but he needed the money more than all of them combined.

"Yo, I gotta take a leak," Chris said as he got up and walked toward the bathroom. Instead of going in, however, he passed by it and went outside. Pulling out his cell phone, he sent Antwan a text asking if he could meet him out there.

Knowing that it must be something that Chris didn't want to discuss in front of the rest of the crew, Antwan pretended that someone was calling him and he had to take the call outside.

"Yo, what's up, dawg?" Antwan asked when he met Chris outside.

Chris was listening very carefully when Antwan told them that he and Temp would start off the rock-slinging mission, and that when they had everything situated, they would call the rest of the team in. But Chris had other ideas. He needed to make bread, and he needed to make it fast. "Yo, man, I need to be out there with y'all when y'all first hit the trap. I need that bread, man."

"Dude, we all need to make this paper," Antwan told him.

"Nah, you don't understand, dawg. I really, really need to get some major cheese in my life, man."

Antwan looked at Chris closely. He saw something in his friend's eyes. It was a look he'd never seen before. "Yo, what's up, playa?" he asked.

Chris turned around so that his back was to Antwan. The last thing he wanted was for Antwan to see the tears that were forming in his eyes. He couldn't hide them for long, however, as Antwan walked up to him and put his arm around him in a manly hug.

"What's up, my brother?" Antwan asked, now genuinely concerned.

Chris figured that now was as good a time as any to swallow his pride and tell one of his closest friends what was going on in his life. From the minute he found out that his sister had cancer, he'd vowed to keep it away from his friends. He didn't need their pity. But now he was put in a position where it would benefit his sibling to tell one of them what the deal was.

"My sister has leukemia, man," he spit out before he had a chance to change his mind about telling Antwan. "The doctors say she needs a bone marrow transplant, and the shit costs a lot o' money. I mean, a lot o' mutha-fuckin' bread! I need to be in that trap, dawg! I need to make paper bad as fuck!"

Antwan didn't know whether to be pissed or feel sorry for his buddy. "Man, why the fuck you ain't tell us, man?"

"Man, I wasn't trying to talk about that shit with y'all, man. Don't get it twisted though. I love y'all like y'all was my blood, man. But I go through enough shit at home. I wasn't trying to bring it out of the house with me. When I leave the house, I leave the house to get away from that part of my life, 'cause when I go back home, I still have to face the fact that my sister is sick. I didn't need to be reminded of it in the fuckin' streets."

Placing his right palm over his mouth, Chris closed his eyes and took a deep breath. As the tears began to roll, he quickly reached up and used the back of his hand to wipe them away. When the second set fell, he used both hands to remove them. He was doing all he could to stop the tears from rolling down his face, but he was unsuccessful. Not wanting to look soft in front of one of his comrades, Chris gritted his teeth and attempted to will the tears back into their ducts. Antwan looked back toward the restaurant and saw the rest of his friends walking their way. Chris made sure all the tears were gone before they got there.

"Yo, what the fuck y'all niggas doin' out here?" Temp bellowed.

"Just shootin' the shit about a few things. Chris been tellin' me that when he visited his cousin last year, he learned a little about slangin' them thangs," Antwan lied. He didn't want the rest of them to know Chris's business about his sister if he didn't want to tell them. Chris and Antwan gave each other a look that said they understood each other.

"A'ight, check it out. Me, Temp, and Chris gonna roll over to Rhonda's and get this shit poppin'. When we make sure that everything is all good, one of us will come swoop y'all."

"Man, how come all of us can't go?" Niko asked, irritated.

"Cause, dawg, I wanna make sure we can all cake off on this shit. It don't make sense for us to go down there and throw rocks at the penitentiary if the money ain't worth it."

He studied each of their faces to check for signs of fear. And just as he thought, there were none. Antwan knew that he hung with a pack of wolves, and none of their hearts pumped Kool-Aid.

Bishop and Niko shot quizzical glances at each other as old-school Isaac Hayes blared through the car speakers. Meanwhile, Temp sat behind the steering wheel, nodding his head. Using his knees to steer, Temp's eyes alternated from the street in front of him to the cigar paper soon to be filled with weed in his lap.

"Man, why the fuck are we listening to this old-ass shit?" Bishop asked. "Throw some 50 Cent in, and pay attention to the fuckin' road before you crash this muthafucka."

Temp ignored his buddy and continued to bob his head. Shaking his head, Niko took a pull from his own blunt and held it in. Bishop grabbed the blunt from him and stared at his friend for a few seconds.

"Damn, nigga, you gon' blow that muthafuckin' smoke out?" Bishop asked.

After holding it in a few more seconds, Niko half blew, half coughed the toxic fumes into the air. He didn't know if his other friends had seen it, but he'd definitely noticed the troubled look in Chris's eyes. He suspected strongly that it may have had something to do with his family. But unless Chris brought it up, he wasn't going to pry. None of the Young Lionz talked about their family life much. Whenever they got together, it was strictly to have fun getting high or drunk or to go on a paper chase.

"The fuck on yo' mind, nigga?" Temp asked him when he saw him staring off into space. Originally, the plan was for Temp to accompany Antwan and Chris to Rhonda's house. But after getting a call from a girl he'd been trying to bang, he decided to just meet them there. It was just his bad luck that her boyfriend popped up over at her house, and she had to take a raincheck on the dick.

"Huh? Oh, nothin'," he lied. "Just thinkin' 'bout what I'm gonna do with all this cheese we gon' be makin'."

"Shit, I'ma get me another ride," Temp proclaimed.

"Another ride? Damn, man, you just got this one," Bishop reminded him.

"So what? When you a fly-ass nigga like me, you s'pose ta have multiple rides."

While rolling down the street, Temp spotted a young, sexy cutie walking toward the store. Although she looked rather young, that didn't stop Temp from trying to hit on her. "Hey, sexy, where you goin'?" he spat at her.

"You talkin' to me?" she asked.

"Yeah, you need a ride?"

"Nah, I'm straight."

Bishop squinted his eyes to get a better view of the pretty vixen. "Oh, shit, man, hol' up. Ain't that Veronica's sister, Dana?" he asked.

"Yeah, nigga, that's yo' sister-in-law," Temp said, picking on his friend while watching Dana go into the store.

"Sister-in-law? What the fuck that nigga talkin' 'bout, dawg?" Niko asked, confused.

"Oh, you ain't heard, my dude? The li'l homie here been bumpin' uglies with Veronica."

"Veronica?" Niko asked as a pang of jealousy hit him. He too had dreamt of knocking Veronica's boots. "Nigga, how the fuck you pull that?"

"First of all, you can eighty-six that sister-in-law shit, my dude. Ain't no nuptials jumping off around here, homie," Bishop clarified. "Second," he said, looking at Niko, "it's called mackin', baby!"

The three of them shared a good laugh until Bishop realized that they were still sitting in front of the store. "Man, why the fuck we still sitting here?"

"Shit, nigga, I thought that you might want me to give the little heifer a ride home."

Before Bishop could respond, Dana came walking out of the store. Her eyes rolled, and her lips smacked at the sight of them still sitting there.

"Don't trip, li'l mama. We just wanted to know if you needed a ride home."

"Boy, please. I don't get in the car with strangers," she proclaimed, leaning back with her arms folded.

"Number one, that 'boy' shit is dead. Number two, what the fuck you mean strangers? You don't remember us?"

Dana craned her neck as she tried to look inside the car. It took her a few seconds to recognize who they were. "Oh, yeah, that's right. Y'all Tangie's boyfriend's friends." Dana craned her neck again to see if Chris was in the car with them.

"Why you lookin' all in the car like that? You want a fuckin' ride or not?" Temp asked, getting irritated. He was trying to be nice, but this little hot-in-the-ass heifer was testing his patience. When Dana didn't see Chris inside, she backed away.

"Nah, I'm straight. I'ma walk. Thanks for the offer, though."

"Man, why the fuck you think she was looking in the car like that?" Niko asked.

Temp looked at him like he was the dumbest dude on the earth. "'Cause she's a bitch, nigga. That's what bitches do. They nosy as fuck!"

"Yo, man, while we're in front of this store, I'ma run in and get a six pack," Bishop said as he hopped out of the car.

While Bishop was in the store, Temp noticed a familiar car driving toward them on the opposite side of the street. He recognized it as the car driven by the dudes they got into it with over at Tangie's house. The car slowed down as it approached. When it looked like they would stop, Temp reached into his glove compartment and took out his pistol. Niko couldn't do much of anything since he'd left his pistol at home. The four men made eye contact once their cars were parallel to each other. Jermaine and Erik kept on driving as Temp held the gun up so they could see it.

"Pussy-ass niggas," Niko said as they drove by.

Niko stumbled out of Temp's car feeling nice. Bishop had said that he was going in the store to buy a six pack of beer, but he'd come back with a fifth of Absolut, some cranberry juice, and some cups. The three of them proceeded to drink and smoke for the next forty-five minutes. When Temp pulled up to Niko's house, Niko had a nice little buzz going on.

"Yo, dawg, throw this in the garbage for me," Temp said, handing Niko the empty liquor bottle. After getting out of the car, Niko took the bottle and stumbled up the steps of his front porch.

"Damn, man, you need some help getting yo' drunk ass up the steps?" Bishop laughed.

"Nah, man, I'm straight." No sooner had the words left his mouth than Niko fell and almost busted his ass. Temp's head fell onto the steering wheel as he cracked up laughing.

"Look at this clumsy muthafucka," Bishop said, shaking his head.

"Man, that nigga ain't clumsy. He just drunk as fuck," Temp said as he continued laughing.

Niko gave them both the finger as he got up and dusted himself off. He could still hear them laughing as they drove off down the street. Niko then turned around and headed for the front door. Twice he dropped his key as he attempted to stick it in the lock. Once he was able to unlock the door, Niko staggered through the hallway, feeling nice. He stepped on the bottom step and took a deep breath. The last thing he wanted to do was fall back down the stairs. He grabbed on to the railing and half walked, half pulled himself up the stairs. Once he got to the top, he quickly walked forward.

He wasn't smashed, but he was tipsy enough that he didn't want to stand on the edge and take a chance on falling back down the stairs. Niko leaned and walked at the same time as he approached his mother's door on the right. He thought it was strange that her door was open. He glanced inside as he passed by and quickly turned his head away as he saw his mother sprawled out on her bed, asshole naked. He shook his head in disgust and kept on walking. It wasn't like his mother to leave her door open like that, and he was starting to wonder why.

As he came to his room, he heard noises inside. He reached into his waistband for his pistol, but then re-membered that it was in his room in the closet. Then he looked at the bottle he'd forgotten to throw away and clutched it tight. He looked at the door, which was slightly ajar, and gripped the bottle even tighter. Slowly, he pushed the door open and tiptoed inside.

Anger rushed through him when he spotted James counting up money he'd made with his Young Lionz crew. James's back was turned to him, but Niko could almost see the cocky smirk on his face from the back. He could also see that James had found his pistol. It was lying on the bed. Just as Niko was about to sneak up behind him and take him out, James's cell phone vibrated on his hip. When James decided to answer it, Niko stopped. He wanted to see who the fuck James was talking to and what he was talking about.

"Hello? Hey, baby," James said to whoever was on the other end. "I know. But check this shit out. I just made a come up. This bitch's son must be slangin' or somethin'. This nigga got all kind of bread stashed in his closet. The li'l muthafucka even had a fuckin' gun in there, too."

Niko's rage grew by the second as he listened to James talk to his other bitch about him and his mother.

"Almost, baby. This nigga gotta have about six or seven thousand dollars here, and I'ma take all of this shit. As soon as I get done fleecin' this li'l punk, I'ma meet you at the airport so we can take that trip."

Niko gripped the bottle so tight it almost cracked.

"Nah, I ain't worried about that. I drugged her ass up real good, so that bitch ain't gonna wake up no time soon."

Niko couldn't take anymore. He stormed up behind James and brought the bottle down on his head with such force it knocked James out instantly. Glass exploded and flew through the air.

As James crashed to the floor, blood seeped from his skull and spread out onto the floor. Niko spat on him as he snatched his cell phone off the floor. He put the cell phone to his ear and listened to the woman on the other end as she called James's name over and over again.

"Sorry to fuck up yo' plans, bitch, but James's ass ain't gonna be able to make that trip."

Niko hung up and threw the phone at the wall, shattering it into ten pieces. He then stomped James in the head with his Timberland boots, causing the back of his head to leak blood. He was so mad he wanted to kill James right then. But instead, he came up with another plan. Niko grabbed James by the ankles and dragged him out of the room. When his mother woke up, he didn't want her to think that he had anything to do with James catching a beatdown.

He dragged him to the cusp of his mother's bedroom door and let James's feet fall to the floor. After that, he ran into the bathroom, grabbed a towel, and wet it. He cleaned up the blood that had been smeared from his room to his mother's door. Niko went back into his room and gathered his money and gun, and he packed a few clothes. He walked back out of his room and down the hallway. As he passed James, he spat on him again. He didn't want to see his mother naked again, so he didn't bother to look into her bedroom.

He didn't know what kind of drugs James had used to render his mother unconscious, but he was hoping that she woke up before he did. Niko walked down the steps and stormed out of the house. When his mother awoke, she would find her boyfriend lying on the floor in front of her bedroom. How she found him, either dead or alive, didn't make much difference to Niko.

Chapter 18

"Damn, nigga, who keep blowing ya jack up?" Antwan asked Chris as the two of them made their way to Rhonda's house.

"Just a li'l broad I'm fuckin' around with," he lied. Actually, it was Chris's mother who had been calling him nonstop for the last fifteen minutes or so. He knew that she was going to want an explanation for the money he left for her. She was going to want to know where it came from and if he did anything illegal to get it. Chris wasn't about to get into that with his mother. He had to do what he had to do in order to make sure that his sister got the operation she needed to survive.

"Nigga, stop lyin'. If that was some broad, yo' ass woulda answered the damn phone," Antwan said, laughing.

Chris laughed too. He should have known that his friend would see right through the lie. "Okay, man, you right. That was my mom. I left her most of the money that I had in a bag and hung it on her door. She's probably callin' to ask me where I got the money from." Chris paused for a second. "Man, I ain't trying to hear that right now. The only thing on my mind right now is making enough money to get my sister that operation. Fuck everything else."

"I feel you, dawg. And I'm proud of you, man. Do what yo gotta do to get that cheese and help ya li'l sis, man. Yo' moms might not like the way you get this bread, but I guarantee she'll appreciate it once it helps yo' sis out."

Antwan pulled up in front of the apartment building that Rhonda stayed in. The two of them jumped out and headed toward the building. It was a large, three-story brick building that was the color of burnt orange. Chris looked around and saw fiends walking up and down the street. It was obvious that they were in dire need of a hit. They were scratching and looking around, trying to figure out where their next hit of the pipe was coming from.

Antwan and Chris slowly walked up the steps and into the building. There was no need for Antwan to wait and get buzzed in. The lock on the door was broken, so they could just walk right in. Even if it weren't, it would not have mattered. The window that was next to the door was smashed out, so anyone could have stepped straight through it. Antwan opened the door, and the two of them walked to the elevator and hopped on.

Antwan took out his phone and texted Rhonda to let her know that he was on his way up. After arriving on the third floor, they walked down the dimly lit corridor and made their way to apartment number 303. The hallway was clean, with wall-to-wall light brown carpet. It smelled like roses from one end of the hallway to the other. Antwan knocked on the door and waited about five seconds before a short, thin, baldheaded man opened the door. He had a deep-set scar on his right cheek, and thick, bushy eyebrows. His skin was the color of butter, and his eyes were light green.

"Yo, what's up, dawg?" he asked, not recognizing Antwan or Chris.

"I'm here to see Rhonda," Antwan said, wanting to laugh at the short man who was trying to put bass in his voice.

The man scrunched up his face and rubbed his chin. "Hol' up a second," he said as he closed the door and walked away. When he door reopened, Bo was standing there with a glass of liquor in his hand. He had on a pair of black slacks, and a wife beater covered his upper torso.

"Hey, what's up, my man?" he said, extending his fist to receive a pound from them. "Y'all ready to make this money?"

"You damn skippy," Chris chimed in.

Bo looked at Chris and gave him a once-over. This was the first time he'd met anyone in Antwan's crew other than Temp. "You kinda young to be out here hangin' with the big boys, ain't you?"

"I'm grown enough to make this paper, my dude."

Bo looked at Antwan and then back at Chris. After shrugging his shoulders, Bo stepped to the side and let them come in. He honestly didn't care how old Chris was. All he cared about was the opportunity that he had to make a king-sized profit off of Antwan and his crew. The three of them walked into the living room, where Rhonda was sitting on the couch, rolling a blunt. On the coffee table in front of her was rocked-up and cut cocaine.

It was cut up in dimes and twenties. On the end table was dope still in its powdered form. Rhonda was dressed in a pair of cutoff shorts so tight they threatened to bust at the seams. The tank top she had on was loose and showed much more cleavage than it had to. Antwan felt a twinge of jealousy seeing his woman on the side sitting there like that. But he wasn't jealous enough that he was going to blow making this paper.

"Rhonda, come on, baby. Let our guests sit down."

Without saying a word, Rhonda got up and moved to the beige lounge chair on the other side of the room. She made a point of switching her ass slightly as she made her way across the hardwood floor. Just then, the man who'd answered the door came into the room with a cigarette hanging out of his mouth. He had a bottle of Cîroc vodka in his hand along with some cups.

"Yo, Antwan. This here is my brother, Mario."

"Sup, dude?" Mario said as he walked over to Antwan and held out his hand.

"Sup, man. This my homeboy Chris."

"Sup, young buck?" Mario said, trying to be funny.

"Not much, old man," Chris shot back. After a brief frown, Mario snorted out a laugh.

"Well, let's get down to business," Bo said. "Rhonda, I want you to take Antwan in the kitchen and show him how to whip up a pie. Then I want you to show him how to cut the shit up. Mario, I want you to show Chris the difference in the sizes of the rocks in the bags over there." He paused for a second and then said, "And then take him downstairs and sit on the stoop with him for a minute and show him how to serve these fiends."

Bo expected Chris to get scared. But instead, Chris just nodded his head, signifying that he was more than ready to get in the trap.

"I'ma go back here and take a shower so I can get ready to go out of town for a few days. Mario, I'ma need you to stay here and take care of that thing with T.J. while I'm gone. For some reason, that nigga act like he can't wait 'til I get back."

Bo went into the back to get ready for his trip. Mario led Chris to the couch and showed him the different sizes of the rocks and schooled him on undercover, short payments, and the switch game. Chris soaked the information up like a sponge. Mario was surprised at the amount of information that young Chris was able to retain when he ran a few situations past him.

While Chris was in the living room picking Mario's brain, Antwan was in the kitchen trying to keep from grabbing Rhonda's ass. The way she looked in her shorts had Antwan turning his head when he saw her so that he wouldn't get a hard-on. As Rhonda was busy trying to show Antwan how to cook cocaine, he was busy looking around. When he was sure that no one else was around, he squeezed her tit.

"Nigga, what the fuck wrong with you?" she asked, knocking his hand away. "You tryin' ta get both of us killed up in here?"

"Ain't nobody in here but us, baby."

"Yeah, but my man is in the back, and his brother is right out there in the living room," she said, pointing. Antwan frowned. He didn't like the way Rhonda referred to Bo as her man.

"I don't know what the fuck you frownin' for," she whispered to him. "You asked me to set this shit up, and I did, so don't be lookin' at me like you mad. The last time I checked, you had a bitch at home you was fuckin' on a regular basis, so don't get all pissed off because I got somebody in my life."

Although Rhonda felt she said what she had to say, there was still room in her heart for Antwan if he ever decided to leave Tangie. Antwan just stared at her for a moment. Even though he didn't like the way Rhonda was coming at him, he knew that she was right. He had no right to get salty at her because she was trying to live her life.

"Now," she said, breaking his train of thought, "are you gonna just stand there, or are you gonna come over here and let me show you how to whip this shit up?"

Feeling like a fool, Antwan walked over to the stove and started taking cooking lessons. When they were done, Rhonda put the hard pie of cocaine on a plate. The two of them walked into the living room and sat down on the couch. Antwan looked around for Chris, but he was nowhere to be found.

"Hey, where the hell my partner go?"

"Mario probably took him outside on the stoop. The fiends been going crazy the last few weeks trying to cop some rocks."

Rhonda motioned for Antwan to sit down. Once he did, she commenced showing him how to cut up tens, twenties, and fifties. He was paying close attention until his phone vibrated and diverted his attention. He looked at the screen and saw that it was Temp.

"Sup, nigga. Where the fuck you at?"

"I'm on my way, dawg. I ran into a little delay."

"The fuck kinda delay you ran into that's gon' keep you from gettin' this paper, nigga?"

"Yo, kid, I ran into this broad I used to kick it with, and the bitch felt like givin' me some head," he partly lied. He didn't feel like hearing Antwan's mouth if he told him that he'd been kicking it with Niko and Bishop, too.

"Well, hurry up and bring yo' ass on, man, so I can show you how to do this shit."

"Muthafucka, it ain't like you an expert. You just learning how to cook the shit up ya'self."

Antwan looked at his cell phone and gave it the screw face. "Nigga, do you wanna make this money or not?"

"Hell yeah!"

"Then hurry up and bring yo' ass on!" Before Temp could respond, Antwan hung up on him.

Detective Ramsey decided to toss back one more drink before she left the bar. She felt bad for Yolonda, but she was extremely pissed off that she had died and essentially left her without a case. Now the only thing she could do was go by Temp's house, question him, and hope the young asshole would give himself away. She got up from the barstool and walked out of the bar in a pissed-off mood. Little did she know, her mood was about to get worse.

She had just gotten into her car and started it up when her cell phone rang. Recognizing the number, she answered it right away. After hearing the message that was given to her, she took the phone away from her ear and looked at it. Then she dropped her head and shook it from side to side. She'd just gotten the news that her captain was going on vacation, and he didn't want anyone to conduct any one-on-one investigations until he got back in three days. All the detective could do was shake her head. The way her luck was going, she was never going to crack the case.

"No, the fuck this nigga didn't just hang up on me," Temp said, laughing. "That nigga startin' to act like a bitch."

Temp drove away from the house of the girl who'd just sucked him off, shaking his head. He and Antwan had been friends longer than the rest of the Young Lionz, and they'd never really had beef with each other. They'd had each other's backs on more than a few occasions. Temp shook off the perceived dis by his friend and continued. He was just starting to feel relaxed about his situation. He hadn't heard anything from Yolonda about the beating he'd given her. Temp reasoned that she was probably grieving the death of her mother.

He was certain that her body had been found right along with her lover's by now. He started to pull a blunt out of his console and blaze it up but changed his mind. He wanted to have a clear mind when he learned about making all of the paper Antwan was telling him about. Temp increased the speed to five miles per hour above the speed limit. He was anxious to get to Rhonda's and learn the game. He was so busy counting in his head the money he was going to be making that he never saw the flashing lights behind him.

He yelled a loud obscenity as he pulled over to the curb. Temp knew the drill, so he dug into his back pocket and pulled out his driver's license. Once he got it out, he rolled down the window. The officer walked up to his car and opened his mouth, but before he could say a word, Temp handed him his license, rolled his window back up, and turned his music back up.

"This muthafucka ain't got nothin' else to do but fuck with me," Temp said as the officer was running his license. He was so mad he didn't even bother to look in the mirror as the cop was doing it. In Temp's mind, this little infringement on his time was causing him to potentially miss out on some dough. He opened his cell phone to call Antwan and tell him that he was going to be even later than he originally planned because he was being detained, but before he could, he heard a tap on the window.

Temp turned his head to the left, expecting to see the same ugly-ass cop who had pulled him over, but instead, his dick almost burst through his pants as he laid eyes on the most beautiful detective he'd ever seen.

"Hello, Mr. Green," Ramsey said in a no-nonsense tone that caused Temp to start sweating.

"Hey, what's up?" he said, trying his best to remain cool under the circumstances. He watched as the police car that had pulled him over pulled out from behind him and drove away.

"The officer who stopped you informed me that you were speeding. Now I convinced him to let you off with a warning this time, but you're going to have to watch your driving in a residential area," she said as she gave him his license back.

"Okay, I will. Thanks," he said as he tried to drive away.

"Hold up. Not so fast, youngster. I have a couple of questions for you, if you don't mind."

Ramsey stared into Temp's eyes for a few seconds to see if there was any kind of admission of guilt in them. But all she saw were the cold eyes of a thug. Had it not been for the fact that she'd been involved in another crime scene in the area, she would have been nowhere near where Temp was driving.

"Do you know a Yolonda Bates?"

Temp looked at the cop and knew instantly that she knew the truth. The only thing lying to her would do was make him look suspicious. "Yeah, I know her. Why?"

"How do you know her?" Ramsey asked, ignoring Temp's question.

"I used to screw her."

The hairs on the back of Ramsey's neck stood up. She couldn't believe that Temp could be so cocky as to say that to her. "When was the last time you saw her?" she asked through gritted teeth.

Temp could tell by the look in Ramsey's eyes that she knew something. But he also knew that she didn't have anything on him. If she did, she would be hauling his ass off to jail. "I ain't seen her in about two months," he lied. "You wanna tell me what the hell this shit is all about?"

Ramey's eyes turned into narrow slits. The longer she was in Temp's presence, the more she disliked him. She decided to test the waters and see what kind of reaction she would get from Temp when she told him that Yolonda had died. "Well, Mr. Green, I'm sorry to be the one to have to tell you this, but Miss Bates recently passed away."

"What? Passed away? When the fuck did that happen?"

Ramsey wasn't a rookie. She'd seen enough fake remorse to know that Temp was spitting out a slew of it. From his body language alone, she could tell that he didn't care one way or the other about Yolonda being dead.

"Did you know that at the time of her death she was pregnant?"

Temp stared at her. She was trying to trap him, and it ticked him off. "How, I mean, *how* in the hell would I know that? I just told you that I haven't seen her in two months. How in the fuck would I know that the bitch was pregnant?"

Before she could stop herself, Detective Ramsey reached into the car and grabbed Temp by the front of his shirt. It was obvious that the young man had no respect for the law. It was going to be her pleasure to nail his ass.

"Little boy, I don't know who the fuck you think you're talkin' to like that, but you'd better show the law some fuckin' respect! You fuckin' hear me?" she asked as she tightened the grip on his collar.

"Yeah, I hear you," Temp said with a smirk on his face. He was more confident than ever that the cops didn't have anything on him. When Detective Ramsey released his shirt and stepped back, Temp drove off with the sly smirk still plastered on his face.

After walking Antwan through the cook, cut, and bag process one more time, Rhonda went into the back room with Bo. She'd given Antwan a quarter and told him to cook it up. He wanted to try his hand at cooking up a half, but she told him that he would have to take baby steps first. While he was in the kitchen working on his dope-cooking skills, he heard moans and bed springs creaking from the back room. After three minutes, the noise ceased. Antwan smiled to himself.

No wonder she keep coming back and giving me the pussy. This nigga is a straight minute man. I'ma show that nigga how to beat a bitch's pussy up when he leave.

Shaking away the thought of his side chick getting smashed, Antwan concentrated on the task at hand. He

boiled the water to near perfection as he equally distributed the coke and baking soda into a large jar. Carefully
and attentively, he watched as the product started to do
its thing. When it was all said and done, Antwan was sure
he'd made the perfect pie. He'd just put it on a plate when
Rhonda came out of the bedroom looking frazzled. Bo
was right behind her with a look of pure satisfaction on
his face. It was obvious that his minute-man ass couldn't
handle good pussy.

"Let's see what you got going on out here, youngster,"
Bo said as he walked over to check out Antwan's handi-
work. After looking at the job that Antwan had done, he
nodded in satisfaction.

"Damn, youngster, you look like you a natural at this
shit. Hey, baby, look at the pie this nigga done whipped
up. I'ma have to start calling you the baker, son. Now
let's take this in the other room and see what ya cuttin'
skills hittin' on."

When the three of them got into the living room, Chris
and Mario were sitting back on the couch sharing a blunt.

"The fuck y'all doing in here? Ain't them fiends biting
out there?" Bo asked.

Mario looked at his brother and pointed at the table
where the bagged-up rocks used to be.

"Yo, what the fuck happened to all the shit?"

"Man, this li'l nigga went out there and got that shit off
like Nino Brown. This li'l muthafucka here is a straight-
up beast when it comes to slangin' them thangs," Mario
said, pointing at Chris.

Bo looked at the empty table and then back at Chris.
He couldn't help but think how reckless Chris had been
to get that much dope off in that small amount of time.
He also knew that because of the drought in the area, the
fiends would be flocking to the rocks like wildfire, so he
wasn't ready to anoint Chris the second coming of Tony
Montana just yet.

"Good job, junior," was all he said to Chris. "A'ight, Antwan, let me see what you can do with the rock and razor."

Antwan sat down and went to work. Wanting to learn as much as he could, Chris walked over beside him and observed. Although Mario had shown him how to cut, he figured that he may as well pay attention just in case Antwan did something that Mario hadn't shown him.

"Damn, young blood, you wanna learn everything, don't chu?" Bo said, smiling.

"You damn skippy, cuz."

Bo laughed at the young upstart. But then as quickly as he had started laughing, he stopped. "Hey, I thought you said that your other partner was going to be here," he said, referring to Temp.

"When I talked to him last, he said that he was on his way."

Bo's left eye started to twitch, a sign that he'd gotten slightly nervous. Although Antwan was supposed to Rhonda's cousin, he didn't know him from a hole in the wall. He wasn't about to be caught slippin' and let some masked fools run up in his spot and rob him. For all he knew, Antwan could've been playing Rhonda all along just to get the inside track to jack him. Just as he thought about shutting down shop for the rest of the night, someone knocked on the door.

Mario walked up to the door and looked out the peephole. He'd never seen Temp before, so he didn't recognize him. "Ay yo, I don't know who the fuck this is, Bo."

Bo snatched the 9 mm he had tucked in the small of his back and chambered a round. He figured that it was probably Antwan's other partner, but he wasn't taking any chances. He looked out the peephole and stuck his pistol into his waistband.

"Damn, man, when I talked to you about fifteen minutes ago, you said that you was on yo' way."

"Man, I was until I got pulled the fuck over," Temp said, walking in.

"Man, yo' ass was speedin', wasn't you?" Chris asked, knowing his friend's driving habits. Temp gave Chris the finger and walked over to where Antwan was busy cutting up the pie.

"Rhonda, take tardy man in the kitchen, and show him how to cook a half."

Temp eyed Bo like he wanted to say something but decided to keep his mouth closed for the greater good. But if Bo thought he was going to treat Temp like a stepchild because he was supplying them, he was dead wrong.

Chapter 19

Moonlight cut through Bishop's window like scissors and splashed onto his pillow. He was in a deep sleep before the sexual moans from the room next to his interrupted him. His pillow lay on his head, and as soon as he moved it, the light slapped him in the face like a scorned lover.

Bishop stole a glance at the clock on his nightstand before pulling the pillow back over his head. It was only six o'clock, so it was still dark outside, and he hadn't gotten a full night's sleep.

"I guess they done made up," he said as he listened to the loud moans and groans coming from his sister's bedroom.

After Temp dropped him off at home the previous night, Bishop walked into the house to find the two of them snuggled up on the couch. Jason was kissing Carla on her neck, which had her giggling like a schoolgirl. Bishop just shook his head at the dysfunctional relationship shared by her sister and her boyfriend, and he stumbled upstairs. His head was spinning, and his stomach was threatening to eject the contents inside of it. The last thing he remembered was falling down on his bed and passing out. Now he was lying in his bed, trying to muffle the sounds of Jason and his sister screwing in the room adjacent from his bedroom.

Bishop wanted to get as much sleep as possible before nightfall. On the way home, Temp had told him that he and Niko would be hustling in the trap the next night. Bishop's cell phone went off, and after looking at the screen, he sent it to voicemail. He hadn't been to work in a couple of days. With the money that he was going to be making slinging rocks with his Young Lionz crew, Bishop was thinking very seriously about quitting. It wasn't that he didn't like his job, but it didn't make any sense to him to continue to work there and make pennies when he could hit the block and make thousands. For a very brief moment, he was conflicted as to whether he should continue working and making a legitimate living or risk going to jail for doing something illegal. That mental tug of war didn't last long. The amount of money he would make selling drugs crushed any lingering feelings of doing the right thing. Bishop did feel bad about quitting on Mr. Hanley but, in his mind, he had to do what he had to do in order to make some decent money. His cell phone rang again, and this time the number on the other end made him smile.

"Hey, baby girl," he answered the phone.

"Sup, boo? Hey, I know it's kinda early, but I was wondering if you wanted to go to breakfast," Veronica said.

"Shit, you ain't got to ask me twice," Bishop said as he rolled out of the bed. "Just gimme about twenty minutes, and you can come and pick me up."

"Pick you up? Can't you just come over here?"

"I ain't got no damn car. That was Temp's car I was driving the other day."

"Oh, okay, baby. No problem. Let me get ya address, and I'll come pick you up."

After telling her where he lived, Bishop jumped up and quickly showered. He got dressed and went down into the kitchen where his sister and Jason were sitting side by side, drinking coffee. Bishop and Jay stared at each other for a good ten seconds. This was the first time they had seen each other since Bishop pistol whipped him.

"Sup, nigga?" Bishop said. It was more of a challenging tone than a way of saying good morning.

"Good morning, man," Jason said, not wanting to have a problem with the young hothead. He was still pissed about what Bishop had done to him, especially since he was the victim to begin with. He'd thought seriously about having one of his thug cousins catch Bishop slipping and return the pistol-whipping favor. But since he and Carla had gotten back together and she'd told him that she set her brother straight, he figured he'd just let it go.

"What's up, bro?" Carla spoke to her brother.

"Sup, sis."

Bishop felt strange as an awkward silence hung in the air. Feeling out of place, Bishop walked out of the kitchen and headed for the front door. He would rather wait outside than to feel like an outsider in his sister's house. He sat on the porch for ten minutes before Veronica pulled up in front of the house.

Veronica smiled as she looked out the passenger's side window. Bishop had been on her mind ever since they were last together. She was starting to catch major feelings for him and wondered if now was the time to let everyone know about their relationship.

"Damn, I hope we going to a place that's got some good grub, 'cause a nigga hungry as fuck," Bishop said as he got inside the car.

"Damn, hello to you too," Veronica said.

"Oh, my bad," he said.

Veronica leaned over and kissed Bishop on the jaw. Just feeling his ruggedly handsome skin made her moist. As she drove, she fantasized about Bishop eating her out. Ever since she'd found out that he didn't indulge in carpet munching, she took it as a challenge to get him to do just that. It didn't take long for them to get to the restaurant.

Landmarks sat on the corner of Fifty-third and St. Clair and was one of the most affordable breakfast eatery spots in the city. It was a reddish brick building that looked like it had been well maintained, despite that it had been there for quite some time, around thirty-five years to be exact. Since the area was being remodeled, the place stuck out like a sore thumb. Other businesses in the area had been updated, but the owner of Landmarks felt that there was a certain nostalgic feel that his place brought to the area that made the building priceless.

The inside of the place had two separate eating spaces. On the side where the customers entered was a long bar-like table adorned with metal, backless stools that rotated. Plates sat in front of hungry customers as they dug in. Behind them against the wall were booth-style tables that seated up to four people. On the other side were regular rectangular tables lined against the wall. In the middle of the floor were oval tables that seated six people. Near the back were a flight of stairs that lead downstairs to the bathrooms.

Bishop and Veronica walked into the restaurant hand in hand. They were really starting to feel each other. The waitress sat them in a booth right in front of the window. Bishop looked around and was surprised to see that the place wasn't that crowded. He's heard that the food was fantastic and wondered why there weren't more people inside if the food was that great. While they were waiting to place their order, the two of them engaged in light conversation.

"What you gettin' ya boy Antwan for his birthday?" Veronica inquired.

"The same thing he got me for my birthday: not a muthafuckin' thing," Bishop answered, laughing. "Nah, I'll probably get the nigga a gallon of liquor or a sack of weed. That's something I know his ass won't let go to waste. I just can't wait 'til this party Saturday."

"Party? What party?"

"Antwan's party. You ain't heard that Tangie is throwing him a surprise birthday party this Saturday? Damn, I thought Tangie was yo' homegirl."

"I did too," she said as she took out her phone, prepared to call Tangie and cuss her out. Before she could press a single button, the phone started vibrating in her hand. Veronica popped her lips when she saw that it was Tangie calling her.

"Hello?" she said with an attitude when she pressed talk.

"Bitch, what the fuck wrong with you?" Tangie asked, hearing the tone in her voice.

"Nothin'. What's up?"

Tangie didn't know what her friend's problem was, but she was definitely not in the mood for the bullshit. She ignored her friend's snotty attitude and got to the business of why she called in the first place. "Well, like I been trying to call and tell yo' ass, I'm having a surprise birthday party for Antwan next Saturday. I was gonna do it this Saturday, but he had to go outta town to handle some business for a few days. The nigga probably gonna be all tired and shit when he get back, so I rescheduled the shit."

Veronica nodded. *Yeah, bitch, you betta invite me.* "That's cool. You know I'll be up in that piece lookin' fly as hell."

Tangie noticed a change in her mood when she told her about the party, but she didn't dwell on it. She didn't have time to. She wanted to discuss other things with her friend. "What's up, bitch? You ready to tell me who you been fuckin'?" she said, diving right into it.

"Damn, bitch, you nosy as fuck," Veronica countered, laughing.

"Bitch, stop holdin' out. Spill the damn tea."

"A'ight, bitch, damn. But I don't wanna tell you over the phone."

"Why not?"

"'Cause I want to tell you this shit face-to-face. I wanna see the look on your face when I tell yo' ass."

Right away, Tangie suspected that it was someone they both knew.

"I'll be by later on to let you know what the deal is."

Veronica knew that her friend was going to try to get her to tell her over the phone anyway, so she hung up on her before she had a chance to start begging.

"That was Tangie," she told Bishop as if he didn't know. "She finally told me about the fuckin' surprise party next Saturday."

Next Saturday? I thought she said it was this Saturday. Thirty seconds later, he received a text message telling him that the day of the party had been changed.

When the waitress came over to take their order, Bishop recognized her as Erica, a girl he'd smashed about six months ago. They were never a couple, though. It was strictly a fun thing for both of them, and even though he hadn't seen her in a few months, they were still on friendly terms with each other. Erica was very pretty, with light brown doe eyes and long, shiny hair. She had a dark tan complexion. She was, however, a bit on the thin side.

"Hey, Bishop. What's good?" Erica asked, totally ignoring Veronica.

"Not much," he responded. "Just kickin' it with my homegirl, tryin' ta get some grub."

Veronica got pissed immediately. *Homegirl? I know this nigga ain't tryin' ta play me in front of this anorexic-lookin' bitch.*

Erica placed two menus on the table in front of them and asked them if they wanted anything to drink. Bishop asked for a glass of orange juice. Veronica asked for water in a not-so-friendly tone that wasn't lost on either Bishop or Erica. Erica simply rolled her eyes and walked away. Veronica wasted little time getting in Bishop's shit about the comment.

"Homegirl, huh?"

"Huh?"

"I said, 'homegirl, huh?' Is that what I am now, your homegirl?"

"Ain't that what the fuck you is?"

"Humph. I thought I was a little more than that."

"Look, don't start that bullshit. We ain't even told nobody that we been screwing around yet. And now you want me to claim you as my shorty?"

"Shorty? Nigga, do I look like a damn teenager to you?"

Bishop stared at her like she had insulted his mother. "Let me tell you somethin', Veronica. If you want us to be together, don't be talkin' to me like I'm ya fuckin' child or somethin'. And like I said, we ain't even told nobody that we kickin' it yet, so don't be actin' like we engaged or somethin'."

Veronica didn't like it, but she knew he was right. They had only been kicking it with each other for a few days, so it was unrealistic to think that they were a couple so soon.

"Okay, baby, I feel you. But I gotta ask. Where do you know this broad from?" she asked, referring to the waitress.

"Look, I ain't gonna lie to you. We kicked it a coupla times, but that was like six months ago. I ain't seen her in like three months, so me and her is a dead issue."

Although she still felt a little jealous, Veronica accepted and appreciated that Bishop was telling her the truth. At least, she thought he was. When Erica came back, she too had an attitude.

"Is it okay if I ask him what he wants to order?" she asked Veronica.

Veronica twisted up her mouth and held out her hand toward Bishop, letting Erica know that it was okay to do what she'd asked. After the two of them ordered, Erica turned to Veronica.

"Thank you for allowing me to do my job," she said just before she turned and walked away.

"Don't get spanked, little girl," Veronica said to Erica's back. Erica didn't respond. She just kept on walking. Bishop just looked at Veronica and shook his head.

"What?" she asked, snaking her head like a typical ghetto girl.

"Nothin'," Bishop said, figuring the argument wasn't worth the time. He used to wonder why someone as fine as Veronica was single. He was beginning to see why.

After having breakfast with Veronica, Bishop went home and lay back down. He wanted to make sure that he had plenty of rest before he went to grind. He was nervous yet excited at the same time. Although he'd never sold drugs before, he was confident that he could hold his own in the trap. As he lay in the bed, Bishop wondered if he was doing the right thing getting involved with Veronica. He didn't need the headache of a jealous woman questioning his every move and trying to find out where he was at all times.

Bishop really didn't want to be bothered with a jealous broad. He'd heard enough stories from his friends that being with someone like that was not worth the trouble. Personally, he'd never had to endure such a hardship, and he wasn't about to start now. Even though the sex with her was fantastic, it wasn't good enough for him to put up with bullshit.

Bishop closed his eyes, but he didn't get to keep them closed for long. His ringing cell phone made sure of that.

He ignored it at first, but after it rang twice more, he answered it in an aggravated manner. "What?" he asked.

"Damn, nigga, what the fuck wrong with you?" Temp asked.

"I was trying to get some damn sleep, fool."

"Man, fuck that shit. I'm on my way to get you."

"Now?"

"Nigga, do you wanna make this money or not?"

"Nigga, hell yeah!"

"Then pull yo' ass outta Veronica's pussy and get ready." Temp hung up before Bishop had a chance to respond.

"Jealous-ass muthafucka," Bishop said as he got up, smiling. It cracked him up the way Temp was acting about the whole Veronica situation. If he didn't know any better, he would think that Temp was her man or something. Bishop got up and walked into the kitchen. After grabbing a beer out of the refrigerator, he went out on the porch to wait for Temp.

Chris sat at the bus stop with a huge smile on his face. He was sleepy as hell, but that did nothing to dampen his mood. Temp had offered him a ride home, but Chris declined. He had been on his grind since the previous night. The only reason he even took a break was that he wanted to go home and give his mother some of the money he'd made. He would keep a little for himself, but the rest of it was going toward his sister's operation. He honestly didn't know how much he'd made, but he couldn't wait to get home to find out.

On his way there, Chris thought about how exciting it was to make large sums of money at an accelerated rate. From the time he'd started grinding, he'd come in contact with all types of people. Old men, young men, pregnant women, teenaged girls, even professional-looking men and women all came through looking to get high.

Chris jumped up when he saw the bus coming. He couldn't wait to get home so he could give his mother the money that he'd accumulated hustling. He hopped on the bus and sat down on the first seat he came to. His cell phone vibrated, jolting him out of his daydream. Chris looked at the number and sighed. He knew that he was going to catch hell from his mother for being gone all night long, but it couldn't be helped. He started to let it go to voicemail, but he was going to have to talk to her sooner or later.

"Hello," he said cautiously.

"Chris, where in the fuck have you been all night? Why you ain't been answering the damn phone?" Chris's mother had called him no fewer than six times, and he'd sent her to voicemail all six times.

"I'm sorry, ma. I just went for a walk and ended up over Niko's house," he lied. "After talking to him, I just fell asleep." The line went deathly silent. It was silent for so long, in fact, that Chris thought his mother had hung up on him.

"Do you think I'm stupid, Chris?" she finally asked him.

"Nah, Ma, I don't think you stupid at all."

"Then why are you lying to me?"

"Lyin' to you about what, Mama?" The line went silent again.

"I'm going to see your sister. Be home when I get back. I want to talk to you."

Vivian then hung up before Chris had a chance to respond. Chris sat back in his seat and blew out a long breath. He figured that since his mother wasn't going to be there, there was no sense in him rushing home. He wondered why she hadn't asked him about the money he'd left on her door.

When the bus came to a stop, Chris looked around and saw that he was almost in front of Dana's house. It was a

Saturday morning, so he knew she would be at home. His manhood started to grow as he thought about how good she looked when he was in her room. Just as the bus started to pull off, Chris yelled for the bus driver to stop. The bus driver cursed under his breath and slammed on the brakes. Chris hopped off the bus and power walked down the street to Dana's house.

The closer he got to her house, the harder his dick got. He walked up on her porch and knocked on her door. When he didn't get an answer, he knocked again. After the third knock, Chris figured that she was asleep or had gone with her mother. He turned to walk off the porch and froze when he saw a car coming down the street. His back stiffened when the car came to a stop in front of Dana's house.

"Boy, what the hell you doin' over my li'l sister's house?" Veronica called from her car. When Chris didn't answer, Veronica walked up on the porch and got in Chris's face. "Li'l boy, did you hear me?"

Chris looked at her like she had lost her mind. He liked Dana, but he wasn't about to be checked by her sister or anyone else. "First of all, you can back the fuck up off of me. I ain't yo' muthafuckin' child. So don't be fuckin' talkin' to me like I am." Chris's voice was calm, but his tone was unnervingly deadly.

When Veronica saw the look on Chris's face, she turned on her heel and walked toward the door. Then she turned back to him. "You wanna see my sister? Fine! Come on! I wanna hear what her li'l hot ass has to say."

Veronica unlocked the door and walked inside. Chris was right behind her. Veronica looked around and didn't see anyone.

"The li'l heifer probably still in the bed," Veronica said.

"Yo, can I use the bathroom right quick?"

"Go ahead. I'ma go see if Dana is still sleeping."

As Chris headed for the bathroom, Veronica walked toward her sister's room. She looked at her watch and smiled. Knowing that her sister was going to be as mad as hell if she woke her up, Veronica decided to do just that. Snickering lightly, Veronica burst through her sister's door.

"Wake yo' ass . . . What the fuck?"

Veronica's mouth hit the floor. Her eyes almost popped out of her head at the sight of her baby sister on her hands and knees. Standing in front of her with his pants around his ankles was Jay.

"Oh, shit," he yelled as he struggled to get his dick out of Dana's mouth.

Dana was loving what she was doing so much that she was oblivious to anyone else being in the room. When Jay finally pushed her head away, Dana looked around for the first time and saw her sister. Surprisingly, Dana showed no fear. She simply gave her sister a sly smile and shrugged her shoulders.

"That's what the fuck you get for busting into my room like the damn police," she said smugly.

Veronica looked into her sister's eyes and saw a look she'd never seen before. Then she looked around the room. Her eyes came to a stop when she saw a blunt burning on Dana's nightstand. She didn't mind that. She knew that her sister smoked weed occasionally. But what pissed her off was the bag filled with a white powdery substance that was lying next to it. Veronica stormed over to the dresser and picked up the bag.

"Bitch, have you lost yo' muthafuckin mind?" she yelled. "This nigga got you in here suckin' his dick for a laced-up joint? What the fuck is wrong with you?"

Jay snickered slightly, causing Veronica to turn her venom on him. "Nigga, what the fuck you laughing at? You got my baby sister in here smoking a laced-up joint?

Are you fuckin' crazy? Nigga, get the fuck outta this house!"

Seeing the crazed look in her eyes, Jay quickly headed for the door. He had come over with the pretense of an apology, but that's all it was. Jay knew that Dana loved to smoke weed, so he promised to give her a twenty sack if she would let him come over and speak his piece. She had no way of knowing that he intended to trick her by putting cocaine in the weed.

Jay walked through the bedroom door and turned left. A slow, sinister smile crept onto his face when he saw Chris standing there with tears of hatred in his eyes. Without saying a word, he walked past Chris and headed for the front door.

"Where the fuck you think you goin'?" Veronica yelled at her sister.

Dana ignored her and stormed out of her bedroom, trying to stop Jay. "Jay, wait!" As soon as Dana reached the hallway, her heart dropped. "Chris, baby, I—"

"Get the fuck offa me!" Chris yelled when Dana reached for him. He'd been in the hallway listening to everything being said. "You had me slappin' this muthafucka around, and now you in here sucking his dick? But you a virgin. Yeah, right! Fuck outta here with that shit!" Chris headed for the door. He wasn't so much hurt as he felt disrespected.

"But, Chris, I am a virgin," Dana said, following him. "All I did was . . ." Dana's words lodged in her throat as Chris turned around and looked at her with a death stare.

"I don't even wanna hear what the fuck you about to say!"

Chris then walked out of her house and slammed the door behind him. Dana dropped her head and slowly walked back to her bedroom. When she got there, her sister was standing there, shaking her head.

"What? I guess yo' snitchin' ass gon' tell Mama now, right?"

Veronica didn't say a word. She just snatched up the bag of dope up and walked out of the room.

"I shoulda known that little hot-ass bitch was getting dick from somewhere," Chris mumbled as he walked home. He was starting to feel Dana, and she'd shitted on him. But even though he was pissed about what happened, Chris still wanted to fuck her. An evil smile registered on his face as the ultimate plan of revenge entered his mind. When Chris walked up on his porch, he looked through the window and saw his mother sitting on the couch.

"Fuck!" he said, surprised that she was home. He shook his head as he unlocked the door and walked in. The second he saw her reading her Bible, Chris shook his head. He had almost stopped believing in God. He just couldn't understand how God could allow his sister to suffer like she had been. He walked into the house, went over to where his mother was sitting, and sat down beside her. Vivian never even looked up. She just continued reading the Bible.

"Are you ready to tell me where you've been, or are you going to just keep lying to me?" she asked without looking at her son.

"Ma, I told you, I was—"

Vivian held up her hand to stop her son from lying to her any further. She took off her reading glasses and looked her son directly in his eyes. "When are you going to see your sister?"

"I'm going today, Ma."

"Good, good. I know she will be very glad to see you. Now about this money you left for me. Look me in my eyes, and tell me you got it legally."

Chris opened his mouth, but nothing came out. It was easy for him to lie over the phone, but to do it while staring her directly in the face was something altogether different.

"That's what I thought," Vivian said.

Chris saw the disappointment in her eyes, but he still felt that he was doing the right thing. Unless his mother or anyone else knew where to get their hands on the money for the operation, he was going to continue to do what he had to do in order to save his sister. He decided to bring that into the conversation.

"I'm sorry, Ma, but what do you want me to do? Tracy needs this operation, and if I don't make this money, we're gonna be in debt forever. I gotta do what I gotta do."

A single tear rolled down Vivian's face. She would never tell her son to go out and do something illegal, but she understood his position. Nor would she ever tell him that she was secretly proud of him for going above and beyond to make sure that his sister received the proper care. The last thing she wanted to do was make him feel comfortable about doing whatever it took to save his sister's life. Vivian wiped the tear away and cleared her throat.

"Well, I talked to the hospital, and they told me that I didn't have to pay the whole amount at one time. They said I could put like twenty-five percent down and make the rest in payments. With the money you left this morning, I need about two thousand more to make the down payment."

Chris smiled so hard it stretched the muscles in his face. He quickly reached into his pocket and pulled out the money he'd made from his night of hustling. He took great pride in handing his mother the folded bills. Reluctantly, she took them and started counted the money out. When she was done counting, the total was $3,200.

Tears of joy ran down her face as she fell to her knees. Vivian clasped her hands together and looked up to the ceiling. She thanked the Lord over and over again as Chris stood there and watched. As if having an epiphany, Chris kneeled beside his mother. *It can't hurt,* he thought as he prayed alongside her.

Dear Lord. Thank you. Thank you for making a way for me to pay for my sister's surgery. I know that I'm not getting money the right way, and maybe I'll have to pay for that one day, but for right now, I just want to say thanks.

When Chris opened his eyes, his mother was staring at him with a smile on her face.

Chapter 20

Niko could barely keep his eyes open. He'd been sitting on the stoop for what seemed like forever. Antwan had told him to go ahead and leave after Bishop got there, but Niko wasn't ready to go home after smashing James in the back of the head with the liquor bottle. Niko knew that he had to find some way to show his mother that James was just playing her. Telling her wasn't going to do any good. She was so much in love with him that she would never believe it.

"Nigga, why don't you take yo' sleepy ass home?" Temp said.

"'Cause I don't feel like it. You go home."

"Nah, fuck that shit, my nigga. I gotta make this chedda."

"Well, what the fuck you think I'm out here doin', killin' time?"

"Man, why don't y'all two be cool with that shit?" Mario said.

"Yeah, y'all gon' scare away the fiends," added Bishop.

"Man, I gotta go take a piss," Mario said, getting up to leave.

"Yo, Temp, what you gon' do with that car when you get another one, man?" Bishop asked.

"Probably sell it. Why?"

"'Cause, nigga, if you gon' sell it, I wanna buy the muthafucka, that's why."

"Word? Shit, nigga, I'll sell you that muthafuckin' piece of shit. I'ma buy me a truck."

"Whateva, nigga. How much you want for it?"

"I don't know yet, dawg. I gotta think about it first."

"Ay yo, what time y'all going to Antwan's party?" Niko asked.

Bishop looked at Niko liked he was crazy. "Nigga, that shit is a week and a half away. The fuck you asking us about that shit now for?"

"'Cause I wanted to know, that's why."

Just then, a pregnant woman came walking across the street. Her hair was wrapped in a dingy tan scarf. She had on a yellow oversized shirt with a smiley face on the front. The tight shorts she had on threatened to cut off her circulation. A loud horn blared as a black Dodge truck almost sideswiped her. "Asshole," she yelled after the truck. After finally making it across the street safely, she walked up to the stoop and looked at each one of their faces. Earlier, she had copped from Chris and Mario, but when she didn't see either one of them, it caused her to hesitate.

"What you need, homegirl?" Temp asked. Bishop hit Temp in the arm. "What, nigga?"

"Man, that chick is pregnant," Bishop said.

"So what?"

"Man, we can't serve to a pregnant bitch."

"Nigga, you betta get the fuck outta here with that 'Captain Save a Ho' shit! What you need, baby?"

"Uh, I, uh . . . I want—"

"Look, ain't nobody got time for that shit," Niko yelled. "Either cop somethin' or get the fuck on."

Fearing that she wouldn't get her hit if she continued to waver any longer, the woman quickly reached into her pocket and pulled out a crumpled bill. "Let me get a twenty."

As fast as lightning, Temp dug into the pouch he was carrying and took out a twenty piece. After serving the woman, Temp went and sat back down on the stoop. Bishop started to say something about what Temp had just done but was interrupted by his buzzing cell phone. He looked down and saw that he had a text message from Veronica. Bishop then looked up and saw three men coming toward them from the right. Then he looked the other way and saw two women coming down the street from the left. Bishop jammed the phone back in his pocket. Veronica was just going to have to wait. Bishop had to make this money.

Sweat ran down Antwan's face and splashed on the floor. He and Rhonda had been cooking dope nonstop for the past twenty-four hours. The fiends were coming out in droves and showed no signs of slowing down. As soon as the dope was cooked and cut, one of the Young Lionz came up the stairs to re-up. After cutting and bagging up the dope, Rhonda went into the kitchen to see if Antwan was done whipping up another pie.

She stopped and stood in the doorway, staring at Antwan as he put in work. She was proud of herself for the way she'd taught him. He was pretty close to being an expert dope cooker, in her opinion. Rhonda got hot looking at the muscles glistening on Antwan's body. She let her eyes fall to his crotch and licked her lips as she daydreamed about stuffing his pecker in her mouth. Now that Bo was gone out of town, Rhonda wasn't as nervous about messing around with Antwan.

Just as Antwan was finished cooking up another rock, Rhonda crept up behind him and wrapped her arms around his waist. "Hey, baby," she said as she started kissing him on his neck.

"Oh, so now I'm ya baby, huh?"

Rhonda took a step back and looked Antwan up and down. "Nigga, are you gonna start that bullshit again?"

"Nah, I'm just messing with you," Antwan said, laughing.

"Oh, I was about to say," she said, walking back up on him. Rhonda then grabbed his dick and leaned forward to whisper in his ear. "'Cause I would hate for this big muthafucka to go to waste just because you wanna act an ass."

Rhonda got down on her knees and unzipped Antwan's pants. After pulling it out, she hungrily shoved his dick into her mouth.

"Oh, shit," Antwan moaned, throwing his head back in ecstasy. Rhonda devoured Antwan's meat with zest. She reached around his waist and grabbed his ass as her head moved back and forth. It didn't take long for Antwan to bust as Rhonda worked her magic like a porn star.

"Damn, that felt good as fuck," Antwan said, breathing heavily. "I gotta get back to work, baby, but I wanna hit that shit later tonight."

"Oh, baby, we gonna have to do that somewhere else. I ain't gonna take the chance of getting caught fuckin' in here now."

"Just tell me where and when, baby."

"We'll work that out later. Whip up that last pie. After that one is gone, I'ma shut it down for the night."

Rhonda walked toward the living room with a smile on her face. She'd wanted to suck Antwan off ever since Bo left. Now that she'd gotten her appetizer, she couldn't wait to get him in a motel somewhere and enjoy the main course. The second she got inside the living room, her smile disappeared. Mario just stood there shaking his head. His cold eyes lingered on her for another five seconds before he turned and walked away.

***

Rhonda gripped the flimsy headboard and held on tight. She was in a cheap motel, down on her hands and knees. The bed she was in had cum stain spots all over it and smelled like someone had fucked on it less than an hour ago. Rhonda gritted her teeth as the nine-inch dick slammed into her asshole. Her pussy hole had already been beaten sore. Her jaws were aching because of the thirty-minute blowjob she'd been forced to give.

Now her asshole was being stretched to its limits. Rhonda bit her lip until it bled in an attempt to keep from screaming. She didn't know how long she was going to be able to hold out without tears falling down her face. Just when she was getting used to the sodomy, she was yanked back onto the thick pole. The maneuver caused pain to shoot up through her stomach, which in turn caused her to let out a glass-shattering scream. Just when she thought she couldn't take anymore, hot cum filled up her asshole and ran down the inside of her leg.

Rhonda then fell face-first onto the dingy brown pillow that used to be white. Slowly she turned over on her back and looked up at the ceiling. After catching her breath, she looked at Mario with hatred in her eyes.

An hour after walking out of the bathroom and catching Rhonda on her knees servicing Antwan, Mario gave her two choices. Either she gave in to his desires whenever he wanted her to, or he was going to go straight to Bo and tell him what was going on. Rhonda laughed at him and cussed him out, telling him that Bo would never believe him.

But Mario had the last laugh. In the midst of Rhonda's laughing spell, Mario pulled out his cell phone and showed her the video he'd made of her sucking Antwan off. Fearing that Bo would kick her to the curb and she would no longer be able to live in the lap of luxury in which she was accustomed to living, Rhonda quickly buckled under the threat. When Rhonda asked him why they were going to such a fleabag motel, Mario told her that she didn't deserve to be taken anywhere nice. Rhonda tried to make him feel guilty by mentioning the fact that Bo was his brother.

"How can you do this to your brother?" she'd asked. Mario responded by slapping her and telling her that she had some nerve to try to make him feel bad when she was the one who lied about Antwan being her cousin. Little did Rhonda and Bo know that it was actually Bo's fault that Mario wanted to sample Rhonda's cookies. From the first time he'd fucked Rhonda, Bo had constantly bragged about how good her pussy was.

Mario, being the dog he was, couldn't wait for an opportunity to get a piece of that good ass. The way she dressed only made him lust after her more. Now Rhonda was lying on a nasty bed, disgusted with herself for even allowing herself to be caught up in this web of deceit with her man's brother. As Mario got dressed, Rhonda just lay there with tears in her eyes. When he got his clothes on, Mario walked toward the door. Just before he left, he looked back at her and smiled.

"My brother was right. You got some good-ass pussy, baby. And remember, whenever you give that nigga Antwan some ass, I want some too, unless you want me to show my brother this video," he said, continuing to blackmail her. Mario then walked out the door, leaving Rhonda with nothing else to do but cry.

The sun had just started to dip beneath the earth, providing the city's skyline with a nice hue of orange. Except for a man walking his dog on the other side of the street and an elderly couple holding hands and making goo-goo eyes at each other, the streets were pretty empty. A strong gust of wind swept through, causing the old man's hat to blow off of his head. Before he could bend down to pick it up, however, Niko was on the job.

"Here you go, sir," he said after scooping the man's hat up and handing it to him.

"Thanks, young man," the elderly gentleman said to him, smiling.

Niko was on his way home when his cell phone vibrated. He smiled when he saw that it was Regina. When Niko wasn't spending time with his crew or hustling, he was kicking it with Regina. The two of them had gotten to know each other pretty well over the last few days. He still hadn't told her that he was married to the streets, but he knew that he would have to tell her sooner or later. He didn't want to get too attached to her and then have it all fall apart because he kept secrets from her. Regina wasn't like any of the other girls he'd been associating himself with. She was smart and pretty, and she had a future.

He couldn't for the life of him figure out why she would even be bothered with a dude like her ex-boyfriend, Ricky. But then again, the more he thought about it, people would probably look at him and wonder the same thing. Niko could hardly contain himself as he answered the phone. Her sweet voice sounded like an angel from heaven to him. He was already thinking about telling his crew that he wasn't going to be in the trap later tonight. The last time they were together, Regina suggested that he come over and watch a movie with her.

Niko didn't answer right away, mostly because he was worried about her parents. Regina put those fears to rest when she told him that her natural parents were dead and she lived with her grandmother. This caused Niko to like and respect her more than ever. Most teenagers he knew who lived with their grandparents tended to take advantage of the situation by running over and disrespecting them. Regina told Niko that as long as she did well in school, her grandparents gave her the freedom to date as she saw fit.

"Sup, baby girl?" Niko answered.

"Nothing. Just called to see what you were doing this afternoon."

"Not much. Just lying around the house, chillin'," he lied.

"Really? Because you sound like you're outside," she said.

"Oh, yeah. Well, actually I'm standing on my porch. When I said I was lying around the house, it was just a figure of speech."

"Oh, cool. Well, the reason I was calling was because I wanted to know if you wanted to come over and watch that movie like we were talking about the other day. My grandparents went to play bingo, so they're gonna to be gone awhile. And it's just so lonely over here by myself," she said in a seductive manner.

"Is that right?" he said, matching her tone. Niko looked at his watch and saw that it was later than he thought it was. "Okay, just gimme about an hour, and I'll be right over there."

"An hour?" she asked, wondering why it was going to take him so long.

"Yeah. I gotta jump in the shower. You don't want me coming over there smelling funky, do you?"

"Yeah, you right. Go ahead and jump your musty ass in the shower," she laughed.

After hanging up with Regina, Niko started a light jog. In light of what he'd done to James, he didn't know what was going to be waiting for him when he got home, but whatever it was, he wasn't going to let it stop him from getting with Regina. Niko had found out that he only lived a few blocks away from Regina, so he didn't even have to catch a bus to get there. By the time he got home, he was sweating like he'd just run a marathon, although in reality, he'd only been running for about ten minutes. Luckily for him, Niko was in good shape, so much so that he ran to his house and didn't have to stop to catch his breath at all.

When Niko got in front of his house, he stopped. He didn't know who was going to be here, so he tiptoed up the steps and into the house. He breathed a sigh of relief when he saw that neither his mother nor James was there. He quickly ran upstairs to his room and looked around. Everything seemed to be the way he left it, except that there was a note on his bed. The note informed him that someone had attacked James from behind while he was taking out the garbage and that they were going to stay in a hotel for a few days just to be safe. After ripping the letter up and throwing it in the trash, Niko just stood there shaking his head.

"Let me get this shit straight," he said to himself. "This lying muthafucka tells her that he was attacked from behind while taking out some fuckin' garbage, and not only do she believe this nigga, but she goes to a hotel with him and don't give my ass a second thought!" Niko snatched his cell phone off of his hip and dialed his mother's cell phone number.

"Yo, Ma," he started when she answered the phone. "How you just gon' leave me in a house you think is unsafe and roll out with that nigga?"

"First of all, boy, don't be callin' my phone talkin' to me like you losin' yo' muthafuckin' mind. Yo' mannish ass ain't never there no muthafuckin' way, so what's the damn difference? I know you ain't scared, Mr. Bad Ass."

"Nah, Ma, I ain't scared, but I'm just sayin'. This don't seem right to me."

"Oh, boy, please. If you need me, I'll be in the Marriot downtown."

"But, Ma—"

That was as far as he got before he realized that his mother had hung up on him. Tears welled up in Niko's eyes, but he refused to let them drop. With the back of his hand, he wiped them away before they could even come out of his eyes.

After composing himself, Niko jumped in the shower and washed off the previous night's hustle. He cursed himself for not going shopping like he'd planned on doing. The last thing he wanted to do was go over to Regina's house looking like a bum. He looked in his closet and took out an old shorts set that he'd worn a thousand times. He examined it, saw that it was clean, and decided to throw it on. His checkerboard Timberlands made his gear complete as he walked out the door in a rugged state of mind.

Niko didn't know whether Regina drank, but he definitely needed a drink to calm his nerves. On his way to Regina's, he stopped off at the store and picked up a double deuce of Olde English malt liquor. He hadn't eaten anything since early yesterday, so he stopped a few buildings down the street and picked up a Subway sandwich. By the time he'd gotten to Regina's house, he'd already eaten half of it.

He walked up on the porch and was about to knock on the door until he realized that he had his gun tucked in his waistband. During the time he'd spent with Regina, he still hadn't told her that he often carried a gun. Niko slowly walked back off the porch and looked around for someplace to hide his weapon. On the side of the house, he spotted some shrubbery that would be perfect. He then looked across the street to see a few girls standing on the porch, gossiping. Slowly, he scanned to his right and his left to see if anyone was on the porches of the houses next to Regina's. Regina lived on a cul-de-sac, and there were a couple of kids riding bikes in a circle. Since no one seemed to be paying any attention to him, Niko casually slid around the side of the house and stuck his gun down in the bushes. He then walked back up on the porch and knocked on the door. He was surprised when the door opened slightly.

Damn. Maybe she in there naked and wanna surprise a nigga. Niko knocked on the door once again. "Regina?"

When she didn't answer, Niko pushed the door open and carefully walked in. His back stiffened when he peeked into Regina's living room and saw her on the floor with her clothes half torn off. The sky blue T-shirt she had on was ripped down the middle. Her skirt was torn down the seam. Niko looked around and for the first time saw that the room was in disarray. He was so focused on Regina that he never even paid attention to the room at first. A lamp was lying on the floor, smashed into five pieces. Several pictures that appeared to have been sitting on tables were now resting on the floor. The glass frame that held one of them was shattered. Glass fragments from it were spread across the carpet. She was turned on her side, and Niko could hear light whimpering coming from her.

"Regina!" he yelled as he rushed to be by her side. When he reached her, Niko reached down and grabbed her shoulders. Regina jumped, a loud scream emitting from her throat.

"It's me, baby, it's me. What happened?"

When Regina saw that it was Niko, she threw her arms around him and hugged him as tight as she could.

"Who did this shit to you?" he asked as he picked her up and carried her over to the couch. As soon as he lifted her, Regina's face twisted in agony. Low moans of pain escaped from her mouth. Although he tried his best to be as gentle as possible, Regina's injuries caused her much discomfort.

When Niko laid her down on the couch, he noticed for the first time the damage that had been inflicted on her. Her left eye was puffy and slightly swollen. A few drops of blood trickled from her right nostril. Niko look down at her waist and saw burn marks on her hips.

He looked back over to where she had been lying, and he saw her ripped panties on the floor. He had been so preoccupied with making sure she was okay that he hadn't seen them at first. Niko looked down into her face and saw the fear in her eyes. Whoever did this to her had left an impression that would stay with her for life. He gently stroked her hair as he asked her a second time who did this to her.

"Ri . . . Ricky. Ricky did this shit to me."

Niko got so mad his whole body started to shake. In his mind, he could picture putting his gun in the middle of Ricky's forehead and pulling the trigger.

"Where is your bathroom?" he asked her.

Regina pointed him toward the hallway. Before leaving, Niko kissed her on the forehead. He got a washrag to help her get cleaned up. When he came back, he gently rubbed her arms and legs with the cloth. He didn't want to press too hard for fear of aggravating her already-sore bruises. After doing this, he went back into the bathroom and rewet the cloth. Niko then came back and washed her face. He was careful not to put too much pressure on her eyes. His blood boiled as he wiped the blood from her nose.

"What happened, baby?" he asked when he was done.

"That asshole snuck in through our back door. At first, I thought it was you messing around, but it wasn't."

"The fuck that nigga want?"

"He wanted me to take him back, but I told his ass that I had a new man in my life," she said as she reached up to touch Niko's face. "That's when he went crazy and started tearing off my clothes and shit."

Niko was so mad he was trembling. "Babe, we need to get you to a hospital and—" Niko stopped talking when he noticed Regina shaking her head.

"No, Niko. I'm not going to any hospital."

"Huh? Why not?"

"Niko, do you know how embarrassing it is for a woman to go to a hospital and tell someone that she's been raped? I just don't want to go through that."

"You won't have to go through it, at least not alone. Regina, ain't no telling what kind of injuries that nigga caused. He could have done some major damage, and the only way we're going to know is if you get checked out."

Regina looked into Niko's eyes and saw that he was silently begging her to go. After taking a deep breath and thinking on it a little longer, she relented and agreed to go, but only if Niko could stay there with her until her grandparents got there.

"Baby, you don't even have to ask that," he said, wrapping her in his arms.

While they waited, Regina fell asleep in Niko's arms. His mind was on one thing and one thing only. Revenge.

"Look, I don't why the fuck you keep tryin'a handcuff that damn girl," Tangie told Veronica. "Yo' ass was just as fast as she is when we was comin' up."

"Why the fuck you keep switching the shit back to me? We ain't talkin' 'bout me! We talkin' 'bout her little fast ass!"

Tangie, Veronica, and Cynthia were sitting on Tangie's steps, getting lifted and blitzed. While Cynthia wasn't much of a weed head, she could drink like a fish. She was on her third bottle of Corona while the other two women hadn't even finished their first.

"Bitch, I don't know who the fuck you think you hollerin' at like that. I ain't yo' baby sister."

"Sorry," Veronica said, rolling her eyes. "I'm just sayin'. What I did when I was growing up ain't got nothin' to do with her ass."

Tangie took a puff off the blunt and passed it to Veronica. "I'm just glad yo' snitchin' ass didn't tell on that girl."

"I shoulda told on her ass! What if her ass gets pregnant?"

"Then her ass just gonna have to deal with it. But if you think you gonna stop that girl from having sex, you foolin' the hell outta yo'self."

Tangie noticed that Cynthia wasn't saying anything. She didn't know if she was just trying to feel Veronica out, but Cynthia hadn't said ten words since Tangie had introduced them. "What do you think, Cynthia?"

Cynthia took a sip from her beer and then slowly shook her head from side to side. "I don't know this woman to be gettin' in her business like that."

"Yeah, we just met," Veronica said. "Why you puttin' her all in my shit like that?"

"Whateva, bitch. A'ight, you don't wanna talk about Dana? Fine. Let's talk about how you came to start fuckin' Bishop."

"Damn, bitch, you nosy," Veronica laughed.

"Nosy my ass. If the shit was reversed, you know damn well you woulda been all up in my muthafuckin' business!"

"You gotdamn right," Veronica said, holding up her hand for a high five.

"I ain't slapping yo' muthafuckin' hand until I get some details, bitch."

Veronica just shook her head. She knew her friend well enough to know that she wasn't going to leave it alone until she told her what she wanted to know. Veronica knew how her friend liked to hear it, so she told her how it went down with her and Bishop without leaving out any details. Cynthia remained quiet. She wanted to learn more about Veronica before judging her. After Veronica gave up the goods, a wide smile broke across Tangie's face.

"Get yo' freak on, girl," Tangie said, finally giving Veronica a high five. "I just hope you know what you doin', fuckin' around with that young-ass boy."

"I got this," Veronica said smugly. "And you can't talk, bitch," Veronica said once she thought about it. "Yo' ass is older than Antwan." Tangie didn't have a comeback for that.

"Is the party still on for tomorrow?" Cynthia asked.

"Oh, shit, girl, I'm glad you mentioned that shit. I'm pushin' it back to next Saturday. Antwan been outta town so much, I'ma have to do it next week to make it work."

"Oh, okay. Can I use your bathroom right quick?"

Tangie looked at Cynthia like she was crazy. "You was a guest the first time you asked," Tangie said as she took the blunt from Veronica and took a puff. Catching the hint, Cynthia got up and walked in the house.

"You invited her to the party?"

"Yep."

"You neva did tell me where you met her ass at."

"Oh, shit, that's right. I didn't tell you what happened at the bar the other day." Tangie quickly gave her friend the rundown of the altercation and how Cynthia came to her rescue.

"Damn, that bitch gangsta like that?"

"You betta believe it," Cynthia said as she walked back into the room.

Chapter 21

Ninety-degree heat beat down the city of Cleveland. People were either lying around under the air conditioning or sitting in front of a fan, trying to keep cool. But Tangie was running around like a chicken with its head cut off. The day of the party had finally arrived. Because Antwan and the rest of the Young Lionz crew had been grinding so hard, Tangie felt that she had no choice but tell him about his surprise party.

Antwan had been in the trap twenty-four-seven, and Tangie was afraid that she wouldn't be able to get him to come home for his own party, therefore ruining the surprise. Sweat poured from Tangie's forehead as she raked and bagged leaves in her backyard. Before that, she made sure that her bathroom was clean and her kitchen was spotless. Tangie may have been ghetto, but she wasn't nasty. She couldn't stand when her house was dirty, and she really hated for it to be fucked up when she knew she was going to have company.

It took Tangie ten minutes to finish the yard. After that, she went into her house, walked into her bedroom, and fell face-first into her bed. Before she closed her eyes, she looked at her radio alarm clock and saw that she had another two hours before people started coming over. She had already set her alarm clock to wake her up at that time. She was sure that her guests were going to be late, so she wasn't worried about not being ready when they got there. As she drifted off, she felt a hand creeping up her thigh.

"Get the fuck off of me, Antwan!"

While Tangie had been working herself into exhaustion, Antwan had been lying in the bed, snoring loud enough to wake the dead. It galled her that he hadn't lifted a finger to help her, and now that she was trying to get some rest, he wanted some ass.

"Come on, baby, let a nigga tap that," Antwan begged, stroking his dick.

"Hell nah! I been working like a Hebrew slave while yo' ass been in here dead to the fuckin' world, and now you want a bitch to put out? Fuck that! I'ma catch some Z's before this party! Yo' ass can wait until later or go jack the fuck off!"

Tangie turned her back to him and closed her eyes. Antwan couldn't believe it. He couldn't remember the last time Tangie had turned him down. Tangie had just about fallen asleep when she felt the bed shaking. Five seconds later, she felt something wet splash on her ass. Tangie quickly rolled over and looked down. Her mouth fell open as she eyed Antwan's hand wrapped around his dick.

"Nigga, what the fuck you doin'?" she screamed.

"Shit, you told a nigga to wait or jack off. I didn't feel like waitin'," Antwan said, smiling.

"Muthafucka, I didn't tell you to squirt that shit on my ass!"

"My bad."

Tangie was so pissed that she jumped out of the bed and stomped out of the bedroom. The walls shook as she slammed the door on the way out. Antwan just laughed and fell back on the bed.

"That's what yo' ass get for being stingy," he mumbled to himself.

After going to the bathroom and wiping Antwan's semen off of her ass, Tangie went into the living room and plopped down on the couch. She looked at the clock and saw that she had roughly an hour before people were supposed to arrive.

"Fuck it," she mumbled. "I might as well get my smoke on," she said as she reached into the ashtray and picked up a half-smoked blunt. Tangie suddenly started laughing as she fired up the weed. "I can't believe that nigga jacked off on my ass. Nasty muthafucka."

After taking a few puffs, Tangie set the blunt back down in the ashtray. Her head fell back against the couch as she drifted off to sleep. The next sound she heard was someone beating loudly on her door. Jumping up from the couch, Tangie looked at the clock and realized that she'd slept longer than she intended to. "Damn. I guess I was more tired than I thought," she mumbled. Tangie rubbed her eyes in an attempt to get the sleep out of them. She slowly dragged herself to the door and looked out the peephole. Veronica stood there with her arms folded. Her right foot was tapping the ground at an exaggerated pace.

"What's up, girl?" Tangie said as she opened the door. "Did you get the liquor?"

"Yeah," Veronica said, walking past her friend. Tangie frowned when she saw that Veronica wasn't caring any bags.

"Where the hell is it at?"

"In the car."

"The fuck you leave it in the car for?"

"Bitch, I ain't carrying that heavy-ass bag. You betta tell Antwan to get that shit."

"Damn, you a lazy bitch," Tangie said as she stormed out the door and to Veronica's car.

When she came back into the house, Veronica was sitting on her couch about to blaze up her weed. Tangie set the bag on the kitchen counter and walked back into the living room.

"Oh, bitch, I know damn well you ain't in here firing up my damn weed and I can't even get yo' ass to bring in a fuckin' bag."

After inhaling the smoke into her lungs, Veronica slowly blew the fumes into the air. "Tangie, as much weed of mine that yo' ass done smoked up over the years, I know you ain't trippin' about a fuckin' half a blunt." Veronica held out the blunt for Tangie to take.

"Whateva, ho. Gimme my damn dope," Tangie said, snatching the Dutch out of her friend's hand.

When the two of them got done smoking the rest of the blunt, they went into the kitchen. Veronica poured herself a drink while Tangie took the seasoned pan of ribs out of the refrigerator. She went outside and set fire to the charcoal in the barbeque grill. While she was outside, Antwan came out of the bedroom and walked into the kitchen.

"Sup, Veronica?" he said as he reached into the refrigerator and grabbed a beer.

"What's up, my nigga? Happy birthday."

"Thanks."

"You ready to get this party started up in this bitch?"

"You damn right," he said, giving her dap.

"Where yo' boys at?"

"Shit, I don't know." Antwan thought for a minute and then looked at Veronica sideways. "Matter of fact, what the hell you askin' me for? Yo' ass oughta know where Bishop is. The nigga is yo' man."

"Oh, I know where my man is, Antwan. He's at home. I'm going to pick him up in another hour or so. Y'all been in the trap so much, he ain't been able to get that much sleep."

"I know yo' ass ain't complaining. We're making mad loot pushing that work. And what the fuck you mean, he at home? Y'all done moved in together or somethin'?"

"Nah, boy. But what if he did move in?"

"Shit, I don't give a fuck. I was just making conversation. You the one brought that bullshit up."

"Whateva," Veronica said as she held up her hand and rolled her neck.

Just then, Tangie came back into the kitchen. She rolled her eyes at Antwan as she poured herself a Jack Daniels and mixed it with Coca-Cola.

"The hell wrong with you?"

Tangie ignored him and motioned for Veronica to follow her into the backyard. Antwan quickly downed the rest of his beer, and after pouring himself a large glass of vodka and orange juice, he followed them into the backyard. Tangie and Veronica had started laughing among themselves, and it irritated Antwan that Tangie was ignoring him.

"Yo, Tangie, I don't why the fuck you acting all fly in front of yo' girl, but you betta chill out with that bullshit."

"Whateva, Antwan. You know what the fuck I'm mad at." Before the argument could go any further, Temp walked up.

"What's up, my nigga? Happy birthday!" Temp walked up to Antwan and put him in a playful headlock.

"Man, get the fuck off of me," Antwan said, pushing his friend away.

"Yo, nigga, I know we gon' get fucked up tonight!"

"You got that shit right," Antwan said, smiling.

"Damn, you don't see nobody else out here besides Antwan?" Tangie asked with an attitude.

"Damn, Tangie, my bad. Don't cut a nigga. Hello to you, homegirl. Sup, Veronica?"

"Hey, Temp."

"Yo, Twan, let me holla at you for a minute, dawg." Temp started walking toward the front, all the while pulling a pair of keys out of his pocket.

"What's up, dawg?" Antwan asked when they reached the front yard.

"I just wanted to show you my new ride, playa." Temp jingled the keys and pointed toward the curb. Resting there was a black Lincoln Navigator.

"Damn, the muthafucka nice," Antwan bellowed. Both of them walked over to the passenger's side. Temp opened the door so Antwan could look inside. "Man, this mutha-fucka is the shit," Antwan said as he ran his hands over the black shiny leather. "What did you do with your other car?"

Just then, Bishop came driving down the street in Temp's old car.

"Man, you sold that raggedy muthafucka to Bishop?"

"Hey, he wanted to buy the damn car, man," Temp said, holding up his hands.

"Nigga, yo' ass is foul for that shit," Antwan said, laugh-ing. Bishop pulled over to the curb and parked directly in front of Temp's new truck. After shutting off the engine, he hopped out of the car, clutching a double deuce of Miller Genuine Draft beer in his hand.

"What up, fools?" he said, strolling up to his partners in crime.

"Man, you actually bought this raggedy-ass car from Temp?"

"Man, ain't shit wrong with this damn car. Stop hatin', nigga."

"Whateva, sucker. Ain't you supposed to be at work today?"

"Yeah, but I think I'ma quit, man. I'm making too much money in the trap to be working for minimum wage."

"I don't know if you should do that, man," Antwan advised. "At least working there, if the man caught you with a lot of cash on you, you could say that you had a job, and they couldn't keep yo' bread. When you can't justify where you got the money from, they automatically assume that you been selling drugs and keep that shit."

Bishop looked at Temp and then back to Antwan. "For real?"

"Real spit, nigga. And you don't ever get that scratch back."

Bishop thought about it for a second before shaking his head vigorously. "Nah, man, I'll just take my fuckin' chances. I'm tired of workin' there anyway."

"A'ight, you li'l hardheaded muthafucka. Don't say we didn't try to warn yo' ass," Temp told him.

"Man, y'all act like y'all wishing for a nigga to get caught and shit. What's up with that bullshit?"

"Nigga, ain't nobody wishin' you get caught. We just tryin' to educate yo' li'l ignorant ass on a couple of thangs."

"A'ight. Then how come you two muthafuckas don't get regular jobs and cover ya'selves like y'all tellin' me to do?" Bishop asked.

Antwan and Temp both stood there stuck on mute. Bishop had just hit them both with a question neither of them could answer.

"Yeah, that's what the fuck I thought," Bishop said as he started walking toward the backyard. "Man, let's get this party started," he said as he reached into his pocket and pulled out a sack of weed. "Antwan, I know got you some Dutches around here somewhere. Set 'em out so I can roll this shit up."

Antwan and Temp looked at each other, shrugged their shoulders, and followed Bishop into the backyard. As the three of them made their way to the back, they started to smell the burgers and hot dogs Tangie had thrown on the grill. As soon as they got to the backyard, Veronica ran up to Bishop and threw her arms around him.

"Hey, baby. I thought you was gon' call me when you was ready to come over."

"Nah, I didn't need to. I bought a car."

"A car? When did you buy a car?"

"Yesterday. I wanted to surprise you. Now you ain't gotta worry about coming to pick a nigga up no more."

"Baby, I didn't mind doin' that shit," she lied.

"Well, I did."

"What kind of car did you get?" she asked, pulling his hand toward the front.

"I bought Temp's old car. He just bought a new truck."

Veronica stopped dead in her tracks. "You bought Temp's old car?"

"Yeah. What's wrong with that?"

Veronica stared at Bishop for a few seconds and threw both her hands up. "Nothin'," she said as she went and sat back down. *I can't believe he bought that raggedy muthafucka.*

"I thought you was cookin' ribs," Antwan said to Tangie.

"I'm gonna put them on last. It don't take as long for these to cook. That way, if anybody get hungry, these will already be done."

"Cool. Hey, did you invite yo' friend what's-her-name today?"

"Yeah, I—"

"Hol' up," Temp interrupted. "Y'all got another broad coming over here today?" Temp rubbed his hands together like he was getting ready for his last meal.

"I don't think she yo' type, Temp," Veronica told him.

"Do she got a pussy? Then she's my type."

"Nah, nigga, that ain't what the fuck I'm talkin' 'bout. She got a kid, and you know how you hate kids, nigga."

"I never said that I hate kids. I just don't want none of my own."

"Well, she has one, so unless you ready to sponsor her ass, you need to stop drooling," Tangie added.

"Well, I hope her ass got good car insurance, 'cause all I want to do is hit and skip, if you know what a nigga mean. And as for me sponsorin' a seed, fuck that! That's on her baby daddy. He gonna have to supply the bread. All I got for her ass is hard dick and bubble gum, and I'm fresh outta gum."

Antwan was slightly giggling as Temp let it be known how he got down, while Bishop was cracking up.

"The fuck so funny, Bishop?" Veronica asked with a frown on her face.

"Yeah, y'all hear somethin' amusing?" Tangie said, eyeing Antwan.

"Hey, he's the one talkin' bullshit. Don't put us in that shit," Antwan said. "And oh, I invited someone too. My nigga Bo coming through today."

"You gonna invite somebody here who we ain't neva met before?" Veronica asked with a screwed-up face.

"The last time I checked, yo' ass didn't pay rent here."

"Whateva, boy," Veronica said, waving her hand.

Everyone's head snapped around when they heard a car horn blowing. Antwan walked around the side of the house and saw Bo pulling down the street in an old-school Chevy Impala. It was gold with whitewall tires on it. Bo was coming down the opposite side of the street. It took all of his driving skill to hit a U-turn and have enough room to park without backing up. Once he parked, Bo got out of the car and walked around to the passenger's side.

His long frame seemed to glide as he reached down and opened the door for the lady he was with. She was tall for a woman, standing a shade over five feet ten inches. She wore a blond wig and had large gold hoop earrings hanging from her earlobes. Her huge D-cup breasts looked like they were going to pull her to the ground any second. Both of them looked like runway models as they strolled up the sidewalk.

"What's up, dawg?" Antwan called out to Bo.

"You the man, playboy."

The two of them gave each other a pound as they met up. After Bo introduced Antwan to his friend, whose name was Crystal, Antwan led them to the back of the house and introduced both of them to Tangie, Veronica, and the rest of his crew.

"Yo, Antwan, let me holla at you for a minute," Bo said, pulling Antwan to the side. "Yo, dude. I know Rhonda's ya cousin and all, but Crystal is my baby mama. She know all about the illegal shit that I do, so I gotta cater to her a li'l bit so she won't get salty at a nigga and put the man on my ass."

"Don't worry about it, my dude. Do you. I'm pretty sure that Rhonda knew what time it was when y'all got together."

Bo was surprised that Antwan wasn't pissed off because he'd brought another female to his house instead of his cousin. "Damn, good lookin', my dude."

The two of them walked back over to where the rest of the Young Lionz were passing a blunt around, and they joined in. They all greeted Bo with either fist pounds or nods.

"Yo, Twan, where the beer at, man?" Temp asked.

"Shit, I don't know."

"Nigga, you don't know if you got beer in the refrigerator?" Temp asked.

"Muthafucka, go see."

Temp gave Antwan the finger and walked in the house.

"Man, I don't see no barbeque sauce out here, dawg," Bishop bellowed. "I know damn well you ain't out here Q'ing with no barbeque sauce."

"Man, we don't eat that shit too much. We like it plain."

"Well, I like my shit kinda dressed up, so I'ma run to the store to get some Open Pit, my dude."

Bishop dashed around the side of the house, hopped in his car, and headed toward Giant Eagle. Veronica thought about how Temp would probably be all over Cynthia, and she started on a hate campaign.

"Girl, I hope you don't plan on introducin' Cynthia to that cock-hound-ass nigga."

"I ain't worried about Cynthia. That bitch done showed me she can handle herself."

Right on cue, Cynthia walked up. "What's up, girls?"

"Damn, bitch, we was wonderin' where the fuck you was," Veronica said.

"I was waitin' on my mother to bring my son back. But of course, she decided to keep him at the last minute. You know how grandmothers are. They never wanna bring ya kids back when they get hold of them."

"Girl, I don't what the hell that's like." Veronica beamed. "I ain't nowhere near ready to put no beans in this oven." Veronica twirled around like a model and held her hands up in the air. "You bitches wish y'all looked like me, don't y'all?"

"Yeah, right, bitch," Tangie said, laughing. "Girl, sit yo' chunky ass down somewhere," she laughed.

"Chunky? Bitch, you on some hellafied drugs to think some shit like that," Veronica responded.

"Oh, shit," Tangie yelled as she ran over to the grill and tended to the food she was burning up.

"I knew yo' ass was gonna burn up the damn food," Veronica laughed.

"Whateva, bitch. Ain't nobody burnin' up shit. You two hoes come here so I can teach y'all how to cook."

Veronica and Cynthia laughed to one another as they made their way over to the grill. A few seconds later, Temp came out of the house with a bottle of Corona in his hand.

"Comin' out feeling about ten pounds lighter." Temp sang the old Ice Cube song as he made his way down the steps. "Yo, Veronica, put somethin' in the air, my . . ."

Temp's words caught in his throat when he saw who was standing near the grill. An evil scowl made its way onto Cynthia's face when she laid eyes on her former lover.

"The fuck is she doin' here?" he yelled.

"Nah, nigga, what the fuck yo' trifflin' ass doin' in here?"

Everyone else looked at each other, confused. They had no idea what was going on.

"Y'all know each other?" Veronica asked.

"Yeah, I know this asshole," Cynthia said through gritted teeth. "He's my son's father."

Temp dropped the beer to the ground, causing it to shatter. A deathly silence hung in the air as everyone stood there in stunned silence. It wasn't until the gunshots rang out that they all snapped back to their senses.

Chapter 22

Chris sat in the waiting room with his mother, thanking God that his sister was able to find a donor so quickly. They had been told that it could take anywhere from a week to a year to find a bone marrow donor. They also told them to pray for the best. Even though they didn't say it, Chris and his mother knew that if their loved one didn't undergo the operation as soon as possible, she was going to die.

The operation took well over four hours to complete, and when the doctor came out, he looked exhausted. Chris held his breath. He was well aware that any operation posed a great deal of risk. The closer the doctor got, the tighter Vivian clutched her Bible. She'd been either reading it or rubbing it ever since her daughter went into surgery.

"Well," Dr. Ewing started, "the operation was successful. She's in recovery now."

Chris and Vivian hugged each other tightly. "Can we see her doctor?" Vivian asked.

"Not now, I'm afraid. She's heavily sedated so she will probably be out of it until tomorrow."

Vivian was sad that she couldn't see her daughter until then, but she was overjoyed that her daughter came through the operation in good shape. Although she didn't like where Chris had gotten the money to put down on the payment, she was more than happy that he came through for his baby sister. As the two of them started toward the hospital exit, tears of joy rolled down Vivian's cheeks. They continued to flow as they made their way to the bus stop.

A friend of Vivian's had taken them to the hospital, but she couldn't stay. Vivian didn't want to bother anyone, so instead of making a phone call, she chose to ride public transportation home. The twenty-minute bus ride seemed to last longer than the actual surgery. Vivian cried all the way home. People were staring and pointing, but she couldn't care less. All she knew was that her baby girl received a new lease on life. By the time they reached their front porch, the front of her shirt was soaked with tears. With a surprised look on her face, she looked at Chris and smiled.

"What?" he asked.

"Oh, nothing." It wasn't until Chris looked in the mirror that he realized he'd been crying himself.

Chris had to make sure that his mom was okay before he got ready to go to Antwan's party.

"Baby, I'm fine now. You go on to your friend's party and enjoy yourself. I'm just gonna sit here and read my Bible some more and thank the Lord that He saw fit to spare my baby's life."

"You sure, Mama? I can stay here with you if you want me to."

"Boy, go 'head on. I know you've been under just as much stress as I have. Go ahead and enjoy yourself. I'ma be okay."

Chris kissed his mother on the cheek and ran upstairs to get ready. Temp had told Chris to call if he needed a ride. Chris took his phone off of his hip and started to dial. Halfway through the numbers, he changed his mind and decided to just walk. After getting dressed, Chris went into his closet and got his gun. He didn't foresee any problems with his crew, but the way they laid the smackdown on the rest of the hood, he had to be ready at all times.

Chris walked out of his bedroom and darted toward the front door. Just before he walked out, he peeked in on his mother. Just like he thought, she was in her favorite chair, still reading the Bible. Chris smiled and walked out the door. His mood instantly turned sour when his cell phone rang. Looking down at the screen, he gave his phone the finger when he saw it was Dana calling him. He hadn't talked to her since he'd found out that she was in her bedroom giving Jay head. He was done with her. He didn't want anything else to do with her.

As Chris bent the corner of Antwan's street, he started thinking about the fun he was going to have hanging out with his boys. It had been a while since they'd all gotten together to just kick back and get toasted. He was just about to head into Antwan's backyard when his back exploded in pain.

Bishop drove down the street, slightly tipsy from the three beers he'd consumed before leaving for the store. Seeing Veronica in those tight shorts she had on had him horny. As soon as he got back, he was going to try to creep her down into Antwan's basement for a quickie. Bishop did a double take into the rearview mirror. He could have sworn that he saw someone following him. Bishop quickly shook the feeling off, chalking it up to the buzz he was feeling. He pulled into the Giant Eagle parking lot and parked.

"Damn, it's hot out here," he said to himself as soon as his Timberlands hit the pavement. Bishop gangsta walked into the store and made his way to the aisle with the barbeque sauce. After paying for his item, Bishop started to walk out of the store and ran right into Eddie.

"Well, well, well, look at the dude who don't wanna come to work no more."

"The fuck you worrying about it for?"

"'Cause I'm the one who's been working by himself the last week, nigga, that's why."

"Man, get the fuck outta my face," Bishop said, brushing past him.

Eddie swung his right hand and backhanded Bishop upside the temple. Bishop responded by punching Eddie in the face. He then tried to follow up with a left hook that Eddie ducked. Eddie rushed Bishop and grabbed his legs. While Eddie was trying to lift Bishop off the ground and slam him, Bishop was busy kneeing him in the face. That's when both of them were bum-rushed by security.

"Hey, what the hell is going on here?" the 300-pound guard asked when he ran over. For the second time in the span of a week, the fight that had been brewing between the two of them had been interrupted.

"Yeah, next time, you bitch-ass nigga," Eddie yelled as he was ushered away.

"Fuck you, nigga," Bishop retorted.

Now Bishop couldn't wait to get back to the barbeque. His nerves were shot, and nothing was going to calm them except smoking a blunt. Bishop stomped back to his car and slammed the sauce on the seat. He wanted to go back into the store and stomp a mud hole in Eddie's ass, but he knew that doing so would only result in him getting arrested. The last thing he wanted to hear was his sister's mouth when she had to come and bail him out. Bishop was just about to pull out into the street when he was cut off by a dude in a blue Camaro.

It suddenly dawned on him that it was the same car he'd seen in his rearview mirror just before he'd pulled into the parking lot. A light-skinned dude with a shiny bald head jumped out and started walking toward his

car. Bishop reached into his console and took out the
.38 Special he had stashed there. The dude was smart
enough to not walk up to Bishop's door, as he stopped
about ten feet short of it.

"Yo, nigga, yo' name Bishop?" he asked.

"Muthafucka, why?" When he saw that the shiny head
wasn't going to come any closer, Bishop set the gun down
on the passenger's seat.

"'Cause if you is, I wanna talk to you about somethin'."

Bishop got out of the car and walked toward the dude.
He was kind of short, which caused Bishop to look down
at him when he got up on him. "Yeah, I'm Bishop. The
fuck you want?"

"Nigga, I wanna know why the fuck you put yo' hands
on my fuckin' brotha, muthafucka."

Bishop looked at the short, baldheaded dude like he'd
lost his mind. "What? Nigga, I know you ain't jumpin'
in my fuckin' face about slappin' yo' bitch-ass brotha
around! You tell that muthafucka to keep his hands off
my damn sister and I wouldn't have to beat his muthafuckin' ass!"

The two of them stood there and stared at each other
for a few seconds before the dude backed away. The comment about Jason hitting her surprised him. Apparently,
his bother hadn't told him the whole story.

"Yeah, a'ight, nigga," he said as he got back into his car
and drove away.

"The fuck wrong with these silly muthafuckas today?"
Bishop asked himself.

Bishop jumped back in his car and pulled off. *Now
I really need a fuckin' blunt.* Bishop pulled out of the
parking lot and headed back to Antwan's. He slowed
down when he spotted an unmarked police car coming down the other side of the street. As soon as the car
passed him, it made a U-turn and got behind him.

Bishop grabbed the gun, put in the glove compartment, and locked it. Bishop wasn't a lawyer, but he knew that the police couldn't force him to unlock it without a search warrant or reasonable cause. Bishop drove slowly. He didn't want to give the pigs any reason to pull him over. His efforts were in vain, as the car's light started flashing and rotating.

"Man, what the fuck?" he screamed.

With a pissed-off look on his face, Bishop pulled over to the curb. He was ready to get his party on, and the boys in blue were putting a serious cramp in his plans.

"Damn, it would a damn woman detective," he said when he saw the female cop stroll toward his car in high heels.

Detective Ramsey smiled as she walked toward the car. She tapped lightly on the window and waited for it to be rolled down. When she saw the driver's face, she became confused. She knew that when she pulled the car over a week ago, it belonged to Temp. After a deep sigh, Ramsey asked for Bishop's driver's license. She was hoping to harass Temp into making a mistake and giving her something she could use to nail him in the murder of Yolonda and her child.

Her captain had strictly forbidden her from arresting Temp until she had something concrete. Ramsey let her eyes fall to something peeking out from underneath the driver's side seat. A wicked smile slowly made its way onto her face as she told Bishop to step out of the car.

Bishop got out, wondering why he was being told to do so. Ramsey reached into her pocket and pulled out a handkerchief. Ever so slowly, she reached down and wrapped the handkerchief around the butt of the pistol and picked it up. Bishop's mouth fell open as Ramsey dangled the gun in his face. She reached back into her pocket, pulled out a plastic bag, and dropped the gun into it.

Bishop threw his head back and closed his eyes. *No, this muthafucka didn't leave this fuckin' gun in here!*

"Turn around," Ramsey commanded. Her gut feeling told her that the gun was Temp's, but since Bishop was caught with it, she was going to use that to her advantage.

"You have the right to remain silent. Anything you say can and will be used against you in a court of law . . ."

As Bishop was read his rights, all he could think of was choking the shit out of Temp when he got out.

Two days after raping Regina, Ricky began to relax. After the incident initially occurred, he was nervous as hell, knowing that he'd let his anger and lust get the best of him. It was around five o' clock, and he was now hanging out in the park with his friends, doing what he did best: lying on his sex game. They were all seated on the benches as he stood in front of them like he was giving a lecture.

Ricky turned up the can of Budweiser and nearly drained the whole can. It was the first time he'd been out in public since he'd raped Regina. He had let his bruised ego get the best of him. Taking rejection was something he'd never been good at. He'd been sweating bullets for the past week, fearing that the police would show up at his home and haul him off to jail. He didn't know why they hadn't yet, but since they hadn't, he was starting to think that he'd gotten away with it.

"Man, I'm tellin' y'all niggas, she was beggin' me for this dick," Ricky lied. "I couldn't get in the door fast enough before that bitch was reachin' for a nigga zipper."

"Nigga, you lying," his boy Binky said. "That bitch ain't gave you no pussy. She barely speaks to yo' ass!"

"Yeah, nigga," his other friend Buck jumped in. "You betta leave that ho alone before that young-ass nigga she fuckin' with split yo' muthafuckin' wig."

"That muthafucka ain't gon' do shit but get fucked up."

"I know that's right," Binky agreed, holding his fist out for a pound. Binky had spotted Ricky coming out of Regina's house rather quickly. Since he'd heard that they had broken up, he questioned why he would be over at her house in the first place. Ricky surely wasn't about to tell his friend that he'd gone over to Regina's house to beg her to take him back. And he would have been a fool to tell him that he'd just committed rape. He did what any asshole of a man would do, which was lie about the woman.

"Man, that bitch got some good-ass pussy. But I think I'ma let her go."

"Nigga, if the pussy that good, why the hell would you talk about kickin' the bitch to the curb?"

"The bitch just too clingy for me," he continued lying.

"Shit, nigga, if the bitch that sprung on you, then use that shit to yo' advantage, and see if you can get her to fuck us all before you get rid of the bitch," Buck suggested.

"Yeah, nigga, have her set that shit out for all of us," Binky said.

"Man, I don't know about that," Ricky said, trying to get out of being found out. "I don't think she would go for that shit, dawg."

"Nigga, if the bitch as sprung as you say she is, then you shouldn't have no problem gettin' her to set that ass out," Buck said. "Matter of fact, let's go to her house now and fuck her."

Before Ricky could come up with a reason why he couldn't do it, he was saved from having to make up another lie when the three of them were distracted by a very curvaceous young woman walking across the park. She was about five feet six inches tall and weighed around 125 pounds. Her skin tone was the color of dark honey, and her hair hung loosely and freely from her shoulders. A knock-off Gucci handbag hung over her shoulder as she sauntered past them.

"Damn, baby, can I go with you?" Ricky asked, his voice dripping with lust. The vixen got a few feet from the woods that separated the park from the street, and she looked back.

"You can if you can keep up," she said. That's all it took for Ricky to sprint toward her and try to get his mack on.

"Damn, you fine as hell, baby," he started when he caught up with her. "What's yo' name?" he asked.

"Brandy," she said in a sensual manner. As the two of them continued to walk and become acquainted with each other, Ricky started wondering how long it would take him to get into her pants. A woody grew in his pants as he eyed her plump, juicy ass. When they got halfway through the woods, Brandy grabbed Ricky by the hand.

"Baby, I am really feeling you," she said, looking into his eyes.

The moment their lips met, Ricky's dick pointed toward the sky. His heat index rose as she slipped her tongue into his mouth. Brandy then reached down and grabbed his zipper. After freeing his dick, she started stroking it, causing pre cum to ooze out. Ricky responded by palming her left titty. All of a sudden, excruciating pain shot through his mouth. Brandy bit into his tongue so hard that blood shot out of the side of his mouth. Brandy released him and pushed him away. Ricky was in so much pain, he couldn't even scream. Tears welled up in his eyes as he fell to one knee.

Brandy stood there with her hands on her hips, smirking devilishly. Ricky tried to speak but couldn't. Rage grew inside him as he got up and took a step toward Brandy. Before he reached her, however, pain shot through his head and his lights were turned out as a result of a baseball bat to the back of the head by Niko. Brandy, who was

Regina's cousin, then pulled out a pair of scissors and kneeled down beside Ricky. His body jerked reflexively as she cut off his dick. Niko and Brandy then jogged back to Regina's house. It would be another five minutes before Ricky's friends would come and try to sneak a peek at him screwing Brandy. Buck threw up at the sight of his buddy bleeding to death.

Chapter 23

After leaving Regina's house, Niko made his way toward Antwan's. He felt vindicated by the fact that Regina's cousin had helped him exact revenge on the girl he had started to care about deeply.

Brandy had come over to Regina's house while she was recovering from her injuries. While Regina was the good girl who was on her way to college, Brandy was just the opposite. A violent girl by all accounts, Brandy was quick-tempered and always down to set someone up to be robbed. After seeing what had happened to her cousin, she caught Niko as he was leaving and told him that if he wanted to get even with Ricky, she was more than willing to help him. Niko then scouted around and found out where Ricky liked to hang out. He took to the streets the following day and even greased a few palms to get a lead on his adversary. He got lucky when a dude who'd gotten into it with Ricky heard about his search and hit him off with the information.

Niko knew he was late to Antwan's party, but this was something he had to do. He wasn't going to go at first, but Regina told him that she was okay with him going. Brandy was there with her, so she wasn't worried about anything. Reluctantly, Niko agreed. Since he had to pass his house to get to Antwan's, he decided to go home and take a quick shower. He didn't want to go to his friend's party smelling like he'd just played a full-court game of basketball.

As he walked up on his porch, he heard loud arguing coming from his living room. Niko walked in the house just in time to see James backhand his mother to the floor.

"Hey, muthafucka!" Niko rushed James and threw a wild right hand at him. James ducked and picked Niko off the ground. James then slammed Niko to the floor, causing him to hit his head on the hardwood floor. A knot quickly formed on the back of Niko's head. Niko was slightly dazed as James wrapped his hands around his throat. Doris tried to intervene, which resulted in her being hit again. Niko took advantage of James briefly taking his attention off of him by rolling James over and getting on top of him. Niko then peppered James with lefts and rights. No matter how bad Doris treated Niko, she was still his mother. Once again Doris jumped in, grabbing her son around the neck and pulling on him with all her might.

"Niko, let him go!" she screamed.

With one mighty tug, Doris yanked her son off of James. Both of them fell backward onto the floor. James jumped to his feet. But instead of trying to get to Niko, James made a beeline for the couch. Niko knew right away that he was going for the gun that his mother kept between the cushions. As quick as lightning, Niko got to his feet and tackled James just as he got the gun out of the cushions.

The two of them struggled with the gun until they both tripped and fell on the floor. For the third time, Doris got involved in the melee.

"Stop it, please, stop it!" she yelled as she ran over and tried to snatch the gun from both of them.

With all three of them on the floor trying to gain control of the weapon, it went off twice. An ear-splitting scream could be heard all the way to the corner.

***

After hearing gunshots followed by a scream, Antwan and Temp took off running around the side of the house. Both of them had their pistols in their hands. Cynthia, Veronica, and Tangie were right behind them. Bo and Crystal brought up the rear. When they got halfway to the front, their hearts sank. Lying on the ground bleeding was their friend and fellow Young Lionz, Chris.

"Chris! Chris!" Temp yelled in shock.

Antwan ran to the front of the house just in time to see a black Nissan Sentra peel off down the street. Antwan fired off a couple of rounds but didn't come close to hitting the car. When he ran back to the side of the house, Temp had his cell phone in his hand. Tears were in his eyes as he dialed 911.

"Who the fuck did this shit to you, man?" Temp asked.

"I don't know, man," Chris answered.

"Did you see who it was?" Temp asked Antwan.

"Nah, man, I didn't recognize the car."

Veronica and Tangie were bawling their eyes out. Tears had also crept into the corners of Antwan's eyes. Crystal had her head buried in Bo's shoulder as he stood there shaking his head. Minutes later, the ambulance pulled up to the curb. Without a second to waste, the EMT workers jumped out of the truck, grabbed a gurney, and rushed over to attend to Chris. Immediately, they began checking his wounds.

"Okay, we need to stop this bleeding and fast," one of them said. The other one nodded his head in agreement as he dabbed at Chris's wounds with towels.

"Oh, shit, man. I can't feel my legs, man," Chris said. They carefully loaded him onto the gurney. "Man, somebody call my mom," Chris said weakly. The blood loss was beginning to make him lose consciousness.

"What's yo' house number, man?" Antwan asked, taking out his phone to dial.

When they transported Chris to the hospital, Temp rode in the ambulance. He refused to leave his friend's side. Antwan and Bo followed them in their cars. On the way there, Veronica called Bishop to tell him what had happened, but she got frustrated when he didn't answer.

Vivian sat in the hospital with her head hanging to the ground. For the first time in her life, she was seriously starting to lose her faith. She just couldn't understand how the Lord could play such a cruel joke on her. It had to be a joke. Or maybe she was dreaming. That's what she kept telling herself over and over again. She wanted to believe that. But every time she lifted her head up and saw Chris's friends sitting in the same room as her with tears running down their faces, she knew that she was wide awake. This wasn't a dream. Her son was lying on a table, fighting for his life.

Vivian was starting to wonder if she should just buy a cot and bring it into the hospital along with a blanket and a pillow. She had spent so much time there that she thought they were going to start making her pay rent. After realizing that her situation was not a dream, she let her head fall back down and hang to the floor. Tears fell from her eyes in waves and hit the marble with sickening silence. Vivian's hands were shaking as she got up and walked outside. Her tears continued to flow freely as she thought about doing something she hadn't done in the last ten years. Vivian then walked back into the hospital and headed toward the coffee machine. She stood there for quite a while before turning around and walking away from it, deciding that the last thing she needed was caffeine.

When she got back into the waiting room, the doctor was making his way through the doors. He slowly made his way over to Vivian. Chris's friends quickly walked over to see what was going on. Bo and Crystal had already left, Bo telling Antwan that he had some business to take care of. The doctor rubbed his long, angular face. He opened his mouth to say something but changed his mind. Seeing the look in Vivian's eyes caused him to hesitate. It pained him to have to tell her the news about her son.

"Hello, Ms. Morrow. My name is Dr. Richards. The bullet that struck your son nicked his spine and lodged into his back. As of right now, he's paralyzed, but it may not be a permanent situation."

"Oh, my God!" Vivian cried out. Tangie put her arm around her and held her tight. Vivian had no idea who these people were comforting her. She didn't know any of Chris's friends except Niko. But one thing she was quickly finding out was that they cared very deeply about her son.

"Is he awake?" Temp asked.

"No. I'm sorry to tell you he's slipped into a coma."

Vivian collapsed. Temp turned around and stormed out of the hospital. He was walking so fast he almost knocked down a woman who was coming through the door.

"Damn, excuse you," the woman said, snaking her neck. Temp stopped in his tracks. Slowly he turned around and shot daggers at her. He was just about to say something foul to her when Antwan, who was following him, grabbed him by the arm and ushered him outside.

"Come on, man. Let it go," he said, throwing his arm around Temp.

As the doctor continued to talk to Vivian, Veronica tried to call Bishop again. "He has to be back at Antwan's by now," she mumbled. Just as she was getting ready to dial, her phone went powerless. Veronica wanted to scream. She couldn't believe that at a time like this, her cell phone was out of power. It wouldn't be until later that she'd find out about the text message Bishop had sent her.

Temp and Antwan stood in the waiting room, digesting the bad news. Had it not been for the fact that there were at least four other people there, both of them surely would have broken into tears. Seeing their comrade lying on the ground bleeding like that tore them apart. Temp quietly eased over to Antwan and placed his hand on his shoulder.

"Yo, man, you sure you didn't recognize the whip them shots came from?" Temp whispered to Antwan.

"Nah, man. I ain't never seen that ride before."

"Well, I know one muthafuckin' thing. Whoevea did this shit gon' pay!"

"You muthafuckin' right!" Antwan agreed.

"Wait a minute," Temp said all of a sudden. "Where the fuck is Bishop? I know he done got back to your house by now."

Temp took out his cell phone and dialed Bishop's number. He got a bad feeling in the pit of his stomach when he didn't get an answer.

"Man, that nigga ain't answering. We need to go back to your house and see if something done happened."

Before leaving, Antwan gave Vivian his number and told her to call him if there was any change. Antwan then gathered the rest of his crew and told them that it was time to leave. Before they left, they all gave Vivian a hug. Each of them struggled to hold back tears as they headed for the door.

***

Doris sat down in the waiting room and shook her head. The turn of events that happened less than an hour ago had shaken her to the core. For the longest time, she had ignored James's adulterous behavior. Even though they were not legally married, Doris had put up with enough from him to call him her own. She was loyal to him. She loved him unconditionally and would do anything to protect him. She had never strayed on him, and foolishly trusted him when he told her that she was the only woman for him.

She had her suspicions but gave him the benefit of the doubt when it came to infidelity. She wanted to believe everything he said. She worshipped him. And he thanked her by giving her the monster. That's why they were having such a heated argument when Niko walked through the door. James had accused her of sleeping around. But Doris was 100 percent certain that she couldn't have concocted the deadly disease from anyone but him. Now part of her wished that whoever attacked him in her hallway had killed him. And when she told him so, he slapped her to the floor. The look in his eyes when he did it scared her.

That's when Niko came in and quite possibly saved her life. Only minutes after Niko was shot, James ran out of the house to avoid being questioned by the police. Now here she was sitting in the chilly hospital waiting room to see if her son was going to live. Doris felt so alone sitting there. Doris looked across from her and saw a woman sitting there with a Bible in her hand. The Bible was open, but the woman didn't appear to be reading it. Every few seconds, a tear would fall from the woman's face and stain the holy paper.

Doris more than felt her pain. She didn't know what the woman's plight was, but she could tell that it was something gut-wrenching to have that kind of effect on her. Doris then got up and went to the bathroom. When she came back, she took a seat right next to Vivian. After exchanging hellos, the two women started talking about their respective issues.

"You know, I'm really proud of Chris," Vivian stated as tears ran down her face. "Even though I didn't approve of what he was doing, I did appreciate that he was willing to do whatever he had to do to make sure his sister's surgery was going to be paid for."

Doris nodded her head as she looked at Vivian with sad eyes. She could almost feel Vivian's pain leaking from her heart and seeping into her pores. Placing her hand on Vivian's, she rubbed it gently. Vivian responded by placing her other hand on top of Doris's.

"I'm so sorry about your loved one," Doris said sympathetically. "Will he be okay?" Although Doris was dealing with her own crisis, she couldn't help but be sympathetic to Vivian.

"I don't know. I pray to God that he will be." Vivian looked at Doris with sad eyes. She could tell that she also has something heavy on her heart. "Are you okay?" she asked Doris.

"Not really. My son is in there fighting for his life, and to be honest, I kind of blame myself."

"Why?"

Doris opened her mouth to speak, but nothing came out. Even though she felt she needed to talk to someone, she'd just met Vivian, so she didn't feel comfortable sharing her story. Doris knew that her man was no good. She'd even thought about leaving him a time or two, and now she wished she had. But what really made her feel like shit was the way she'd treated her son. She treated him like he was a piece of shit, and now she may never be able to make it up to him.

Even though Chris and Niko were friends, the two women didn't know each other from a can of paint. It wasn't until they started talking that they realized both of them had children in the same hospital fighting for their lives.

When Antwan pulled up in front of his house, he and Temp jumped out of the car and eased around the side of the house. Both of them had their guns down by their sides. They didn't know if whoever shot Chris was going to come back and sling slugs at the rest of them, but they weren't taking any chances.

While Veronica and Tangie waited in the car, Antwan and Temp crept toward the backyard in murder mode. Antwan stopped Temp when he looked around the corner and saw someone at his back door.

"Freeze, muthafucka!" Antwan yelled as he jumped out and pointed his gun at the perpetrator.

"Don't shoot, man!"

"Mike, what the hell you doin' back here?"

Mike was a 13-year-old hothead who couldn't stay out of trouble. Antwan would sometimes pay him the run to the store for him or Veronica. He had small, beady eyes and his hair was very nappy. "Man, this is the fourth time I been over here. I woulda called yo' cell, but I forgot yo' number."

"What's up, Mike?"

"Man, I was ridin' my bike from Giant Eagle and saw some bullshit. Ya boy Bishop was being hemmed up by a plainclothes."

"What?"

"Yeah, the bitch who got him was looking all smug and shit."

Temp's eyes got wide. He didn't know for sure that it was the same woman detective who pulled him over, but he had a hunch it was. "Bitch? A bitch cop pulled me over a few days ago. What she look like?"

"To be honest, the bitch was fine as fuck. Long hair. Brown skinned."

Temp reached into his pocket and took out a $20 bill. "Thanks, dawg," he said, handing the money to Mike.

"One more thing, man," Antwan said. "You know anybody 'round the hood who drives a black Nissan Sentra?"

Mike thought for a second and then snapped his fingers. "Yeah, that nigga named Truck drives one. I be seeing him cruisin' around with his boy Dillon sometimes."

"A'ight, thanks," Temp said. The two of them headed back to Antwan's car. "Yo, we need to find them niggas and let 'em hold something hot," Temp said heatedly.

"I feel you, man. Them muthafuckas need to feel the pain."

After ushering the women out of the car, they all went into the house. Once they got inside, Veronica called the police station to find out if Bishop had been charged yet. When she was told no, they realized all they could do was wait.

"Ay, we need to talk," Temp said to Cynthia.

"Yeah, I guess we do," she answered. Temp walked back outside, and Cynthia followed him. So much had happened that it had all of a sudden hit Temp that Cynthia was accusing him of being a father.

Temp and Cynthia had met over a year ago at a cabaret that Antwan had gotten Temp into. They weren't in the place twenty minutes before Temp saw Cynthia and made up his mind that he just had to have her. That's where Antwan had seen her before.

He didn't get a clear look at her because she never came over to the table where he and Temp were sitting. Temp made it his business to go to her. One thing led to another, and the two of them ended up hooking up. They were together for about three months and had a tumultuous relationship. Temp discovered that he couldn't control her like he could some of the other girls he'd been with. Toward the end of their relationship, Temp ended up getting Cynthia pregnant. In keeping with his MO, Temp agreed to pay for Cynthia's abortion. Cynthia was all for it until she visited a friend of hers who had just had a baby.

Cynthia took one look at her friend's child and decided that she couldn't go through with it. Cynthia tried to get in touch with Temp to tell him that she'd changed her mind, but he wouldn't take her calls. Cynthia's mother told her that if Temp didn't want to be a part of her child's life, then she shouldn't beg him to do so, so she stopped calling him. Temp, figuring that Cynthia had gotten the message because she'd stopped trying to call him, never even knew that Cynthia had had the baby until her statement earlier.

"What do you want to talk about?" she asked with a smirk on her face.

"You know what the fuck I wanna talk about! Yo' ass was supposed to have a fuckin' abortion!"

"First of all, I don't know who the hell you think you yellin' at like that! I ain't one of those thot bitches you probably used to fuckin' around with, nigga!"

"Yo, I ain't tryin' ta hear that bullshit! Since you ain't get no abortion, I want my fuckin' bread back!"

"Charge it to the game, nigga. And don't worry about me coming after you for child support. Me and Brian don't want a muthafuckin' thing from you! We doin' just fine, sperm donor."

With those parting shots, Cynthia walked back into the house and left Temp standing there wondering about the son he never knew he had.

Chapter 24

Bishop sat at an interrogation table with a frown on his face. He was thoroughly pissed off that he was being held without bail. It was bad enough that the police had found Temp's gun under the seat. But it got much worse when they searched the car and also found his gun in the car. The detective had already informed him that they were planning on charging him with gun possession. But the thing that worried Bishop the most was that when they ran ballistics on Temp's gun, it was sure to come back dirty.

Ain't this a bitch, he thought. *I'm supposed to be at the party, gettin' fucked up and gettin' ready to put the dick to Veronica later on, and here I am in muthafuckin' jail.*

Bishop looked at the door and frowned even harder when he saw Detective Ramsey walking through it. Confidently and smugly she strolled into the room and sat directly across from Bishop. She leaned back and took a deep breath. In her heart of hearts, she was certain that at least one of those guns belonged to Temp. But what she really wanted was to scare Bishop into giving her something on Temp. She didn't know if he knew anything about Temp beating Yolonda, but she was more than willing to take a chance to find out.

"Look here, Mr. Bernard Simmons, I've got you on gun charges that will put your ass away for a long, long time. Now you told me that the car you were driving is yours, but it's registered a Mr. Tempton Green."

"It used to belong to him. He sold it to me."

"Is that right? Well, my friend, that may be too bad for you. Because if it was still his car, we could charge him with the guns. But since it's your car, it's your ass in the fire."

Ramsey tried to stare Bishop down. Bishop stared right back at her. Ramsey then leaned across the table and let her elbows rest on it.

"Look, I don't know if you're aware of this, but your friend Tempton brutally beat a young girl by the name of Yolonda about a week ago. Yolonda was pregnant. She and the child died."

Bishop thought for a second. He did remember how Temp was acting in Antwan's backyard when they were there talking about getting revenge on the bitches who'd jacked Temp. But then he thought a little more. *If this bitch had something on Temp, then she woulda been picked his ass up, so she must ain't got shit.*

"If I get Tempton down here, I'm sure that I can get him to slip up and tell me something about Yolonda. I want his ass . . . bad! Now, like I said before, since the car is still legally in his name, it's still his car, and I can charge him as such. But since you told me that it's your car, I can use that against you. One of you is going down. It's up to you to decide who it will be."

Ramsey then got up and walked out of the room. The right side of Bishop's brain said, *snitches are bitches.* The left side of it said that he would be a fool to go to jail for Temp. The mental tug of war continued well into the next day. That's when Ramsey brought him back into the interrogation room and told him that ballistics proved that one of the guns they confiscated from the car killed two people and shot another.

"Now I know that 'no snitching' is the code of the streets. But do you really wanna go to the electric chair for something Tempton did? Because if I can't get Tempton on the murders of Yolonda and her daughter, I'll get him on the other murders. And if you want to take the blame for killing people, we both know you didn't kill, then like the saying goes, 'Stupid is as stupid does.'"

Ramsey got up and walked out of the room, leaving Bishop sitting there shocked beyond belief.

One Week Later

Vivian and Doris both knelt down in front of the alter at Morning Starr Baptist church. They both had been through terrible ordeals. They had experienced the most painful feeling that any parent could feel. From the moment they met, Vivian had been telling Doris to trust in God. They would forever be joined at the soul because of the events that had transpired in their sons' lives just one short week ago.

While Doris was sitting at Niko's bedside wondering if she would ever be able to tell her son that she was sorry for the way she'd treated him, James had the nerve to show up. Before he could even open his mouth to speak, she told him that he had ten seconds to get out of her sight before she called the police. James, who didn't give a shit about Niko in the first place, just shrugged his shoulders and left. The only reason he was there in the first place was that his sister kicked him out and he didn't have anywhere else to go.

Vivian's feelings continued to flip-flop. While she was extremely overjoyed that her daughter had come through her operation in good shape, it tore her up that her son, the one person on the earth who was the most responsible for her daughter getting a new lease on life, was fighting for his.

The two mothers grabbed each other's hands and clutched tight. Tears flowed freely from the eyes of both women. One woman's tears were rivers of joy. The other woman was crying for an entirely different reason.

The End